CHANNEL ASSAULT

Also by Godfray Amy:
Horseplay, The Book Guild Ltd.

CHANNEL ASSAULT

Godfray Amy

The Book Guild Ltd.
Sussex, England

This book is a work of fiction. The characters and situations in this story are imaginary. No resemblance is intended between these characters and any real persons, either living or dead.

The Book Guild Ltd.
25 High Street,
Lewes, Sussex.

First published 1993
© Godfray Amy 1993
Set in Baskerville
Typesetting by APS
Salisbury, Wiltshire.
Printed in Great Britain by
Antony Rowe Ltd.
Chippenham, Wiltshire.

A catalogue record for this book is available from the British Library.

ISBN 0 86332 776 1

To Gilberto Franco

PROLOGUE

The public gallery was filled to capacity. The buzz of whispered conversation heightened in anticipation, as resumption of this most crucial of debates grew imminent.

Below, the debating Chamber of the States of Jersey, formed a semi-circle of oak pews facing a central dais. Upon this stood two hand-carved chairs, set throne-like, one twelve inches higher than the other, and presided over by a carved obelisk.

The perimeter walls were panelled in oak, and each section held a red leather escutcheon upon which the Royal Crest of Jersey, three rampant lions, was emblazoned in gold leaf.

Above the panelling a dentiled oak cornice formed the base to the carved and latticed balustrade of the public gallery. A vaulted ceiling, richly enhanced with intricate plaster mouldings, swept up to eight stained glass fanlights each divided hexagonally in colours of green, bronze and purple. A large copper chandelier hung from centre point, its tiers carrying ten moulded glass shades.

The House had assembled, and apart from three absentees, all twelve senators, twelve constables and twenty-nine deputies were in attendance. Some cast their attention towards the gallery as a middle-aged, well-dressed man eased his way along a crowded bench.

Finding a space, he remained standing as the House rose to receive the Bailiff, the Lieutenant Governor, and the Greffier who led the procession carrying the heavy gold mace, symbol of authority and of judicial power.

The Bailiff, dressed in the scarlet robes of the Court, took the higher of the two seats, and the Governor, in a sombre grey suit, sat to his right. The Greffier clipped the mace to the dais and sat at the desk in front as Members, press and public took their seats. The House was called to order and Senator Hetherington was asked to sum up the case against the proposition.

The Senator, a man of working-class origin, delivered a clear and well-defined speech. He had been vehemently against the Defence Committee's proposition from the start. The very thought that a Home Service Force of 150 men should be raised to defend key installations against Russian special forces known by the Soviet acronym Spetsnaz was too absurd to imagine. 'This,' he said, 'is a load of rubbish and an absolute joke.' A rumbling of feet against foot rests signified the approval of many Members. 'It's one of the most obnoxious pieces of propaganda for many years,' – more foot rumbling.

The Senator continued in fine voice. He exploited the weakest points of the speech for the proposition made earlier in the day. He ridiculed those who had spoken for it. 'Why are the Defence Committee seeking to isolate the Soviet Union as the only possible enemy? Islanders are getting fed up with stupid and outrageous ideas imposed on them by us politicians.' He paused for effect, looking around the hushed chamber. 'I am totally against this Home Force, this "Dads' Army" ... it would serve no purpose in any war of the future. For this reason, Members of the House, I ask you to vote against the proposition.' The Senator retook his seat amidst rumbling approval. Senator Bougourd was now called to sum up on behalf of the proposition.

A diminutive man of fifty-three, he stood up slowly, put

on his glasses and for a moment studied his notes. Looking around the House, he addressed his critics.

'Recently my committee invited a military team from the UK to identify areas and installations that should be regarded as key points.' Listing them he continued: 'As a result of that visit it was decided that, to provide twenty-four-hour protection, we would require an organisation of 150 officers and men. Recruiting will be from the twenty-to-fifty age group with compulsory retirement at sixty. Recruiting will be carried out initially among islanders who have had some period of military service.

'The force would be equipped with the standard Territorial Army weaponry – the 7.62 self-loading rifle, the stirling sub-machine-gun and the light machine-gun. We believe that 90 per cent of all training could be accommodated within the island using suitable areas such as Les Landes and the sand dunes in St Ouen's Bay.' The Senator paused to study his notes and took a sip from a glass of water. He resumed, listing wartime roles of the Soviet Spetsnaz. 'These forces,' he continued, 'carefully study the language and customs of the country they will be operating in and are said to pose as tourists in order to familiarise themselves with their potential targets. My committee's view is abundantly clear. Jersey should have its own independent defence force and I therefore move that the proposition be carried.' The Senator sat down; the majority of the House seemed unimpressed. There was a rustle of papers and movement as Members relaxed and prepared to make their decision.

Thanking the Senator, the Bailiff instructed that a vote be taken. The Greffier bowed and began reading out the names from the roll of attendance. He started with the senators: 'Senator Bougourd.' The answer was returned loud and clear: 'Pour.' 'Senator Hetherington,' and a equally loud 'Contre' reverberated around the chamber.

9

The ten remaining senators, the twelve constables and twenty-six of the twenty-nine attending deputies were each called in turn, their answer returned either as a 'pour' or 'contre'.

The last name called registered a final 'contre', and the House remained silent as the Bailiff made the tally.

Looking up with a wry smile he gave the result. 'We have eleven "pours" and thirty-nine "contres", the proposition is defeated.' Hushed conversation and rustling of papers filled the chamber as the House was called to order and moved on to the next item on the agenda. The day's business of island government would continue. Members previously at loggerheads unrestrained by party politics might now unite in the campaigning of some common cause.

With an inward smile, the man in the gallery rose from his seat. The island's defences would remain vulnerable, their vulnerability publicised to all and sundry. In these uncertain times he thought it incredible that Jersey's abundant wealth should remain virtually unprotected.

He felt adrenalin coursing through his veins, and once outside walked briskly towards his bank.

1

Joseph Mullings said goodbye to his wife and walked down the path. He'd laid the stone flags over the weekend and was proud of his work.

'They've set nicely, Joyce,' he called. 'No movement in them at all.'

'That's good, dear, hurry now or you'll miss your train.'

Joseph waved without looking back. He was well aware he had six minutes before the 7.08 train was due. He was equally aware that his walk to the station would take four minutes and forty-five seconds. He didn't need Joyce to tell him whether he'd miss the train or not. He'd not missed a train in the three years they'd been living here and he was not likely to miss it this morning either.

At precisely 8.57 Joseph entered the dimly lit hallway of the ministry building, the lift doors were already open. He removed his Homburg, acknowledging the two other occupants.

In answer to an enquiring look, he asked for the third floor, and, never having been permitted higher than his own supervisor's office on the fourth, he gave a knowing and subservient bow of respect when he realised they were continuing to the eighth.

The automatic doors opened and, offering thanks, Joseph stepped out. He turned to his right and made his way down the long corridor. There were few people

11

about. The rush was yet a full fifteen minutes away, when hordes of secretarial staff, clerks and personnel would arrive in time for the official 9.15 start. Joseph could not abide crowds and was happy to be safely behind his desk by 9.02.

This single small office was his domain. He was neither bothered nor bullied, here in this small back room. A room that gained little daylight from its single sash window set only a few feet away from the windowless wall of an adjoining building.

Joseph hung up his hat and brolly, slipped off his overcoat and placed it carefully over a wooden hanger. Smoothing imaginary creases out of his black jacket, he sat down at the desk in front of the window and looked at his watch. It was 9.04. Uttering a deep and contented sigh, he spread his hands over the smooth surface of the desk devoid of any modern trappings. He opened the drawer and, without removing the magazine flicked through the pages, stopping at a photograph of a young blonde model bending over an armchair. Her white panties, pulled to one side, revealed everything that Joseph so desperately wanted. He swallowed, his mouth suddenly dry. He wanted to masturbate, but there was no time just now. Pushing the drawer shut he sought to regain his composure. There was a knock at the door. 'Come.' The sound didn't register properly. He cleared his throat. 'Come in.'

'Ah, good morning, Ralph.'

'Morning, Mr Mullings' said the acned youth.

The boy pushed a trolley into the room stacked high with daily newspapers and magazines, packed and bound with string in piles of twenty. He lifted one of these and placed it on the desk.

'Mr Perkins given his notice in. Just told me.'

'Mr Perkins leaving? I don't believe it. Where's he

12

going?'

'Don't know, he looks pretty happy about it though.'

'Well, well. Thank you, Ralph. Thank you.'

The youth pulled his trolley out backwards and closed the door. Joseph Mullings talked to himself. 'Perkins leaving after twenty-five years, the boy's having me on.' He reached into his pocket for the silver penknife and cut the string. Here, piled in front of him was his day's work, work at which he was considered expert; 'no one better,' someone had once said. How long ago had that been? Joseph couldn't remember. Anyway he enjoyed skimming through the text and small ads, searching for anything subversive in which his superiors would have interest.

Taking the red felt pen from his breast pocket, he started to read.

☆   ☆   ☆

It was 12.37 when he spotted it. Joseph Mullings, a nothing person, a no one, a nobody. But he was expert in his own field. In room 367 he was highly regarded. Outside room 367 he was totally ignored. He was known by his number, 'the chap in 367.' He had 'scored' several times over the years and today he was sure 367 had scored again. His find was important enough to take to his supervisor; something he had not done for eighteen months. Normal procedure would be to circle suspect text ready for collection at 4.15.

Joseph felt a sense of achievement; it was always exciting taking the lift to the fourth floor.

'Come in.' Joseph entered an office twice the size of his own. An attractive secretary brushed past him on her way out, he breathed in her perfume.

'Well, Mullings?' enquired the bald-headed civil servant, peering over the top of his metal-framed glasses.

'I thought you should look at this sir; you know I would never bother you ....'

'Yes, Mullings, let me see.'

Joseph handed him the newspaper folded to the 'personal' advert columns. The insertion ringed in red, was considered in silence. Mr Albert Tinkler looked up at Joseph then returned to the text.

1010011. 1001111. 1001100. 1000100. 1001001. 1000101. 1010010. 1010011. 1001111. 1000110. 100110. 1001111. 1010010. 1010100. 1010101. 1001110. 1000101. 1000001. 1010000. 1010000. 1001100. 1011001. 1010001. 1001111. 1000010. 1001111. 1011000. 1001110. 1001111. 0111000. 0110111. 0110011. 1000010. 1000001. 1010100. 1001000.

'What is it, Mullings?'

'It's machine language, sir, computer language. It's called ASCII CODE.'

'Have you interpreted it then?'

'Yes sir, of course, it reads: "Soldiers of fortune apply P.O. Box 873 Bath."'

'How available would this code be to the public?'

'Easily available, sir, it would be listed in most books on computer studies.'

Albert Tinkler thought for a few seconds, before looking up. 'Why did they bother to put it into code? We've seen hundreds of these adverts in the past; no one's ever bothered to code one before.'

'Exactly sir, that's why I've brought it up to you. It's obviously meant for a selected group of people.'

'OK, Mullings, thank you. You may well have picked up something of significance here. Carry on now, there's a good chap.'

Joseph nodded, accepting the rare compliment from his superior with pride. He thanked him profusely, and returned to his office.

☆ ☆ ☆

Tinkler picked up the phone, and dialled extension 817.

'Could you allow me a brief interview with Major Jackson please? . . . As soon as possible. I have something that may be considered of some urgency . . . fifteen minutes . . . thank you.' Tinkler replaced the receiver. He returned his attention to the coded text and copied it together with the translation on to a large white pad. He lay back in his chair and considered the possible implications. He stopped himself short; these matters were beyond his brief. No use in clouding the mind, he would not be permitted to voice an opinion.

Tinkler was ushered into the large reception room with three secretaries. They looked towards him, displaying neither recognition nor welcome.

Tinkler swallowed hard, he was nervous. Distracted he suddenly realised that he was being spoken to.

'Mr Tinkler . . . the Major and his committee will see you now. Please follow me.' Tinkler, note-pad in hand, passed through the double doors into an elegant room beyond. The doors closed behind him.

Six men were seated around a large circular table with copious papers and documents scattered in front of them.

'Ah, Tinkler, what have you got for us this time? Why the urgency?'

'Well, sir, 367 spotted it and brought it up to me this morning.' Tearing the top sheet from the pad, he passed it to the Major. 'It's binary code sir; computer machine language. As you see I've printed 367's translation above each series of numbers.'

Tinkler addressed himself to the others as the Major studied the translation. 'It reads: "Soldiers of fortune

15

apply P.O. Box 873 Bath." ' The Major looked up.

'A little mundane wouldn't you say, Tinkler? I mean we've seen this sort of thing many times before.'

'Certainly we have, sir, and such recruitment for work in foreign parts does not concern us. The situation as I see it is that the reason for placing the advert in code may well indicate a domestic situation. I feel sure that this must be secondary to some other, placed previously, and that it is directed towards a specific group of people already known to the advertiser.'

The Major looked up. 'Is it a sophisticated code?'

'No sir, any computer enthusiast could decode it.' The Major passed the paper to his colleagues. He thought for several moments.

'You may leave us now ... and thank you.'

The doors opened and Albert Tinkler walked out briskly. He felt very pleased with himself.

✩ ✩ ✩

'Well, gentlemen?' asked Major Jackson, 'what's your opinion? Is it a nonsense or do we view it with some concern?'

'I think it needs looking into, sir, in fact I agree with Tinkler, it could be a recruitment for something close to home.'

'Thank you, Jason.' The Major turned to an elderly man on his right. 'What is your opinion Colonel Wyatt?' The old boy thought for a moment. 'Can't ignore it old chap. If you do it's bound to blow up in your face. It does seem a bit *Boys Own* stuff to me but ... check it out. We must.' The Major looked around the table looking for further comment.

'Anyone else? ... Yes, Hamilton.'

'It's impossible to assess one way or another sir, unless

16

the department can link it to any other previous communication. I think this has to be a job for one of our "icemen".' The Major nodded his approval.

'We've got at least ten agents who've not been operative for three years or longer. As you are all aware, we have devised a life-style for each, whether activist, criminal, financial or sexual. If you approve I will get the department to find a suitable candidate with credentials likely to prove acceptable to these people . . . . Are you in agreement?'

The five members of the committee murmured their consent.

'I believe that we have to be very quick and that this advert must be answered within the next two days. May even be too late now. I think it will depend very much on whether we have someone available with the necessary background; someone who might prove to be irresistible to them. Now, gentlemen, have we any other business?'

2

Half light fought its way through the partly pulled curtain hanging precariously from the detached rail. An early-morning drizzle clouded the glass; a broken joint in the gutter outside trickled a rhythmic pattern of sound on to the sill below. Inside the room an alarm clock, by the side of a small double bed, ticked in counterpoint. A hand reached out and disengaged it, some fifteen minutes before its abrasive reveille. A sleepy form switched on a small bedside light. He half sat up against the backboard and ran fingers through his hair.

Holding his palms against forehead he thought of the day ahead; it depressed him. He looked towards the window and slid back down under the duvet. Had he ever reached such a low point in his life before? Was this really where all his efforts and specialised skills had brought him? He gave a deep sigh and fought for some reserve deep down that might provide renewed strength. It just seemed that every endeavour over the last three years had ended in one disaster or setback after another. And now today . . . 'Bloody bastards they wouldn't, they couldn't. No way!'

Feeling a spirit and passion welling up from deep inside, he threw back the cover and swung his legs on to the pine floor-boards. They felt cold and refreshing to his feet. He put on a tee-shirt and underpants, went into the bathroom, relieved his aching bladder, cleaned his teeth and shaved off a two-day growth of whisker. He already felt better. He looked into the mirror and ran a hand over his thinning hair, smoothing it into place. He touched the scar, a light furrow from cheekbone to temple, healed now and hardly discoloured. Three years ago, and every morning since a reminder of what had been.

Quietly, he crossed the landing and opened the door to the bedroom opposite his own. He paused for a moment and walked over to the two single beds pulled close together. He sat on the edge of the nearest and gently pulled the silky blonde hair from the face of the occupant. For a few moments he marvelled at her beauty before stroking the little girl's cheek.

'Samantha, darling, wake up. Jennifer, come on, time to get up.' The little girl opened her eyes and after a brief moment put her arms around his neck. He breathed in the smell of her hair and kissed her gently. 'Come on, love, up you get.' Reaching across to the other bed he gently shook the sleeping form. 'Jennifer, breakfast ready in ten minutes. Come on now.'

'What are we going to do today, Dad?'

'We've got someone coming at eleven. Someone who wants to see whether I'm looking after you properly.'

'Why, Dad?' Samantha looked up at him, head cocked to one side.

'Because Mummy's gone away, and dads aren't supposed to be very good at looking after children.'

'Jennifer helps to look after me, Dad, she always makes sure I eat my lunch at school.'

'Yes I know, love. Just you make sure she gets up whilst I'm getting breakfast.'

Minutes later the three of them were seated at the table... Samantha a bubbling, energetic six-year-old, and Jennifer seemingly wise and mature for her nine years, the complete opposite to her sister; reserved and

19

very responsible.

Ronnie Brownlowe loved his daughters. He loved them so much it hurt. Because he wanted so much for them, he sometimes felt painfully inadequate.

He started to clear the breakfast things.

'Jennifer, you take Sam upstairs and get her to put on that little blue dress and you put on a dress too . . . and see you both wash yourselves properly. I'll come up and check you over in a few minutes.

'Do we have to Dad; just 'cos this lady's coming to see us?'

'Don't argue, there's a good girl. You want to put on your pretty blue dress don't you, Sam?'

This all-important visit by the Social Welfare Officer was something he had been dreading all week. Why had Francine decided to leave him, to walk out like that? Well – he knew why – God! Not many women would have stuck by him as long as she had. Everything he'd touched over the last three years had turned into a disaster. Every business venture, and every opportunity. Twenty-three thousand pounds he'd started with, and the house already paid for, and now, nothing – no money, no future.

☆　☆　☆

The doorbell rang. Ronnie's heart missed a beat.

'Now girls, you just get on with your new colouring books, and please be good.'

He paused with his hand on the front latch, and tried to collect his wits.

A man and a woman stood at the doorstep smiling. The man in his mid-forties, bearded, looking rather like a schoolmaster, the woman attractive, in her late twenties with auburn hair and light freckles. She wore little make up . . . .

'Hello, Mr Brownlowe, I'm Janet Sinclair, this is my supervisor George Matlock .... May we come in?'

'Yes, of course – I'm sorry – please – come in.' Ronnie showed them into the sitting room, there was an awkward silence.

'May I take your coat, Miss Sinclair? Sit down please.' They obliged, she on the edge of the seat. They held their silence as if putting him under some pre-planned psychological test.

'Look, I don't really know what this is all about. My girls are really well cared for, you know.' Miss Sinclair stood up.

'I think I'd like to see them, Mr Matlock wishes to discuss other issues with you.'

'What bloody issues?' Ronnie was losing his patience, he jumped to his feet. 'Why don't you just leave us alone?' His face was transformed by aggression. Miss Sinclair touched his arm; she looked him straight in the eye.

'Captain Matlock has something of great importance he wishes to discuss with you. Don't worry, we are fully aware of the love and care you give your children. Now, where are they?'

Ronnie was confused but her manner visibly calmed him. He led her to the kitchen. The two girls looked up, apprehensively. Janet Sinclair smiled and within seconds was chatting amicably with them. Ronnie, realising they felt secure once more, returned to the front room. As he entered, the man got to his feet.

'Look ... I'm sorry about all this cloak-and-dagger stuff, Brownlowe, but it's time to put you back in the picture. We've made hell for you over the last three years. The business failure; the reason you lost your jobs; the bank deciding to repossess this house after you'd been forced, out of dire necessity, to remortgage. It's all been

21

the Department's doing.' Ronnie sat down, and he put his head in his hands.

'I might have known it – I half guessed it. You bloody bastards, why? – For God's sake why?'

'Look, this is as difficult for me as it is for you.' Matlock played for time . . . . 'Have you a drink in the house, I'm sure we could both use one?' Ronnie poured out two large measures of Johnny Walker. He returned to his seat and looked at the man opposite – an ordinary and very unmilitary figure. Ronnie took a gulp of the liquid, and felt the warmth flow through him. For a brief second he wanted to mutilate that mean anonymous face, but restrained himself. His expression softened into a request for an explanation. The Captain responded.

'Look, it's not that bad you know. We've been paying £20,000 into a numbered account of a Swiss bank, for each of the three years you've been away from us. That's yours, it's yours whenever you need it. Further, we have an agreement with your bank to repay the monies owing on the mortgage you took out last year. There will be no further pressures made upon you from that quarter.' Ronnie shook his head in disbelief.

'You mean you made me suffer for three years . . . . You emasculated me – do you know that . . . you took away my manhood. Why? Christ I know why, its fucking obvious isn't it? What do you call us up there in your ivory fucking tower? "icemen"; that's what they call people like me, isn't it? I've been made one of your fucking icemen, haven't I? Put away in cold storage, ready for the day when the department is ready to use me again. Of use now, only because of the dire straits and the deplorable situation I've been pushed into. Jesus Christ! And what about my wife? Have you got her too?' For a moment Matlock looked embarrassed.

'We are extremely sorry about that. No, we had

nothing to do with your wife leaving you. However, we know where she is and one of our personnel has made contact with her.' Ronnie took another gulp of whisky.

'Go on – tell me . . . . You're expecting me to agree to do some job for the Department aren't you? Christ, I don't believe it, and I thought I'd turned my back on you lot . . . you conniving bastards.' The Captain pressed forward.

'Yes we do want you, you are the most qualified to help. The Department has allocated £100,000 to be paid over to you or placed in trust to your wife and daughters. In return, we require that you infiltrate a particular organisation whose activities we are most anxious to monitor. This is the situation as it stands at the moment.' Matlock explained how the Department had already applied to the box number on his behalf. A P.O. box had been arranged at an Islington post office to which it was hoped that the persons behind the advert would reply. Ronnie listened intently neither interrupting nor querying the Captain's assumption that he would co-operate.

Matlock passed him the coded advertisement with its translation and a paperback entitled *Computer Studies.*

'Presumably I would have decoded this myself.' The Captain indicated he should turn to the back of the book. Each letter, both alphabetically and numerically was listed against the binary code.

'It's just simple computer language,' added the Captain, 'you don't have to claim to be an expert; just read the book. An inkling of knowledge will be enough, and here . . . a copy of the reply we've sent on your behalf.' Ronnie read the typed words as the Captain closed and locked his brief case.

RONALD BROWNLOWE. FORMERLY SERVED WITH BRITISH PARACHUTE REGIMENT. RANK CORPORAL. LATER TRANSFERRED TO BRITISH

AIR SERVICE CREW COUNTER-TERRORIST COM-
MANDO: INVALIDED OUT OF SERVICE WHEN
WOUNDED DURING STORMING OF IRANIAN EM-
BASSY 1980. PRESENTLY IN GREAT FINANCIAL
DIFFICULTIES. LONG FOR ACTIVE SERVICE. NO
QUESTIONS ASKED. IMMEDIATELY AVAILABLE
CONTACT P.O. BOX 117 ISLINGTON LONDON.

'And what am I supposed to do if they take me in?'

'Keep us informed if you can old man .... If you can't make contact for any reason you'll just have to play it by ear.'

'And my girls, what's supposed to happen to them?' The Captain leaned forward and placed his hand on Ronnie's knee; it was brushed away with some vicious- ness. 'Don't touch me, you fucking bastard. Who do you think you are coming in here as if nothing's happened? It's not just me you've put through hell you know, it's my whole family who's suffered.' Once again having given vent to his anger, he visibly calmed. 'Go on tell me what arrangements will be made for the girls.'

Matlock looked relieved. 'As far as your neighbours are concerned they will be taken into care. What will actually happen is that Miss Sinclair will take them up to Scotland where your wife is presently living with her sister. As I said previously, we have already been in contact with her and she has agreed to take them.'

'And how have you explained my incapacity to her. Where does she think I've swanned off to?'

'You, my dear chap, have been pronounced as incapa- ble. Your wife was given the option of either letting them be taken into care or providing them with the proper attention they deserve. She decided of course on the latter.' The Captain finished his drink in a final gulp of self-satisfaction.

24

'You bloody wankers think of everything, don't you?' scowled Ronnie.

'We do, Corporal Brown, we do.'

✧   ✧   ✧

Three days later his girls were taken from him. Miss Sinclair had called as arranged and after tearful goodbyes they were driven away by car. Ronnie felt utterly desolate, worrying that if Francine really believed Matlock's lies it was unlikely she would ever agree to return them.

Twice already he'd been to Islington, only to discover an empty post box, and a long walk home. Having asked Matlock for some cash to tide him over, he'd been refused.

'Now then, Corporal, if you were suddenly seen to have come into money it would rather spoil the special effects we've created. Don't you think?'

'Bloody bastard of a man. As if a few quid in advance would have made a hap'orth of difference.

More like they'd never even received his application or even more likely they'd received it and, because of his past exemplary service record, considered him too great a security risk to enlist. What did it matter, either a reply would turn up or it wouldn't.

Ronnie ran up the post office steps, and waited his turn.

'Have you any mail for Box 117?' He handed the clerk the identification ticket.

'Won't keep you a moment, sir.' A minute later he was back. 'No sir, nothing for you today.' Ronnie thanked him, surprised at his own disappointment. For the first time he worried that contact might not be made.

Calculating the length of time it would have taken for his application to be processed, he supposed at the very earliest it could have arrived yesterday. If contact wasn't made within the next three days the whole venture could be deemed a non-starter.

Into the brightness of the street he turned to make his way home. Immediately he felt uneasy – instinct, not drawn upon for so long, warned him that he was being followed. Adrenalin heightened his senses; he walked on briskly and purposefully. Contact was about to be made; he decided it should be on his terms, not theirs.

A moment later he saw his opportunity. A mini-cab pulled to the side of the road some twenty yards ahead; the occupants were paying their fare.

The driver was about to close the nearside door when Ronnie sprinted the few remaining yards and jumped inside. 'Finsbury Park station, please.' The driver pulled away from the kerb, and from the rear window Ronnie spotted a man in a denim jacket attempt to give chase. Timing his move to the precise moment, Ronnie opened the offside door and screened from his pursuer by a double-decker bus, jumped out into the centre of the road. He rolled over in one athletic movement and alighted on his feet. The man, trying to regain his breath, now stood in front of him.

Ronnie walked up behind. 'Looking for me, son?' The man – in his thirties, slim and tall – looked visibly shaken.

'No, Mr Brownlowe, not looking for you, I was supposed to be following you.'

'Christ, I might have known it. They can never just let one get on with a job alone, can they? Are you supposed to be protecting me or checking on my movements? Not that you are capable of doing either.'

'I was just supposed to keep close until a contact was made, that's all. They weren't too sure whether you would see it through or not.' Ronnie caught the man by the front of his jacket and lifted him on to his toes.

'Look you scruffy little wimp; you go back and tell those fucking pigs that I'll see it through all right ...

26

providing I'm left alone .... You're all I need. You've probably fucked the whole thing up already. What if they're watching us?' Ronnie released his hold; the man readjusted his jacket. 'Now piss off and if I see you again I'll break your face for you.' Ronnie caught sight of an angry cab driver approaching on foot and darted away into the crowd.

☆　☆　☆

The following day, feeling listless and depressed, he again waited his turn in the queue, this time to be recognised by the clerk. 'Good morning, sir, Box 117 wasn't it? Won't keep you a minute.' Ronnie looked up at the clock on the wall – it was 11.50 – the days seemed endless without the kids. He refocused his attention, nostalgia only depressed him. The look on the clerk's face was heartening. 'We're in luck today, sir, I hope it's what you've been waiting for.'

Ronnie took the manilla envelope and slipped it into his pocket. Once outside he set off at a brisk pace and within forty minutes was in the privacy of his own home. The message on a single piece of cheap lined notepaper was brief, concise and hand-written in capitals; he read it out loud.

> *'Within the next 7 days you will be collected. Be ready*
> *but not waiting. Operations will extend 12–14 weeks.*
> *Tell no one. Your life may depend on it .....'*

'More bloody cloak-and-dagger stuff,' thought Ronnie. He hoped it wouldn't be too long before they came for him. Should he inform the Department? Well he should, but would he? He decided not to. What had he to tell anyway? If he did they'd only stake out the house and screw everything up before it even started. The others had

27

obviously checked him over already. Waste of time taking out that box number, it had obviously been no problem for them to discover where he lived. Crumpling up the note and envelope he threw them into the empty firegrate. The note would be found in a week or so and the Department would know for sure that things had finally got underway. He'd be well out of their reach by then.

Ronnie went to the kitchen and made himself a coffee. He sipped the hot bitter liquid; it felt good to be back doing the job he knew best. A job where the simple act of survival meant experiencing life on a higher plane than the average man knew existed, and in stark contrast to the living death he'd been forced to endure over the past three years. He smiled, and realised his depression had lifted. He felt good, he felt sharp, he felt hungry. He scavenged the remnants of the fridge and put together a makeshift meal.

✩   ✩   ✩

The afternoon dragged by slowly. Ronnie spent some time packing a large canvas duffle bag with everything he might need. It was difficult without knowing what to expect; what the operation was, over what terrain and in what climate. He decided it best to take warm clothing; he could always strip off.

Between a pair of black cord trousers, a heavy grey sweater and a black light-weight pullover, he packed his mask and respirator, two small canisters of compressed air, his grey anti-flash hood and a flak vest.

He took the open combat holster from the bedside cabinet and removed his Browning Hi-Power 9mm pistol. He ran his fingers over the cold steel and felt the thrill of it run deep into his body.

Shaking away the sensation, he retrieved the magazine

28

and a box of ammunition, loaded fourteen rounds, and slipped the magazine into the pistol. He cocked it to place one round into the chamber, flicked on the safety catch and eased the loaded weapon back into the holster. Ronnie wrapped a clean hand towel around it, and placed it deep into the bag.

He decided to sleep in the front room. They might come at any time, at any hour and when they did come he wanted to be ready for them. Survival in his book meant being one second ahead of the action.

He took a bath, then bedded down fully dressed on the settee, covering himself over with one of the children's duvets. He was soon asleep, secure in the knowledge that his newly aroused instincts would startle him awake at the first unfamiliar sound. He slept on uninterrupted until 7.30 and wondered what the hell he was going to do with himself for the rest of the day.

☆   ☆   ☆

The doorbell rang. He checked his watch, it was 10.37. He looked through the spyglass, but saw no one. Opening the door, he recognised a small child whose parents owned the newsagents on the corner. The little boy held out an envelope. Ronnie took it, and without a word of thanks returned to the kitchen.

Inside the envelope was a note and a membership card to a Kings Road night-club. The note read:

> *'Proceed to The Squeeze at 23.15 where contact will be made sometime during the evening. Leave your gear at reception. Do as the lady suggests.'*

He read it several times over. They were certainly taking great precautions. The greater the precaution the more audacious must be the mission. Ronnie felt greatly relieved that they hadn't attempted to collect him from home. He knew very well that if they had, he would have acted defensively and probably would have been over-aggressive; the house had too many fond memories to allow such intrusion.

It was another beautiful day, fresh and crisp; Ronnie decided to go out. He walked, not aiming to end up anywhere in particular; he needed to relax and prepare himself mentally for the task ahead.

An hour later he was sitting on a park bench watching children and their mothers feeding the ducks at the edge of the water. Many times before he'd brought Sam and Jennifer to this very spot. Strangely he found himself thinking of Francine and not so much of the children, realising with a jolt that he still really cared for her. It was good to learn she was with her sister and not with some other bloke. It had been hell not knowing, so much so, he supposed, that he had just stopped thinking about her as part of a device he had learned long ago. Even so, the one issue he refused to dismiss was the children, however much their absence tore him apart. Perhaps he could also allow Francine back into his thoughts, now that he knew where she was. Perhaps when this was all over he'd go up to Scotland to try and sort something out.... Things could be different with enough money to provide for them properly.

Ronnie decided he'd better contact the Department, to inform them of the latest developments and to secure the payments that had been promised.

He continued his walk along the path edging the lake until he came to a solitary phone box at the rear of the park café. Ronnie took out the last £5 note from his inner pocket, and read off the number he'd written on the top left-hand corner. He placed a 50p coin in the slot and dialled. A woman's voice answered. 'Ladybird Fashions, good morning, can I help you?'

'This is field officer 36 calling. My code connection is ASCII. I wish to make a report.' Ronnie, utilising the information passed to him by Matlock, sought to reach his security-protected contact. There was a slight delay as the woman checked his clearance. Ronnie could hear the data being keyed into the computer. 'I'm putting you through now sir.'

'Hello 36 ... 36, I have been designated to your operation, I shall be your station officer for the duration of this exercise. You may identify me as Arthur.'

'God forbid!' answered Ronnie, 'Arthur ASCII, I don't believe it. You chaps been watching too many Bond movies.' Relating the designated time and place he'd been asked to attend that night, he specifically requested that no one should be placed there to check or follow him. 'I'll make contact again when I feel able to,' he added and went on to request that an interim sum of £10,000 be paid into his wife's account, with the balance to his own numbered Swiss account previously secured for him by the Department. 'Is that clear?' he said finally.

'Yes 36, very clear.'

'And if the promised monies do not materialise I ....' The station officer interrupted him.

'I can give you total assurance that the financial arrangements will be completed forthwith. I have computer clearance on the screen in front of me at this very moment, 36. I look forward to your next report.' Ronnie felt greatly relieved, and replaced the receiver.

Outside he breathed fresh air deep into his lungs and began jogging his way back alongside the lake. He felt fitter and more like his old self, a smile creased his face into rugged good looks. 'Arthur bloody ASCII!' Ronnie gave out a loud shout of aggression and sprinted the remaining distance to the end of the path.

31

Breathing hard he came to a stop, and for a moment felt slightly dizzy. Then, having regained his breath he continued his way home at a brisk walk.

Ronnie Brownlowe was a man restored.

3

Ronnie locked the front door and placed the key in an envelope stamped and addressed to Francine. He dropped it into the post box and as soon as he'd done so, wished he'd included a note to the kids. He breathed a sigh of missed opportunity, then, seeing a bus at the top of the road, broke into a run. It started to pull away from the kerb. With an extra effort Ronnie sprinted the few remaining yards, caught hold of the rail and jumped aboard.

'Sloane Square please, mate.' The conductor handed Ronnie his ticket. 'Sixty-five pence please sir.' Ronnie rummaged through his pockets, eventually making up the fare, and was left with just 23p plus the £5 note.

He took it from his inner pocket and memorised his contact's telephone number. He tested his memory making sure it was indelibly etched on his mind, before tearing it off with the corner of the note. He hoped that £5.23 might be just enough to buy him a couple of drinks at the club. He folded the note and put it deep into his pocket.

Twenty minutes later the bus pulled over to stop just beyond the Royal Court Hotel, Sloane Street. He crossed over on to the square itself then again to the pavement beyond and started to walk up the Kings Road. A few yards on he spotted a small engraved plate by the side of a heavy panelled door.

Ronnie was greeted by the solid beat of loud music. He

paused for a moment adjusting his eyes to the dim light. The door closed automatically behind him.

A staircase carried down to reception where an attractive blonde of about twenty-five sat behind a small counter. She made no sign of welcome. Ronnie placed his membership card on the desk, and she keyed his number into a computer. He expected a reaction but there was none.

'Thank you, sir. Would you like to leave your bag?'

She placed it on the floor under the counter, and he wondered whether it would be searched. He had taken the precaution of attaching a piece of black silk thread from the eye of the zip to the baggage tag holder, and if anyone did go through his belongings he'd certainly know about it.

Behind a pair of heavy velvet curtains stretched a bar the full length of a narrow room separated from another, similarly shaped, by thick walled arches. Through these he could see people seated for dinner and at the far end a small dance area.

The club was not over-full but well attended. The clientele seemed mainly to consist of well-heeled working people aged between twenty-five and thirty-five with a sprinkling of others both younger and older. Ronnie did not feel out of place. It was an atmosphere in which he felt comfortable. The last time he'd been to a club was Francine's birthday eighteen months ago. He suddenly remembered it was his own birthday in two weeks time. April 4, his forty-second. It could well be a birthday to remember for some years to come – if of course he managed to survive it.

Purposefully he walked up to the bar and ordered a vodka and tonic with ice. He made no effort to pay, hoping there would be some system of account that enabled settlement at the end of the evening. Sure enough the barman wrote something on a card under the counter.

'Mr Brown is it, sir?' Ronnie nodded. 'Your account will be taken care of, sir, would you like to have dinner?'

'A little later perhaps, thank you.' Ronnie leant against the bar and sipped at the ice-cold drink. He wondered how he'd been recognised, but then a good barman would know all the regulars by name. Any stranger on his own would stand out, and he'd obviously been expected. Ronnie's thoughts were distracted by a heady perfume and a movement to his right.

She wore a full-length dress, high at the neck and virtually backless, exposing a gymnastic curve from shoulder to buttock. Her dark hair, swept to one side, cascaded over her right shoulder, its fullness contained by two diamante clips. Her large dark eyes looked up at him, cheekily appealing.

'Mr Brown, I've been asked to look after you . . . I hope you don't mind. My name is Sarah.'

'Not at all, my love. Would you like a drink?'

She asked for a dry Martini; Ronnie caught the barman's eye and was served. He handed the delicate crystal glass to the girl. She thanked him and took a sip, her shining lip gloss leaving a red kiss mark on the rim.

Ronnie tried to estimate her age – perhaps twenty-one? twenty-four? It was hard to judge.

He asked whether she worked for the club and she explained that she was with an escort agency. 'I normally come down here if I get a night off. I was really glad when they told me to meet you here. You must be very important, Mr Brown.'

'Why do you say that?'

'Because they paid double my normal fee, I've been told to take you home with me and to give you this.' She opened her little shoulder bag and took out a sealed envelope. Inside was a hand-written note giving instruc-

35

tions to accompany the girl home at the end of the evening.

'Do you fancy having something to eat?' he asked. 'As everything appears to be on the house we might as well take advantage of it.'

'And will you take advantage of me, Mr Brown?' The girl linked her arm through his as they made their way through to the dining room. 'That,' said Ronnie, 'may well depend on the people who've set this up.'

'Can you tell me what it's all about?' she asked.

'No, love, I can't. Let's just enjoy ourselves while we have the chance, shall we? And you had better call me Ronnie.'

A smartly dressed woman in her late thirties showed them to a table. They sat down and ordered. Ronnie was enjoying the girl's chatter and was attracted by her appealing personality. She had a brightness generally not evident in most girls of her suspected trade. It had been so long since he'd been in the company of an attractive young woman, and this one possessed a certain vulnerability, probably the reason he felt so drawn and protective towards her.

They chatted on over a pleasant meal after which they ordered coffee. Ronnie now relaxed with a large measure of Calvados, she sipped lovingly at a Cointreau on the rocks. He looked at his watch, and called over the head waitress. It was 1.35.

'A very enjoyable meal, we wish to leave now. Would you like me to sign the bill?'

'That's quite all right, Mr Brown, everything has been taken care of. I'm glad you had a good time. We hope to see you again soon.' She smiled warmly at both of them as she removed the empty cups. Ronnie drained his glass.

'Are you ready, Sarah?' The girl smiled and nodded, 'I'll just get my coat from the back office. Will you wait for me here?'

'No, love, I need some fresh air. I'll wait outside.' He touched her white neck in a gesture of affection then walked through the bar into reception. The same girl was still behind the desk.

He took his bag without thanking her. He'd met too many like her in the past. What was it that made nightclub doormen and female receptionists so bloody moody? Outside the air felt good. He lifted his bag to examine the zip – the thread had been broken, it was to be expected. He hoped they'd not removed his pistol or any of his equipment. He felt a great sense of attachment to those items of combat which had aided his survival so often in the past. It would be tragic to lose them now. His mind was diverted by an approaching taxi. He waved and shouted at it, but it drove on, oblivious to his needs.

Sarah linked both arms through his and raised up her face; he kissed her on the cheek. Her perfume and affection released feelings of some deep emotion within him. He questioned his reaction and tried to put it into perspective. He shouldn't feel anything for this girl, it was against everything he had been taught. Emotion of any kind clouded concise judgement. In his line of business, occasional instantaneous and reflex decisions had to be made, often making the difference between life and death. Right now however, sexual desire predominated, and as if reading his mind, she gave his arm a squeeze. 'Come on,' she said. 'We can walk, it's only a few minutes.'

☆   ☆   ☆

Ronnie regained his self-discipline and observed every passing car and pedestrian with equal intensity. Contact would soon be made and there was no particular reason to suppose it would be friendly.

They had crossed over the Kings Road and continued walking towards the fire station. Before reaching it they turned into a narrow side street. Sarah stopped in front of a small terraced house and swung open the iron gate. She rummaged in her bag, holding it open towards the street light.

Ronnie waited behind her, feeling for some reason rather sheepish. She found the key and beckoned him to follow her down the granite steps to the basement flat. Without fumbling she unlocked the front door. The light from the hall spilled out into the darkness. She turned towards him, unbuttoning her coat. 'Go into the sitting room and make yourself comfortable, I want to change out of this dress, I won't be a minute.' She gestured towards the door opposite, giving him a sultry lingering look as she went into her bedroom. Ronnie immediately became suspicious; taking into account the natural way she had behaved previously that departing expression had seemed totally false and unnecessary.

It was the only mistake she had made all evening. He cursed himself for being such a fool. It made him realise just how long he'd been isolated from his profession. It was a lesson well learnt and learnt in time. From this moment he would concentrate on seeing this thing through to its conclusion, and clear his mind of all emotion, nostalgia or sentimentality.

Ronnie slowly turned the knob then gently pushed open the door, screening himself from the view of anyone inside. A warm light flowed out into the hall. Ronnie smelt cigarette smoke and eased himself cautiously into the open doorway.

The light issued from a small table lamp in the corner, two armchairs with high backs faced away from the door, hiding the occupants; cigarette smoke curled its blue haze to the ceiling.

38

Ronnie waited, not moving, every nerve tuned ready for explosive action if demanded. He felt an atmosphere charged with tension, and remained silent and detached. The heavy silence seemed interminable.

'Come in, Mr Brown, would you like a drink?' The man stood up as he spoke and turned to face the door; the other remained seated. Ronnie walked into the room accepting the offered glass. Both men were simply minions; their demeanour carried no authority but a persuasiveness of underlying physical presence derived from the gymnasium.

'You boys been waiting long?' asked Ronnie affably.

'No, not long, but long enough ... You ready then?'

'Yes, I'm ready.' Ronnie knocked back the whisky in one gulp. The two minders drained their own glasses. The spokesman continued.

'We'll go out the back way. Never know who's watching from the street. You stay close to me, Brucey will bring up the rear.' Ronnie nodded and followed the brute into the hall. He looked wistfully towards Sarah's bedroom door and cursed the missed opportunity.

Passing through a small kitchenette and out into the backyard, they jumped up and swung over a five foot wall to drop down into a narrow alley. This ran the full length of the properties that backed on to it and eventually brought them out into an adjacent side street.

Brucey went to the back of a Thames van parked immediately opposite and unlocked the rear doors. Ronnie was pushed forward roughly and locked in.

An iron grille separated him from the cab, and he wondered whether it might be an old post or police van; whichever made little difference, for he was firmly imprisoned for the duration of the journey.

Feeling about in the dim light he discovered the floor had been covered with a soft rubber material. He tapped

39

on the grille to attract their attention.

'Have we far to go?'

'We've a long drive ahead. I'd get some sleep if I were you; we won't get there until the morning.' Ronnie would like to have taken his advice, but he needed to know which direction they were travelling. He decided to take a bearing once they were clear of London. If this could be established and length of time the journey took, he would be able to calculate an approximate location.

Ronnie opened the bag and felt through his clothing; the pistol and holster were intact. Everything seemed to be there, except the compass. His respect for the organisation was growing; they seemed to be operating in a most professional way.

There was nothing more he could do until daylight, so he pummelled the bag into an acceptable head rest, and made himself as comfortable as he could.

✧   ✧   ✧

Waking stiff, cold and for a brief moment totally disorientated, Ronnie sat up and eased his aching body. It was nearly dawn. Brucey was asleep in the passenger seat while his mate drove on with grim determination.

From the little Ronnie could see through the front windows, they appeared to be in deep and hilly country, and travelling on a minor road. It was by now a wispy pale morning and the driver was having some difficulty in keeping the windows from misting up. There now seemed little hope of spotting a signpost. The van was being pushed to its limit; the revs screamed to their maximum and the whole vehicle shook and vibrated to stresses never intended.

Suddenly they rounded a tight right-handed bend, and Brucey was thrown hard against the door. He woke up and immediately shouted obscenities, calling the driver by name for the first time. Harry kept silent, allowing Brucey's temper to cool. He had not reacted in any way to the abuse, but carried on driving at the same reckless pace. Five minutes later, he slowed the vehicle and pulled over to the side of the road. He turned off the ignition and brought his hands up to his face, rubbing his temples.

'Sorry mate, give us a fag, will you?' Brucey took a cigarette for himself and offered the packet to his mate. They lit up, totally ignoring their passenger.

'About another hour from here I reckon . . . . Any coffee left?' Brucey reached down beside the seats and eased out a thermos flask.

The steam from the hot liquid rose up, carrying with it the rich smell of roasted coffee. Ronnie moistened his dry lips and watched greedily as Brucey drained the flask into the cup. He took a sip and passed the remainder to the other who downed it in one gulp. 'Let's be making tracks. We're expected at 9.25 and I don't fancy the risk of being late – so no more gripes about my driving.' Harry started up and within seconds was again driving flat out.

The vibration and the bumping tortured every nerve in Ronnie's body. He felt cold, stiff and hungry. He longed to relieve his aching bladder which hurt with every jolt. With at least another hour to endure, he wedged himself tight into the corner, his knees to his chest, pushing with his feet to secure his back firmly against the side of the van.

Ronnie closed his eyes and fed the ducks by the side of the lake. '*This one's for you, Sam; that one's for you, Jennifer; this one's for all three of you. Francine, this is the last time, the last job; the last time. You'll never have to go looking through church jumble sales to find the girls their winter coats. You'll never again have to make do with that same old dress when we go dancing on your birthday. Things are going to be so different for all four of us.*'

41

He opened his eyes. The van had slowed. It turned off the road and passed under an imposing arch. They proceeded at a leisurely pace, along a tree-lined drive with acres of grass on either side. The drive ran on for a mile or so then spread itself into a large gravelled forecourt. The van stopped. Harry and Brucey got out and stretched their weary limbs. One of them walked to the rear of the van and unlocked the doors. Ronnie scrambled out, tried to stand up, but doubled over with stomach cramps. 'Jesus, I've got to have a piss.'

'That's all right mate, go behind the pillar there,' said Harry, affably. Ronnie relieved himself against the red brick buttress that rose high above, offering its support to the imposing Victorian mansion.

The house had a general air of decay. Gutters hung loose from the eaves, paint curled away in flakes from the tall window frames and a green moss clung to innumerable areas of brickwork which were visibly saturated from broken gutters and downpipes. Weeds and tufted grass had also forced their way through the gravelled forecourt, adding to the atmosphere of dereliction and abandonment.

Harry walked towards the front entrance and indicated that Ronnie should follow him, whilst Brucey drove the van through a pair of high oak doors into a quadrangle behind the house.

Gracious curved steps carried them up to the front entrance and, without knocking to indicate their arrival, they entered into a spacious hallway. Harry's footsteps on the marble floor echoed through the house and the door, with a noise loud enough to declare their presence to the world, slammed shut behind them. Harry motioned to remain still and raised his eyes to the ceiling. Four video cameras trained upon them, each with a red light at its base. He spoke, directing his voice upwards.

'It's Harry. I was expected at 9.25,' he checked his watch, 'and I now make it 9.28. May I bring the applicant up?' They waited as an electrical whir broke the silence as one of the cameras adjusted to a new angle. The four red lights at their base changed in an unsynchronised pattern to green; indicating the order to proceed.

Walking across the unfurnished hall, they continued up the generously proportioned staircase that divided to right and left at a mezzanine landing. Each of the continuing flights converged to a first-floor landing and corridor. The uncarpeted stairs and wood floors resounded to their every step.

Harry stopped in front of one of numerous panelled doors, highly French polished and making stark contrast to the faded paper that peeled away from the adjacent walls. Harry knocked gingerly at the door and Ronnie realised that it was here the man's responsibilities ended. He knocked again, this time with more authority.

The door opened. A diminutive man in his late twenties offered a thin smile. A narrow aquiline face with blond hair receding at the temples, gave no hint of his nationality. He spoke in near-perfect English, but in a brittle precise manner, clipping the ends of his words. Ronnie had heard similar accents many times during his specialised training, and placed him at once as German.

'You have done well, Harry. Leave us now. You may have breakfast.' Harry raised a hand in half-embarrassed recognition of the compliment and turned away without speaking. The German stepped aside and beckoned Ronnie in.

It was a magnificent room. Tall windows permitted the morning sunlight to cascade across the maple-leaf floor. Devoid of conventional furnishings, numerous books, maps, pencils, pens, markers, several unwashed plates, mugs and cutlery were scattered untidily over a makeshift

43

trestle table. A fire burned energetically within a classic Adam fireplace; a pile of irregular-sized firewood had been stacked alongside.

Three men scrutinized Ronnie as he approached. Two were seated on folding camp chairs, the other stood with his back to the fireplace. Ronnie's acute powers of observation, having already taken in the room, now assessed its occupants. He addressed himself to the older of the two men seated.

'Thank you for seeing me so promptly. My name is Brownlowe.' The man nodded, the other spoke in a heavy Welsh accent.

'We've been expecting you, please ... grab that chair and sit at the table. Would you like a coffee?' The man poured from a large white pot which had been resting on the hearth. Ronnie sipped at the hot liquid. It tasted good – real good.

'Corporal Brownlowe,' the man continued. 'We know quite a lot about you. However we're not prepared at this stage to inform you of our own background, except to say that we have international contacts, are highly organised and have the administrative skills necessary to plan and execute the operation we have in mind.'

'Are you able to tell me your plans at this stage and do I have any option open to me now that I am here, to accept or refuse?' The man considered Ronnie's question. He turned to look at his companion, seeking support. It was given. The spokesman continued: 'We will permit you to make your own decision. But should you decide not to join us, we would insist that you remain here until sometime after we vacate.'

'That's understandable,' Ronnie answered, 'I accept that, but first I must know the full extent of your intentions.'

'Mr Brownlowe,' the older man leant across the table

44

speaking for the first time. 'Our scheme is threefold. The first will be to secure the arms and equipment required to execute the remaining two. We had recruited all the men necessary before receiving your application, but we considered your previous training and service record too useful to ignore. We are hoping you will agree to lead a small group of specialists on this first and most important phase.

Depending on its outcome you will be given the option to lead the second phase and, finally having proved yourself, the chance to participate in our most daring of adventures. I will be straight with you; it will mean a full military incursion and in all probability some loss of life. You will need to accept this.' The man paused and leant back in his chair. Ronnie was aware of cold calculating eyes searching his face for sign of emotion or reaction. He was convinced that none could have been detected and continued unflinchingly to return his interviewer's gaze.

The man, in order to emphasize the next question, leant forward.

'Are you prepared to kill, Mr Brownlowe?' Ronnie considered his reply, choosing his words with care.

'I'm a military man, as I imagine you to be ... I have been trained to kill and have done so several times, but only in the service of my country. Over the last few years however I have come to feel that my country has deserted me. I am therefore prepared to risk my own life and would take life in the course of a military-style action – provided the rewards justified the risk.' Ronnie rested his elbow on the table. He sipped at the coffee, he appeared relaxed and secure.

'Let me introduce you to my colleagues.' The man touched the shoulder of the person next to him. 'This is Ashley Jones.' Ronnie leant over and shook the Welshman's hand. 'This is William Sobbard.' The aristocratic figure who had remained standing gave a curt nod of acknowledgement. 'I am Commander Teal and that is Reinhard Mueber.' The small German clicked his heels. Commander Teal continued: 'I can assure you Mr Brownlowe that the rewards will justify the risks. We will pay you £20,000 on the successful completion of the first mission, £40,000 for the second and, if you decide to join us on our final incursion and we achieve our objectives, a guaranteed £150,000.

You may have free option to terminate your association with us, after either phase. However, we sincerely hope that if the first two phases are successfully accomplished you would agree to see the whole thing through.'

The Commander pushed back his chair and stood up. He walked over to collect an armful of firewood and placed each piece tidily upon the fire. He then stood with his back to the warmth.

Ronnie sensed the man's authority and considered that anyone under his command could feel confident of his leadership. There was a noticeable pause, each man making his own assessment of the other. Ronnie was the first to break the silence.

'Can you tell me what the three phases entail?'

'Just the first at this stage. We'll tackle one issue at a time.' The Commander walked over to the table and picked up a folded newspaper. He pointed to the headline ARMS FOR IRAN INTERCEPTED. Ronnie scanned the report of how the French Navy had intercepted a German trawler carrying a cargo of arms bound for Iran. He looked up at the Commander enquiringly.

'That trawler is being held at this very moment in St Malo. Its cargo is intact pending diplomatic moves on whether the boat may be impounded or allowed to proceed. That is yesterday's paper. Your mission, Mr Brownlowe, is to secure from the boat enough arms and ammunition to equip one hundred men .... Are you with us?' Ronnie returned his attention to the newspaper and read the report thoroughly. He looked at each of the men in turn.

'Provided the planning of the mission is discussed and agreed between us, and that I feel confident that I have the necessary support, I agree.' Ronnie immediately sensed an air of relief. Each of them came forward to shake his hand. The Commander indicated that the meeting was terminated.

'Reinhard will show you to your quarters, then you'd probably like a good breakfast. We'll meet again later this evening perhaps ... and thank you.'

Ronnie followed the German downstairs and through a corridor to the back of the house. The German stopped in front of one of the many doors, unlocked it and pushed it open.

'This will be your room. You will notice the windows are barred from the outside and when we turn in at 9.30 you will be locked in. Please understand, it is for security.'

Ronnie threw his bag on to a single camp bed, the only piece of furniture in the uncarpeted and curtainless room.

'Now,' added the German, 'I will show you to the canteen.'

Ronnie followed into an old-fashioned Victorian kitchen. A swathy, dark-haired foreigner stood over a large gas cooker. Ronnie's stomach ached at the smell of the bacon sizzling in the pan. The cook turned towards them, a huge grin spread over his face.

'You eata de breakfast?'

'I'd love some thank you, I'm very hungry.'

'Please I bring you, *uno momento*.' The cook, still smiling broadly, nodded his head up and down like a clockwork toy and returned his attention to the stove.

Ronnie followed the German through a pair of swing

47

doors into a large dining hall, probably fifty to sixty foot long. Two tables, constructed from trestles and scaffold boards, ran virtually the full length of the room. There were at least sixty chairs set at each table. The German noticed a reaction.

'The majority of the men have not yet been summoned, they are not due for two or three weeks. I will leave you now. Perhaps you will eat and then wish to rest in your room. You may walk outside but please stay within fifty metres of the house. We will call for you when we are ready to discuss your involvement in closer detail.' The German turned on his heel and left Ronnie to sit at the table in splendid isolation. His eyes wanted to close; he felt heavy with sleep.

A clatter startled him to alertness as the little Italian kicked open the swing doors. He carried a plate of eggs, bacon and sausages in one hand and in the other a huge mug of steaming hot tea. He placed them on to the table, then rummaged in the stained pouch of his apron for a knife and fork.

'You wanta sugar?'

'No sugar, thank you,' answered Ronnie. The Italian stood by quietly, observing with great satisfaction as Ronnie tucked into the delicious breakfast. After several mouthfuls he was asked how many people had been cooked for that morning.

'My name is Renato,' was the reply, 'and I must not talk too much, but I tell you. I cook for ten. You eata now and enjoy.' Ronnie returned the little man's warm smile and was left to himself.

Several minutes later with such a good meal inside him, he felt much better and returned to his room. He eased off each shoe at the heel, took the folded blanket from the foot of the bed, lay down and pulled it over him.

Within a few seconds he had fallen into a deep and restful sleep.

4

Ronnie woke with a start; someone was knocking at the door. He glanced at his watch, it was 3.25 and he didn't feel too good. He sat up and leant against the wall. 'Come in.' He'd spoken too quietly. He cleared his throat and tried again. 'Come in.' It was Brucey.

'Major Teal wants to see you at four o'clock. You know the room, don't you?'

'Yes, thanks.' Ronnie answered. 'Is there a bathroom or somewhere I can have a wash?'

Ronnie slipped into his shoes, took the towel and toiletries from his duffle bag, and followed Brucey to a white-tiled communial shower room. Slatted benches lined one side, with a row of hat and coat hooks above.

'Used to be a school, this place.' Brucey offered an insight. 'Don't know how hot the water'll be, all depends whether the Itie's remembered to stoke up the boiler. You'll find your own way up to the Commander then?'

'Yes. Thanks, mate.' Brucey nodded and left the room.

Ronnie placed his things on one of the benches, undressed and with soap in hand stepped into one of the showers. He shifted an ivory-clad lever to HOT and waited as a trickle of brown water emerged from the large rose fitting above. In a few seconds the rust cleared, and full pressure was restored. Ronnie put his hand out to gauge the temperature. He stepped under the spray and felt it massage his tired shoulders and limbs. He lifted his

50

face to receive its invigorating therapy, running his fingers through his hair and down his neck. After a thorough wash he turned the ivory handle to OFF, stepped out and towelled himself dry.

Half-dressed in tee-shirt and underpants, he shaved at one of the twelve basins, dried his face and finished dressing. He felt a different person, rested, clean and alert, and in total readiness for whatever might lie ahead.

☆   ☆   ☆

Ronnie knocked on the committee room door, and was beckoned inside by the German, Reinhard. The fire still burned brightly; the table had been tidied; dirty plates removed. Jones and Sobbard were seated on either side of Commander Teal.

The German walked over to re-stoke the fire, then took a chair to the far end of the table. The Major spoke.

'We have no time to lose. We were aware of the contents of the impounded ship before it left Rotterdam. We informed the French of its existence, but we have no way of telling how long it will be held. You are to leave tonight.' The Major paused and handed Ronnie a large sealed envelope. 'All your instructions are in there.'

Ronnie started to open it but the Major restrained him. 'Not now. After we have discussed the plan, you'll have time to go over it in the quietness of your own room. Now, let me introduce you to the other two chaps who'll be travelling with you.' Reinhard stood up and went to the door. 'By the way,' continued the Major, 'for the sake of this operation I shall introduce you as Captain Brown.'

'Thanks for the promotion,' quipped Ronnie and turned in his seat to view the two men walking towards them. They stopped short of the table and stood to attention. The Major made the introductions and Ronnie stood to shake hands. 'This is Franco Gilberto, former sergeant and Portuguese commando; served in Angola 1974.' The stocky well-built ex-soldier grabbed Ronnie's hand firmly. 'And this,' continued the Major, 'is Jackson Rae. Former Private Royal Marine Commando, special boat squadron. Previously based at Poole, Dorset. Has not been involved in combat action.' Rae was probably no more than twenty-four to twenty-five years old, lean, agile, and in build a complete opposite of his Portuguese companion. The Major indicated they should sit down, and over the next hour the plan was discussed in minute detail. By the end of the briefing Ronnie felt a healthy respect for the way it had been thought through.

The Major picked up a large briefcase and placed it carefully on the table. He took out three oversized holsters and from one of them drew a stainless steel pistol with attached silencer. He held the barrel in the palm of his hand and gave an enquiring look. Ronnie seized the opportunity to show off his recognised speciality in weaponry.

'US Navy Mark 22, model O silenced 9mm pistol, manufactured by Smith and Wesson. Known as the "Hush Puppy," initially designed for use against enemy guard dogs. Also used extensively against humans in Vietnam. Slide lock action using special subsonic ammunition. An extremely effective and silent killer. The over-sized holsters designed so that the Hush Puppy can be carried with silencer affixed.'

'Excellent, excellent,' beamed the Major and handed the Portuguese and the young Englishman each a box of ammunition and the holstered pistols. He replaced the remaining pistol into its holster and passed it to Ronnie. 'You two chaps cut along now and meet up in the hall at 2000 hours and we wish you the best of luck . . . . No, not you Captain Brown, just a word.' The two men left the room, the Major continued. 'Those two won't let you down, they have each been issued passports in fictitious names. If you could let Reinhard have yours I think it would be opportune to alter it. Have you got it on you?' Ronnie took the battered, much-travelled document from his jacket pocket and passed it over.

'I'll have this back to you within the hour. Now, you have ample money, tickets, documentation, everything you need in that envelope. I suggest you go down to your room, check its contents, then go and have a slap-up meal in the mess.'

The Major stood up to shake Ronnie's hand. 'Good luck, Brown. If everything goes well, we'll see you back here in three days' time. If things do go wrong, we'll put our contingency plans into operation. Please realise, you're very much on your own and if you are caught we will expect complete discretion. In return, we would pay one half of your fee to your wife and family. Good luck Brown .... We look forward to seeing you on Saturday.'

Sobbard and Jones followed the Major with firm handshakes murmuring their support and best wishes. Ronnie thanked them and was summarily dismissed.

☆   ☆   ☆

Once in his room Ronnie opened the envelope and spread its contents over the bed. He replaced the items individually, retaining the twenty 500 franc notes (which he carefully folded and placed inside his jacket) and the six foolscap pages of typewritten text which he read thoroughly.

The whole plan was set out in hourly detail and, try as he might, he could find only one issue of contention. Theoretical planning in such detail usually bore little relation to practical application. The more detailed the plan, the more adaptable he would need to be. It was still a useful document to work through, and he felt increasingly confident.

The final page gave instructions that the document would be collected before departure, so he read it through again, imprinting on his mind names, times and places.

There was so much content, it was almost too much to take in. He decided to have another go after his meal.

The Portuguese and the Englishman were already seated. Ronnie sat opposite, glad of the opportunity to eat with them. It was essential that within a short space of time they form a relationship of particular understanding.

The project was discussed at length and in detail, each expressing his own opinion, hopes and fears. Ronnie found the Portuguese to be friendly, outgoing and relaxed. The other, Jackson Rae, was reserved and introvert, needing to be drawn on every issue.

Their attention was diverted as Renato kicked his way through the swing doors. He carried before him a steaming dish of Osso Bucco which he placed with great pride on to the table. He stood back and waited for their reaction.

Ronnie broke a large piece from a freshly baked loaf and dunked it into the rich gravy. He ate hungrily, then looked up at the Italian.

'*Il mangiare ... molto buono.*'

'*Grazie tante,*' beamed the Italian and with great aplomb returned to his kitchen.

The three men finished their meal as Ronnie summarised the plan, intent on implanting confidence into the minds of his collaborators. Over coffee, they exchanged past service records, special skills and any particular specialisation that might prove invaluable to the enterprise ahead.

✩ ✩ ✩

At 19.55 Ronnie, dressed in black, and carrying no baggage, waited in the hall. A single light bulb at the end of a twenty foot flex hung from the ceiling creating an eerie and surrealistic atmosphere.

Within minutes he was joined by the others, each clutching a holstered pistol and ammunition. Reinhard came down the staircase, he handed Ronnie his passport and the missing compass and led them outside.

A large animal transporter had been parked in the forecourt. Harry jumped from the driving seat as they were taken to the rear. He unscrewed the wing-nuts and was helped to lower the tailgate.

Forty penned sheep, thinking they were about to be released, began to bleat from the dimly lit interior. The three men followed the German up the ramp and into the lorry.

At the far end, set against the driver's cab, was a three-tiered bunk arrangement. The German pulled it towards him and half the backing wall to which it was fixed moved with it, revealing the steel cab lining, some two feet beyond. The German took the weapons and ammunition from each man and placed them into the recess. He pointed out the purpose-built rack to which twelve stun grenades were securely clipped, then pushed the bunk unit and locked it back into place.

Ronnie selected the bottom bunk, realising that the heat and smell of the sheep would most likely rise above him. Franco climbed on to the top and obviously thought he'd got the best spot. Ronnie couldn't help a smile; he already felt a great liking for this genial character. In contrast, his dislike for the German intensified when, without a word of encouragement, the rear was slammed shut and they were left in total darkness. They could hear only the squeak from the securing bolts and a muffled exchange of words. The cab door banged; the engine

55

started. Ronnie felt a sensation of movement, gear changes and then the throb of the powerful diesel engine, its steady rhythm and vibration enticing sleep. Soon he too had joined the sheep in passive acceptance of their fate.

☆　☆　☆

Ronnie woke suddenly. The sheep bleated loudly, the ramp was being lowered and yellow light spilled into the interior from the compound lighting. A figure walked up the ramp, instantly recognised as Harry by his purposeful gait. Franco and Rae eased themselves down on to the floor and stretched their aching limbs. They seemed slightly unsure of what was expected of them. Ronnie took the initiative and they followed him outside.

'These sheep have got to be fed and watered,' said Harry without a word of greeting. 'I'll do it with you now so you know how to go about it. The boss said it's to be done regularly in case you get stopped by animal welfare inspectors.'

The feed and containers of water were stored in compartments on each side of the lorry's exterior and within ten minutes each animal was given a measured portion.

Harry told the three 'mercenaries' he'd be there waiting when they drove off the boat on Saturday morning. He wished them luck and, without looking back, disappeared into the darkness beyond the fringe of the compound lighting. Ronnie and Franco closed the ramp and Rae secured the bolts. It was 4.30.

It had taken seven hours to get to Portsmouth. Ronnie was almost sure they had been somewhere in Wales.

He suggested they find somewhere for coffee. The passenger reception building was shut, so they walked back through the compound and out of the dock area to look for a tea kiosk or an all-night café. Nothing seemed to be open so, reluctantly and somewhat depressed, they retraced their steps.

By the time they got back, the reception building was open, deserted except for an old man cleaning up behind the canteen. After a heated argument he eventually served them coffee and a couple of bars of chocolate which Ronnie paid for with the £5 note. The old man examined the torn-off corner and reluctantly handed him two £1 coins and some small change. Ronnie purposely refused to offer a tip and joined the others at their table.

Whilst sharing out the chocolate, he decided that now was a good time to re-establish contact. Keep the Department happy, prevent them taking further action over which he might have no control.

'You chaps wait here. I'm going back to check no one's nosing around the lorry. Be back in a few minutes.' Ronnie walked out of the building. He looked behind in case he was being followed, then made for a group of call boxes.

Selecting one hidden from direct view of the reception centre, he slipped a coin into the slot and dialled; the call was answered almost directly.

'Ladybird Fashions,' Ronnie allowed the formal reply to prattle on; he waited for the bleep to signal his input. 'Field Officer 36 calling. My code connection is ASCII. I wish to make a report.' He could hear the automatic digital connection.

'This is Arthur. Please make your report, 36.' It was a different voice. No doubt on that particular extension all shift officers would be code-named Arthur. Ronnie spoke briefly and concisely.

'Tomorrow morning at 0200 hours we are going to board the German vessel presently impounded in St Malo. Our objective: to secure enough arms and ammunition to equip one hundred men. I specifically request that no serious attempt be made to prevent us achieving this mission. By ensuring our success I will gain the confidence of the organisation and will be instructed as to their ultimate objectives. In order to save taking lives unnecessarily can I have your guarantee on this?' Ronnie awaited the reply. 'Did you read me?'

'Yes, 36, message received and understood. Can we get back to you? I am not cleared to make this decision.'

'No, I can't be contacted,' Ronnie answered, now wishing he'd left things well alone. 'It's imperative that I secure these weapons and I will, with or without your assistance.' Arthur now proved himself to be more than just a nuisance. 'Look here, 36, if we are able to get the Frogs to play ball, we'll have the ship's engines idling as a sign of their collusion. If not then you are on your own . . . . Good luck, 36.'

'Thank you. I'll be in touch.' Ronnie replaced the receiver.

Within half an hour passengers and uniformed personnel began to trickle in. The canteen was now properly staffed and operating efficiently. The morning papers arrived and Ronnie skimmed through the *Daily Mail*. He found what he was looking for on page five, and read it out aloud.

> 'The German-registered trawler held by French authorities under the Anti-Terrorism Act of 1969 was subject to diplomatic moves from the Iranian Embassy, questioning the validity of this action and seeking to have the restraint lifted. A decision by the French Government is expected within the next 36 hours.'

Before it could be discussed, an announcement boomed over the loud speakers that foot passengers should proceed

58

through passport control for embarkation. Drivers were asked to return to their vehicles.

☆   ☆   ☆

The cab was a three-seater. Franco and Rae climbed into the passenger seats as Ronnie started up the motor. An official came to the window and asked for tickets; he tore out the counterfoil and placed a small red sticker in the corner of the windscreen. Ronnie edged up behind a large container truck and moved on slowly towards passport control.

The three passports were checked individually, 'Thank you, Mr Green.' The officer handed them back. 'Can I see your licence to transport livestock and the veterinary certificate?' Ronnie smiled, and thought: 'Green – a rather unoriginal alias.' He had never been keen on his own surname. On one occasion years ago, the Department had given him the alias of Brett-Thompson; he'd rather liked that.

He pulled the documentation from his pocket; the official scrutinized the paperwork and handed it back. Gesturing that everything was in order, the barrier was lifted and they were directed towards the loading ramp.

The rattle of the steel slats distressed the sheep and they started to bleat as Ronnie drove down and through the cavernous bow into the hold. He parked where directed, close behind the container truck, turned off the engine and pulled firmly on the handbrake.

As the three men got out, dockers were already chaining the wheels to large hooks welded into the deck. Ronnie locked the cab and led the way through a heavy steel hatchway and up two flights of stairs into the reception lounge. He passed their tickets over the desk.

'Green, Schoefield and Rodriguez,' he gave their pseudonyms. 'You have a cabin reserved for us.' The purser looked down his lists.

'Yes sir, thank you,' he beckoned to one of the stewards who led them through a companionway to a three-berth cabin with a shower and loo. 'Would you like breakfast in your cabin, gentlemen, or would you prefer the restaurant?' 'We'll eat in the restaurant, thank you,' Ronnie answered. 'How long before we leave?'

'Three-quarters of an hour, sir. We cast off at 7.30.'

Ronnie gave the steward a pound coin and decided to take a shower.

Holding his face up to the gentle spray he washed away the sleep from his eyes and the smell of the sheep from his nostrils. He felt refreshed and when finished he suggested the others do likewise. Franco declined, saying he'd leave it till later.

'See that you do,' quipped Ronnie, 'otherwise those guards on the trawler'll smell you coming.' Franco dangled his legs over the edge of the bunk and smiled broadly.

'Only Maria, when I get back to Lisbon, she smell me coming . . . I take a shower after breakfast.'

'Okay, you rogue,' chuckled Ronnie, 'we'll wait whilst Rae takes his, then go up for a meal.'

The dining room was quite luxurious; the head waiter in white jacket and black bow tie showed them to a table where they had a good view of the quay.

There being no guarantee from where or when their next meal was coming, they indulged in a hearty English breakfast washed down with several cups of tea.

Conversation flowed easily until they noticed movement on the quay below. Dockers disengaged mooring ropes and the ship's engines previously pulsing at a steady idling speed suddenly increased their revolution. Vibration could be felt through bone and limb as side thrust pushed the ship's bow away from the quay. The tempo of the engines changed again and the ship eased forward.

All three men were silent, each deep within his own thought and personal nostalgia.

☆   ☆   ☆

Ronnie needed some fresh air. 'You chaps go back to the cabin. I'm going to take a walk round the deck, I don't feel too good.'

Making his way out on to the promenade deck he felt the fresh wind and salt spray sting his face. The decks were empty. The cold dampness of the early-morning mist and the heavy rolling swell encouraged passengers to seek the comforts and warmth of their own cabins. He leaned against the ship's rail and gazed out into the grey abyss, glad nevertheless of the opportunity of being alone. It was time to re-assess his loyalties.

Though detesting the secret service, he loved his country dearly. In the past, issues had been clear-cut. Increasingly he was finding that the present situation was not quite so simple. Whilst attempting to form an understanding with his fellow adventurers in order to succeed in a relatively dangerous mission, he was expected to denounce them and their employers at some time in the future. The Major and the other two had seemed neither criminal, cruel nor subversive. Better had they been more like the unpleasant Reinhard, providing a clear definition between right and wrong, good and evil.

There were also financial aspects to consider. If brought to a successful conclusion there was a guaranteed minimum payment of £210,000. The Department's own contribution would already have been made, Francine's account credited with £10,000 and the balance paid into his Zurich account. Darling Francine, if only he could see her face when she checked her next statement. At first

61

she'd wonder whether the bank had made an error, but eventually she'd realise where the money had come from. Even the bank in Zurich might be surprised to find his own account resurrected. Surprises for everyone, but some surprises he could do without. This sudden need to question loyalties!

Previous missions had either been made in the company of men from his own unit, or he'd acted alone and on his own initiative. This operation fell into a different category altogether; it required deceit and betrayal.

Ronnie thought long and hard about it. So much would depend on those who were actually backing the organisation. The Major had mentioned 'international contacts.' They had been able to make contact with the French Government, they'd previous knowledge of the trawler's illegal cargo. These international contacts were most likely financing the operation.

If it were the IRA or some international terrorist organisation the decision would be made for him. If, on the other hand, it were simply a group of high-powered individuals planning to relieve the finance industry of a million or two then it was an entirely different matter. For the moment the issue would remain unresolved. At some time over the next two or three weeks circumstances would hopefully provide the answer.

Having thought the issues through Ronnie felt relieved. He shivered and returned to the warmth of the cabin.

Rae, propped up in the top bunk, was reading the newspaper; Franco was in the shower. No word was spoken. Ronnie settled into his bunk and thought through the brief exchange he'd made with London. There had been so much left unsaid. What if the French did not agree to co-operate? Might they then reinforce the guarding of the vessel? The key to success was in surprise. Ronnie felt sure London would recognise this point, but there would be no half-way measures now, whatever was decided. Either things would be twice as difficult or twice as easy.

Enmeshed as he was in the unwelcome role of double agent he trod a dangerous path of indecision. Yet again he felt confused and lethargic. It was to be a long and boring journey.

5

It was 4.25 in the afternoon when passengers were called to rejoin their vehicles. The nine-hour journey had seemed an eternity. The three men made their way down to the hold and climbed into the cab.

The grinding winches pulled the ship hard against the quay. A scraping and clanking echoed through the ship as the bows opened. A cold grey light spilled into the hold. The ramp was secured and vehicles started to move out.

Ronnie coughed against putrid fumes as a huge pall of blue smoke puffed from the exhaust of the container truck in front of them. The truck moved off and they followed it out on to the ramp and up into the freight compound beyond.

The half-light that heralded the end of a cold and unfriendly day silhouetted the grey granite walls of the enclosed town beyond. Ronnie felt a chill run through him. The fortress town generated an atmosphere of foreboding and invincibility. It needed a conscious effort to rid himself of the sensation. He pulled up behind the truck and turned off the engine.

'Right, lads; whilst waiting for customs, you feed and water the animals. I'll freshen things up with clean straw.'

Whilst Franco and Rae attended the sheep, Ronnie shook out the bales and spread the straw in generous quantity on top of the original bedding which had by now become wet and foul. Something caught his attention and he noticed two uniformed officials observing them from the ramp. Each beamed obvious approval. Ronnie walked forward smiling and was asked in perfect English for the required documentation.

The papers were duly provided and without serious scrutiny the counterfoils were torn out and the top copy returned. In a polite and courteous manner, the Frenchman instructed that they should now proceed to passport control after which they would be free to leave. Ronnie, careful not to show his relief that no effort had been made to search the van, thanked them.

Franco and Rae remained unaware that the concern shown to the animals at that particular time had been part of the plan. The timing had been impeccable but it had been achieved rather more through luck than precise judgement.

Closing the ramp, they drove over to passport control where they were again cleared without question.

Ronnie looked at his watch; it was 5.25. He drove on towards a compound well away from the jurisdiction of immigration or customs and parked.

He locked the doors and padlocked the securing bolts to the ramp. Everything was safe and secure, and now seemed a good opportunity to reconnoitre. At his suggestion they set off at a brisk walk.

The harbour area encompassed a large marina, full to capacity even though it was still early season. The three men passed by the yacht club and turned left towards the deep-water quay. The adjoining main road and promenade were busy. Traffic and pedestrians streamed in and out of the town through several deep archways placed strategically within the sixty-foot perimeter walls. Ronnie stopped in his tracks as he recognised the magnificent high masted 'J'-class yacht *Valsheda* moored against the quay. His own father had sailed aboard her before the war. Many a time he'd proudly shown his son photographs of the yacht and talked of those happy, exciting times. Built in 1932, she had enjoyed much of the glamour and indulgence of the pre-war era but, with the austere years that followed, had been abandoned and for many years left to rot on the mud flats. Four years ago she had been purchased by the current owner, who had restored the yacht to all her former dignity and beauty. Two young men, dressed in navy blue guernseys and blue cords, were on deck tidying the halyards. Ronnie moved on, worried lest his obvious interest might lead to conversation.

Franco and Rae hung back as Ronnie, with hands in pockets, strolled on alone past a small coastal freighter and the pilot boat. Both were of little consequence but the next ship along Ronnie recognised as *The Eridan* M541, lead ship of the tripartite French/Dutch/Belgian mine-hunter programme. It was fairly obvious that this vessel had intercepted the trawler and escorted her into St Malo, and that she was now standing guard. Beyond her could now be seen the black hull of the trawler and, as he drew closer, interlocking metal barriers guided him some fifteen or twenty feet away from the edge of the quay. A lone sailor with an MAS 5.56mm assault rifle slung over his shoulder stood guard at the gangplank. Two others, similarly armed, were aboard, one at the bow facing the quayside, the other at the stern faced the sea. Ronnie ambled on, determining as far as possible the general layout. The stern hold, covered by tarpaulins, seemed the most probable location of the impounded cargo. Access would not be easy.

Already past, he turned and retraced his steps, meeting up with the others just beyond the yacht. Deep in thought, the three men made their way back to the lorry.

After a great deal of thought and discussion, a suggested plan of action best suited to the situation, and based on the assumption of non-co-operation from the French, was agreed upon. Rae had contributed with several valid observations whilst Franco, in his relaxed matter-of-fact way, seemed happy to go along with anything. It was now nearly seven o'clock and Ronnie agreed to the request that they go into town for a meal.

As they again passed by the yacht club Rae was the first to spot the navy-blue van parked among the members' cars. He discreetly singled it out to Ronnie. Their confidence in the Organisation and its arrangements grew by the hour.

The three men entered the old town through its main archway. Many tables and chairs were set outside the garishly lit bars in the main square. Few people sat there; it was too late and too cold. St Malo at this time of the year came to life only from Friday night to Monday morning when the Parisians motored down for *le long weekend*. Ronnie would have preferred the town to be busier; the more people about, the less conspicuous they would appear. He chose the most crowded restaurant on the opposite side of the square.

La Duchess Anne was warmly lit and inviting, most of the tables already taken. The tinkle of cutlery against porcelain merged with the sound of excited social chatter. Large silver trays of *fruit-de-mer*, garnished with seaweed and supported on silver stands, decorated the red gingham table cloths. Canteens of home-made soup steamed heat into the atmosphere, as French bread, broken from *baquet* by hand, tantalised the appetite.

Franco's face creased in a smile of anticipation as Madame approached them. She showed them to a small table in the far corner laid for two. Franco and Rae sat down; Ronnie waited as she fetched another chair. Offering profuse apologies for the lack of space, she laid the extra place.

The next two hours passed quickly. Feeling relaxed and content, they ate the most delicious food, excellently cooked and presented. No mention was made of the planned mission. Each man felt a need to blot out all thought of the impending action. Ronnie learnt a good deal about his two companions as they talked freely of family ties and previous experiences.

Much of it confirmed his own conception. Franco warm-blooded and gregarious, with a girlfriend in Lisbon and a wife and four children in Madeira; Rae, cool and retiring, divorced and alone.

More wine was requested but Ronnie forbade it. They wanted a brandy but he would not allow that either. Without malice they sipped at their coffee, now silent and deep in thought.

Once finished, the bill was quickly settled and they returned to the lorry to while away the remaining hours.

✿　✿　✿

Ronnie put on his jacket and got out of the cab to rouse the others from the rear.

The ramp was down, and the fresh night air ventilated the interior.

Ronnie had difficulty in picking out the two men and was glad that both were dressed in black. Franco had already pulled the bunk unit away from the cab and was strapping the Hush Puppy holster around his waist. Rae already wore his and having removed his belt was in the process of clipping a fourth grenade to it.

Franco handed Ronnie the remaining pistol, and

68

reached down into the dark recess to retrieve his old West German Airborne MK3 Stiefelmesser boot-knife. He smiled at it with obvious affection and tucked it between sock and leather.

Feeling as ready as they'd ever be, the three men closed the ramp, padlocked it and made their way to the car park. They passed no one, their shadowy progress lit only by the overspill from the main-road overhead lighting. The car park by comparison was in complete darkness; they moved stealthily between the numerous parked cars towards the blue Renault van.

Ronnie went straight to the rear of the vehicle and extracted the key that had been lodged within the exhaust pipe. He unlocked the rear doors; Franco and Rae jumped in. Ronnie closed the doors behind them. He went to the left-hand side of the van, unlocked the driver's door, reached into the glove compartment and removed a torch which he passed behind to Franco.

Rae then took off his holster and grenade belt, and slipped out of his clothes, Franco held the torch and passed him the rubber wet-suit. As Rae struggled to pull it on, Ronnie opened the rear doors and with Franco's help removed the two sections of meshed trawling net, two coils of rope and other sturdy equipment. Rae now joined them and together they extracted the deflated rubber dinghies and dragged them some distance away.

Ronnie pulled the red toggle and with a hiss and a groan the dinghy inflated, unwrapping itself in metamorphosis from an unrecognisable package into a sturdy craft. The remaining equipment was placed inside it as Ronnie inflated the other two. He then fetched the oars and locked the van. The others, each with an empty dinghy on his back, moved quietly and efficiently through the darkness towards the slipway. Five minutes later Franco returned and with Ronnie's help carried the loaded dinghy down to the water's edge. Rae had already launched the others and had tied them together, stem to stern.

The loaded dinghy was slipped into the water and Rae climbed over to secure it to the others. Then, taking the oars from Ronnie, he climbed back into the leading boat and slipped them into the rowlocks. It was five minutes before low tide; the wind had dropped; the water was still.

'Good luck,' Ronnie whispered and without waiting for a reply turned away. Franco gave a grin and a wave, walked backwards three steps and raising his arm in a final gesture of friendship watched as Rae moved off into the darkness.

The two men returned to the van. The engine started on the third turn of the key and they drove off, unhurriedly, towards St Malo.

Minutes later passing under the main access archway they'd walked through just five hours previously, they followed the internal ring-road and pulled up opposite the archway nearest to the moored trawler. Ronnie looked at his watch; it was ten minutes before two o'clock. He turned off the sidelights and ignition and waited silently in darkness for another three minutes, then gestured Franco that it was time. They closed the doors quietly and moved across the narrow road to the archway.

Keeping tight against the wall they peered across the main road towards the quay. Surprisingly the area was not floodlit. Instead, a solitary bulkhead light silhouetted a lone sentry at the foot of the gangplank. Two other lights on the stern and bow winches dimly lit the aft and foredecks; a guard stood at each. Ronnie checked the time once more – two minutes to go! He strained his ears to catch a sound of the ship's engines, and heard nothing. He hadn't really expected co-operation between London and

Paris, but at least it did not appear that the French authorities had been alerted in any way. Either London had made no attempt at an arrangement or someone had handled the matter with tact and discretion.

Ronnie psyched himself up to make the move. Suddenly, his mental preparation was rudely interrupted as early-morning revellers shouted their goodnights. Voices and the sound of laughter echoed and reverberated between the tall buildings and narrow cobbled streets. Car doors banged shut, a screech of tyre wheelspin, and the whine of over-revved engines faded into the distance. The Portuguese placed his hand on Ronnie's shoulder in a further gesture of comradeship. He smiled, and in an instant disappeared through the arch and away to the left.

Ronnie moved to the right. He skirted the perimeter wall for fifty yards then darted across to the other side of the road. Quite openly he walked along the edge of the quay towards the trawler, swaying a little as if under the influence of a hard night's drinking. He hummed the Marseillaise just loud enough to attract attention then bumped into the temporary barrier, sprawling across it.

Fully aware of the guard advancing with the machine rifle pointed menacingly towards him, Ronnie stood up and smiled broadly. He put a cigarette in his mouth and fumbling, struck a match. The sailor walked out of the light and into the shadows. The guard on the foredeck called out to his friend, asking in French if he needed assistance. Whether he heard or not the sailor made no reply. Now just ten feet away he waved the rifle aggressively towards the intruder: '*Allez vite, dépêchez-vous!*'

'It's all right mate,' Ronnie spluttered. 'Don't get your knickers in a twist,' he made a mock salute and stumbled on his way. The sailor called reassuringly towards his friend on the foredeck. '*Ce n'est rien, Jules. Ce'est un cochon Anglais qui m'emmerde!*' He followed the 'drunk' muttering

71

obscenities under his breath and when he reached the gangplank he retook his station, the incident already forgotten, passed off simply as a minor disturbance. He stood to attention and thought of Louise.

☆   ☆   ☆

Once attention had been diverted, Franco made his move. Darting across the road he crouched in the shadows beyond the trawler's stern and crept forward to the edge of the barrier. In a movement of athletic agility, he was on board, pressed against the superstructure, out of view from aft or foredeck.

As Ronnie weaved his way noisily along the quay under close scrutiny, Franco eased his dark form around the cockpit to the port side. Like a black cat, with instinctive guile, silently and with deadly efficiency, he stalked his prey.

Now ten feet behind the distracted man, Franco removed the silent killer from its holster. He could feel the primitive excitement of the hunter stir within him. Two strides on, he sprang, his left arm seizing the man's throat in a vice-like grip, cold steel of the silencer pushed hard against the temple.

☆   ☆   ☆

Placing the oars into the water and with the two other dinghies in tow, Rae pulled away from the slip. Wherever possible he kept close to the cover offered by the harbour walls making wide detours when confronted with a moored ship or yacht.

Water lapped against the rubber bow at each pull of the oars. He heard a car door slam and the revving of an engine echo across the water. He heard the moon as it moved between cloud and clear.

Now he could see the white shimmer of the *Valsheda* and the minesweeper beyond, Rae paddled at his left blade and steered into middle water. He was now having to take a stronger pull. The tide had turned and was beginning to flood.

Despite the chill of the night air, his body felt hot and clammy under the rubber suit. He rowed on past the minesweeper. Internal lights radiated from its portholes and sent ripples of gold across the undulating tide towards him. He crossed over them returning to darkness, the water now black and uninviting. He could see the aft light of the trawler, now the foredeck light. Rae continued another hundred yards and turned the craft towards the quay. The dinghies now ran with the tide and needed little propulsion. He steered his silent path to the bow of the ironclad craft.

Catching hold of the front anchor chain he secured the dinghies. He could hear muffled voices from above. Quickly he buckled on the holster and grenade belt, took the heavy link between hands and feet and climbed resolutely upwards.

With great effort he stretched his arm far above, locked his fingers around the gunwale and lifted himself just far enough to peer over the foredeck. The guard was facing away from him and called out to someone on the quay. Waiting a few seconds, Rae heard the reply and eased his body over the gunwale and on to the deck. Removing the Hush Puppy from its holster he closed distance between himself and his adversary, moving one step at a time, slowly, silently. The man started to turn, but before he had a chance to defend himself Rae was on him. He pushed the pistol hard into the man's throat, deep into a pressure point. The guard froze, incapable of further action.

Franco, speaking fluent French, ordered his captive to remove the magazine from the rifle. The guard unclipped it from behind the trigger and pistol grip, and surrendered the rifle. Franco placed it on the deck together with the detached magazine, then told the man to feign illness and call to the guard on the gangplank for help.

He was young and only too willing to oblige. Beads of sweat ran from his forehead. He was frightened – terrified; one wrong move and he was dead. He wanted his mother. Franco goaded him into action with a sharp tap on the temple with the side of the barrel.

'*Fernand, ici un moment ... Fernand*!' He called out just loud enough to reach his friend without attracting anyone aboard the minesweeper.

Franco withdrew to the gunwale and crouched in shadow, holding the sailor in the sights of his pistol.

The young man feigned a severe attack of stomach cramps; he sank to his knees.

'*Fernand, s'il vous plaît. Je suis malade. Venez vite*!'

Believing the drunken English swine offered no further threat, Fernand left his post and on reaching the aft deck immediately became concerned over the condition of his friend.

Concern was short-lived, his sensibilities removed with a vicious karate chop to the back of the neck. Ronnie took the rifle, detached the magazine and placed them on the deck alongside the other. 'Well done, Franco. Get them to pull that tarpaulin off. Make sure they realise one false move and they're dead men, and tell them quick – quick!'

As Ronnie helped the dazed man to his feet, Rae appeared, pushing the guard from the foredeck in front of him.

The three captives stood together, sullen-faced, as

Franco translated Ronnie's orders and, encouraged by three pistols pointed menacingly at them, they moved towards the covered hold. Franco cut the securing ropes and the tarpaulin was pulled aside.

Much to Ronnie's surprise and relief it revealed an open hatchway set within the fabric of the heavy wood slats that bridged the hold. He peered down inside and signalled the three reluctant guards down the iron ladder into the dark chasm below. Franco disappeared after them.

'Rae, bring the dinghies this end and get the ropes and net aboard. I may want those three battery floodlights too. There's probably no light down there.' Ronnie looked back into the hold; Franco called from the darkness.

'I've found a switch. Cover the opening again before I switch on.' Ronnie pulled the tarpaulin over the opening and squeezed under himself, finishing the job from the top of the ladder. Franco threw the switch. The bright bulkhead lighting revealed the precious cargo.

Numerous boxwood containers were stacked neatly to one side from floor to ceiling. Other containers with lids prized open lay haphazardly over the remainder of the floor.

Ronnie tore off the partially closed lids, revealing virgin weaponry, still caked in a protective coating of grease. He picked out a small compact machine piston just over thirty-three centimetres long and held it up to Franco.

'Polish ... the 9mm PM-63 machine pistol. Fires 9mm Makarov rounds in fifteen, twenty-five, forty-round magazines. Fully loaded they only weigh 1.8kg. It's exactly what we need, I can't...' Ronnie's enthusiasm was interrupted by a rustle from above. He swung his pistol towards the intrusion.

'It's me – Rae!' Ronnie breathed a sigh of relief. He

realised only too well that the guards' absence from the deck might be spotted at any minute. 'Well done, mate. Chuck the nets down.'

Ronnie unfolded them on the steel floor below and instructed the three guards to remove the weaponry from the crates on to the net. He counted in fifty then folded them over and threaded the net together with the end of the rope which Rae dangled from above.

Ronnie signalled that two of the guards should follow him and climbed the ladder. As Franco doused the lights, Rae pulled the tarpaulin away and the three men scrambled out. Then pulling together they hauled the loaded net and negotiated it on to the deck.

Rae climbed back over the gunwale, took hold of the rope he'd tied previously and slid down it. The loaded net was lowered gently over the side and Rae guided it into one of the empty dinghies, untying the rope.

The exercise was repeated with another netful of fifty guns and then a third load, consisting of ten cases of 9mm Makarov ammunition plus the three 5.56mm MAS assault rifles and magazines taken from the guards.

With the final load successfully negotiated into his own dinghy, Rae pulled on his flippers, untied the fender and slipped over the side into the icy water. He drew a sharp intake of breath against the cold and remained motionless until the water, trapped between body and rubber, warmed to an acceptable level. Catching hold of the painter to the lead dinghy, he floated on his back and guided the heavily laden craft away from the hull.

The current was running strong. A black swirling tide in full flood pushed in from the ocean beyond, carrying before it the flotsam of harbour waste, finally to release it to the stillness of some dark eddy beyond.

☆ ☆ ☆

Ronnie pushed the guards away from the side of the vessel towards the hatchway and indicated they should climb back into the hold. They offered no resistance. He followed them down and after reassuring Franco that all was well up above they unclipped the grenades from their belts and placed one in each hand of the startled captives.

The spring-levered detonators were gripped hard against the cold steel shells and knuckles shone white as Ronnie removed the pins. He then produced a roll of Elastoplast from his jacket and Franco cut off pieces to form a gag.

Switching off the lights, the two companions climbed the ladder and pulled it up after them. They lowered it over the gunwale into the water and let it go to disappear with the morning tide.

Finally they refolded the tarpaulin over the hold and, keeping close to the superstructure, eased their way towards the gangplank. All was quiet; the road and surrounding areas appeared deserted.

Now they moved with speed and agility and crossed on to the quay. Sprinting, they vaulted the barriers and covered the distance to the town perimeter wall in a matter of seconds. No alarm sounded, no voice of authority, no siren, no floodlight.

The two men, pressed hard against the cool granite, moved within its shadow to the relative safety of the cavernous archway. Now they stood erect and walked casually to the van.

Ronnie started the engine with the first turn of the key, executed a three-point turn and drove at moderate speed towards the yacht club.

As they passed through the main gateway, he let out a yell of delight. Franco grinned broadly. Tension previously controlled, ran out of their fingertips and discharged itself into the air they breathed. Everything had gone their way. Luck had favoured them.

They drove into the club car park, switched off the lights and backed up towards the slipway. Ronnie turned off the ignition and allowed the van to run down the incline to within fifteen feet of the water's edge. They got out and stood straining for sight or sound of Rae, worried more for his safety than any possible loss of their prize.

The rising tide lapped at their feet; they moved back a pace. Ronnie thought he heard a sound. He thought he noticed a movement, there . . . beyond!

A muffled explosion echoed across the water, quickly followed by five more, reverberating in quick succession. Seconds later the crack of a flare trajected high above the town, lighting up the harbour and much of the immediate area. Ronnie picked out the silhouette of the three dinghies some fifty yards distant. He could see the splash as an invisible arm sought to guide them towards the slip. Ronnie called across the water. 'Here, Rae, here! Come on lad, not far to go.' The splashing increased with the greater effort required to propel the heavily laden dinghies out and away from the general stream of the current. Franco waded into the water and with outstretched hands managed to catch hold of the painter. Rae swam to the rear and guided the craft in as a wave lifted and surged them on to the slip.

Franco scrambled out, soaked to the waist. He hung on to the rope as the wave subsided, leaving the dinghies stranded.

Rae began to remove the rubber suit. He was shivering with cold and unable to help as the others transferred the guns and ammunition into the back of the van. Once loaded, he was helped inside and sat on a box of ammunition. The doors were closed and Ronnie drove the short distance to the truck, where the arsenal was stowed away and hidden behind the folding bunks.

Franco volunteered to return the van to the club car park. He drove off with a grinding of the gears. Ronnie winced, and climbed into the front of the truck to wait.

In attempting to restore his body temperature, Rae had wrapped himself in blankets taken from the bunks. When he felt able to talk they discussed the operation in detail. It had all gone so well, no lives lost nor even serious injury.

The two men surmised that the guards' absence had finally been noticed, that they'd been found and on reaching the deck had discarded the grenades over the side. The pandemonium raging in the vicinity of the two ships at that very moment was easily imagined. It would not be long before the search would be extended beyond the immediate vicinity.

Ronnie looked at his watch ... it was not quite five o'clock. The next boat was due in from Portsmouth at six thirty. Their departure would coincide with its arrival. They would head away under the cover of the traffic and freight as it rolled out of the compound and away from the town towards the industrial cities that lay to the south.

Ronnie felt tired and weary; he longed for a hot coffee. He began to doze off but was startled awake by the rattling of the cab door handle. He breathed a sigh of relief seeing Franco's strained face peering through the window. He unlocked the door and moved over to make room.

Franco was numb with cold, his clothes saturated from the waist down. Rae offered him the blankets and they wrapped one around his legs, and the other around the shoulders, folding it across his chest.

The Portuguese mumbled his thanks, then rubbed his legs vigorously through the blanket to increase circulation. Partially revived, he lay back and shut his eyes. The others did likewise; no one felt too much like talking, the euphoria had passed.

79

Ronnie dozed off into a dream-laden sleep, which seemed to last only an instant. A ship's siren sounding off close by woke him with a start. It was no longer dark, but the half-light of dawn.

He checked the time, 6.25. Franco and Rae slept on; he waited for the boat to dock, for freight to clear customs.

The intensity of daylight increased by the minute. The sky heralded a crisp spring morning, it was cloudless and the wind had dropped to a whisper.

6

The first lorry to disembark rolled out of the compound. The sound and vibration of the diesel engine woke the others up as Ronnie drove off to edge their vehicle between a large removal van and a container truck.

A gendarme, with the aid of a whistle, stopped oncoming traffic and directed the 'convoy' into the main road. Ronnie followed to the right and two kilometres on joined a dual carriageway heading towards Rennes.

Warmth from the motor circulated through the cab and eased the chill from their bones. Franco rolled up his trousers and rubbed his legs dry with the blanket.

'What time are they expecting us?' he asked. Rae replied. 'Between 9 and 9.30. How far we got to go?' Ronnie looked at his watch. 'Not far... St Malo to Rennes is about one and a half hour's drive; we're likely to be stopped about five miles short. About another forty minutes I'd say. We're ahead of schedule.'

A mile further on they pulled up at a roadside hotel. Franco rolled down his trousers and tried to smooth out the wrinkles.

'We've got twenty minutes,' said Ronnie. 'Let's go and get something to eat.' The three men crossed the yard and entered the eighteenth-century ivy-clad building.

A small group of French farm workers at the bar were engrossed in conversation. An old man sat at one of the tables, a glass of pastis and a half-filled decanter of water

81

in front of him. Ronnie took out a new fifty franc note and told the others to sit down. 'What would you like?' he asked. 'Coffee? Brandy? Croissants?'

'Yes please.' Franco grinned.

Fifteen minutes later, warmed and nourished, they returned to the truck and continued on their way. The road was becoming increasingly busy. Traffic thundered past in the fast lane as Ronnie kept unobtrusively to the nearside, at a steady forty-five miles per hour.

A few miles on the situation changed. Some obstruction ahead was causing a jam. The build-up increased until both lanes were blocked solid. Ronnie eased the truck into second gear and moved forward at a walking pace until they were brought to a standstill.

Traffic began inching forward again and was diverted into a single lane. Ronnie allowed a Mercedes to pull in front of him and continued at snail's pace until at last they reached the obstruction.

A massive Peugeot tractor had been deliberately parked to block the outside lane. Its driver was in the process of painting a slogan of protest across its windscreen. PRODUIT FRANÇAIS OUI. PRODUIT ANGLAIS NON! Behind it, a trailer, another tractor, a battered old van, farm machinery, a lorry. In all Ronnie counted at least twenty vehicles parked one behind the other. All except the leading tractor were unattended. A large group of people milled around. Most of them carried placards bearing anti-English and anti-Belgian slogans. The Mercedes was waved through; the crowd seemed to become more agitated and hammered their placards against the side of the truck. The sheep inside bleated with alarm.

A tractor emerged from a sideroad to block their progress; the banging on the sides increased. Ronnie checked the doors were securely locked; the mood of the crowd was becoming violent.

Someone hammered on the window and indicated that he should turn off the main road. Part of the crowd surged in front of the truck, waving their arms excitedly. Ronnie re-engaged the clutch and eased forward. He pulled into the minor D-road, where another lorry blocked any possibility of escape. Two men lounged against its bonnet.

Ronnie was signalled to wind down his window. He did so, just enough to hear one of the men speak in a heavy French accent.

'Monsieur, we have nothing against you. As farmers on this district we will not allow produce Anglais to be sold in competition with our own. Especially sheep. We will not damage the animals.... It is true you carry sheep?' Ronnie nodded; he unlocked the door and got out as did Franco and Rae who stood behind protectively.

Walking to the rear of the truck as instructed, they unpadlocked the bolts and lowered the ramp. The sheep, wild-eyed, struggled to turn their heads towards the daylight.

Another man appeared from behind the lorry. Strapped to his back, he carried a copper tank and in his hand, a three-foot brass tube. He walked up the ramp without a word of explanation.

Ronnie followed out of curiosity and watched as the Frenchman pumped a lever, held the nozzle towards the nearest sheep and opened a small valve.

With a hiss, a fine mist of red dye showered the coat of the terrified animal. He continued on to the next, pumping the lever spasmodically to restore the pressure. The air became difficult to breathe, and Ronnie went back outside.

Noticing his concern, one of the Frenchmen assured him the dye would in no way harm the sheep, but the factory they were consigned to in Rennes would not accept them. The dye would contaminate the blood and it would be three months before the authorities would pass them for slaughter. 'You may go now,' he added. 'We will not stop you any longer.' Ronnie nodded his acceptance and understanding of the situation just as the man with the spray came out on to the ramp and gulped at the fresh air.

Covered in red dye, he looked a comical sight. His two friends laughed out loud and when he'd recovered sufficiently they walked away together towards the main road.

'What now?' asked Franco.

'We'll wait here for a few minutes, give the air a chance to circulate. Someone is supposed to offer us help. I mean, we wouldn't know what to do now would we?'

They lay down on the grass verge and looked up into the cloudless sky, each grateful for these few minutes of relaxation and the opportunity for the early morning sun to draw the last of the chilling dampness from their clothes.

The sound of an approaching diesel engine refocused their attention; they sat up. A tractor appeared from behind the parked vehicles, two wheels on the grass verge, the other two half-way down the incline to the ditch. It pulled to a stop in front of them, the driver leaned from the cab.

'*Êtes-vous Anglais? Avez-vous des moutons? Comment je m'appelle?*'

Franco looked at Ronnie. 'What's his name?'

'Serge Coutanche, your name is Serge. We have been waiting for you.' The Frenchman nodded and addressed himself to Franco who translated his instructions. 'He says we're to follow him to his farm where we can unload. His wife will give us a good breakfast. He says we're to wait while he fetches someone to move that lorry.'

The lane was quickly cleared and they followed close

84

behind the tractor for a kilometre before turning off into a rough cart track leading to a muddy yard, set within a small group of buildings. A barn and two horse stables formed one side, a cow stable and an open implement shed, the other. Both were linked by a small cottage, its walls covered with an ancient rendering of cow-dung plaster.

Serge swung the tractor into the shed as Ronnie parked in the yard. A boy of about fifteen or sixteen came out of the cowshed and looked on curiously as Franco interpreted Serge's instructions. 'He asks us to back up to the gate over there and we can let the sheep out. The boy is his son.'

Ronnie manoeuvred the truck into position and they lowered the ramp. Serge and the boy grabbed hold of the animals, lifting them out of their pens to send them scurrying into the field with a kick and a shout. Within minutes they had settled and were grazing contentedly.

Ronnie drove the truck back into the yard where Serge directed him immediately adjacent to a pair of high-level doors above the stables. Two pulleys and a light chain attached to a post above the doors carried a platform hoist normally used for lifting bales of straw and animal feed. Serge spoke again to Franco. 'He says we're to put our "cargo" in the loft and to hide it. He's going into the house to see our food is prepared. He apologises but says he doesn't want to see what we've got. He'd rather not know.' Ronnie acknowledged the Frenchman's wishes: 'Please, it is all right. Thank you very much – merci, merci beaucoup.'

Serge smiled, grabbed his boy by the hand, gave a little bow and disappeared into the cottage.

Rae had already climbed the loft ladder; he opened the doors and looked down. 'It'll be quicker to take the guns up by hand. We can use the hoist for the boxes of ammo.'

'You stay there,' Ronnie called up to him. 'Try to arrange things so we have somewhere to hide the gear.'

The two men removed the ammunition from behind the bunks and loaded it on to the platform. Pulling the chains through the pulleys they hoisted it upwards, until Rae grabbed hold and swung it inside.

Ronnie walked into the stable, climbed to the middle rung of the ladder and looked through the trap-door into the loft. The sun shone through an old metal fanlight, casting a ray of light on the loose hay scattered over the floor. He gazed at the scene; for an instant his mind recalled some distant boyhood memory. Dismissing the sweet nostalgia, he forced himself back to the present.

Bales of hay were stacked against the gable wall, a few bales of straw lay at random over the floor and several bags of cattle nuts were heaped close to the doors. He told Rae to pull the hay away from the wall and returned to help Franco with the unloading.

Thirty minutes later the last bale was pushed back into place, concealing the hundred PM-63 machine pistols, the three 5.6mm MAS assault rifles, ten boxes of ammunition, their own three US Navy Mark 22 Smith and Wesson pistols and the remaining stun grenades.

'Quite a little arsenal,' commented Ronnie. 'Now the job's done, let's go and see what Serge's old lady has got to offer.'

A log fire burned within an old-fashioned cast-iron cooking range. It threw a warm glow around the one large room that comprised the entire ground floor. Stone walls, limed white, rose from a cobbled floor. They supported heavy oak beams and joists, black with age. Pitted by worm, they carried the wood floors to the upstairs rooms reached by a small winding staircase. An earthenware sink and timber draining-board stood under one of four small, shuttered windows that overlooked the yard. A single ceiling light covered by an ancient tapestry shade hung over a rough-hewn oak table which formed the centrepiece to the room. Serge sat at its head, a glass of wine in one hand, a stained hand-rolled cigarette in the other. His wife stood at the range, shaking a large black frying pan on the hot plate. She turned towards them as they entered. Serge stood to greet them.

'Come, come in my friends. Please to sit down .... Here.' He fetched three odd-sized glasses and poured them wine from a newly opened bottle. 'This my wife, Suzette.' He gesticulated towards the woman who smiled nervously, quickly returning her attention to the contents of the frying pan.

'What a beautiful little cottage,' commented Ronnie, sipping at the acid red wine. 'It's so cosy .... Serge do you mind if we use your toilet and have a quick wash before we eat?' Serge did not understand until Franco translated. '*Certainement excusez-moi*,' exclaimed Serge and talked on in his own language. 'He says we can wash upstairs but the toilet's outside in the back garden. He says to flush it with the bucket of water that's out there, and to bring it back for the next one to fill up again.'

Each man took his turn in the little brick building at the end of the garden. When Rae returned and gave the bucket to Ronnie he moaned there was no lock on the door. Ronnie turned to him laughing. 'I shouldn't worry about it Rae, Serge and his wife have lived here for twenty-three years and they haven't had a bucket of shit stolen yet!' Rae's normally serious countenance broke into a rare smile. Franco, hugely amused, reached across and ruffled his thinning hair.

Serge was confused but, realising that these men were good friends and *sympathique*, he smiled broadly, pretending that he also understood the joke. When all were eventually seated at the table, glasses were refilled and

Suzette provided three large French loaves and a huge slab of home-made butter. Never would bread taste so delicious again. Never another omelette as superb as those now served straight from the scalding pan. Even the red wine had begun to lose its acidity.

Ronnie asked Franco to thank the Frenchman for his hospitality and to enquire if there was a phone nearby. To his surprise Serge directed him to a modern instrument standing on a small bureau hidden away in a dark corner.

In order to complete the charade, it was necessary to call the factory in Rennes to explain what had happened.

After being put through to someone of authority, Franco held his hand over the receiver and turned to Ronnie. 'They want to know where the sheep are being kept and where we are calling from now?'

'That's okay,' Ronnie answered, 'give the phone to Serge.'

The Frenchman gave his name and address and related with great excitement an embellished account of the morning's events. By the time he'd replaced the receiver, he appeared well satisfied.

'It is good to leave the animals here. They pay me very good until they fetch them in twelve weeks .... It is good with you?'

'Yes,' answered Ronnie, 'it is good for us and we're glad it's good for you.' He looked at his watch. 'We don't have to be at the docks till eight this evening. I think we'd be safer to hang on here until the last minute I don't know about you but I feel like a nap. Ask if we can borrow their spare room.'

Serge led them up the winding staircase and opened one of the two bedroom doors. A huge mahogany bed dominated the simple room. A crucifix hung on the wall above the headboard. Franco made the sign of the cross and spread himself out on the sheepskin rug at the foot of the bed. The two others kicked off their shoes and climbed on to the deeply sprung mattress.

✧   ✧   ✧

Simultaneously they were startled to consciousness by an approaching siren and within seconds were crouched down peering between the louvres of the closed shutters. A blue police van and two motorcycle outriders were making their way down the track.

'Christ!' exclaimed Ronnie. 'We aren't even armed. Can you see how many there are?' The two riders dismounted and pulled the machines up on to their stands. A single uniformed policeman disembarked from the driver's seat of the van. 'There's only three of them,' observed Franco. 'If we can take them by surprise we can probably get away with it.'

'Wait! Let's see how Serge copes. They don't look as if they're expecting trouble.' Ronnie crept across the polished wood floor and opened the door just enough to hear what was going on below. He beckoned Franco to join him.

Serge shouted at his wife to remain calm. He went and stood in the open doorway as the gendarme walked towards him. Franco was unable to pick up the muted conversation.

The 'visitors' entered the cottage and were offered a glass of wine. Someone started to walk up the staircase. 'C'est moi ... Serge.'

The door was pushed open, Serge smiled broadly as he spoke; Franco's relief was immediately apparent.

'They've come to offer their apologies for what happened this morning. They've been instructed to come here by the Mayor of Rennes. Serge wants us to go downstairs and have a glass of wine with them.'

'Bloody hell!' exclaimed Rae.

'Why not?' smiled Ronnie.

'Let's go,' added Franco.

The senior officer rose from the table and saluted them. He offered humble apologies on behalf of the city of Rennes. The Mayor had been mortified to learn of the inconvenience imposed on their English friends. He rambled on into a formal address. Ronnie, Franco and Rae tried hard to conceal their embarrassment.

The officer finished his speech and raised his glass. Serge, beaming friendship placed glasses in their hands and filled them. The three men took a sip and walked over to shake the gendarme's hand.

After a second bottle had been emptied, the officer asked Serge if his guests were ready to return to St Malo. Franco translated, Ronnie checked the time; it was 16.40.

'They want to escort us back to St Malo as a gesture of the Mayor's friendship,' added Franco.

'Christ! Who would ever believe it . . . . Thank him and say we accept gladly.'

Draining the last of the wine from the glass, each man shook Serge's hand warmly.

'Hope to see you again someday soon,' added Ronnie with a secret wink. 'Tell him to thank his wife for us Franco. I hope we haven't caused her too much trouble.'

Ronnie walked outside and climbed into the truck. He started up and struggled to turn it around within the confines of the yard. By the time he'd completed the manoeuvre the police van was ready and waiting in front; the two motorcycles took up the rear.

Franco and Rae jumped into the cab, Ronnie gave two bleeps of the horn and let out the clutch.

☆   ☆   ☆

Within the hour they had reached the outskirts of St

Malo. The blue light of the police van continued to flash and its warning siren was now switched on.

The procession swept its way noisily towards the docks and into the compound, stopping alongside passport control and customs. The senior gendarme went inside. A minute later he walked up to Ronnie's window; he spoke in French. Ronnie smiled at him, hoping Franco would catch the gist of the conversation.

'He says that we don't have to go through customs; the boat has already docked, and we can go aboard straight away.' Ronnie reached down through the window to shake the Frenchman's hand.

'*Merci, monsieur, merci beaucoup. Nos salutations à votre Maire, vous êtes très gentil.*' The Frenchman saluted, as Ronnie re-engaged first gear and moved off towards the ticket barrier.

Soon, they were aboard ship, safe and secure in their own cabin and needing little persuasion to take a hot shower and shave. Fresh-faced and relaxed, they enjoyed another good meal and later when the bars opened celebrated their success well into the night.

Ronnie staggered back to his bunk at 2.15 and slept so deeply that he was not disturbed when the others rolled in some two hours later, vainly attempting to contain their hilarity as they struggled to support and help one another into the upper bunks.

Almost instantaneously they were asleep and when the call came for drivers to return to their vehicles, not one of them heard it. They were woken by a steward, who had come into the cabin to change the bed linen.

They washed quickly, picked up their few belongings and rejoined the truck. The ship's bow opened and they drove out into the grey light of dawn. Drizzle clouded the windscreen.

Half an hour later, without query or problem, they

cleared customs and drove on through to park outside the compound. Harry waited for them inside the reception building. He stood up with an amazed expression on his face as they approached. 'How did it go?' he asked.

No one felt it worth the effort of reply. Instead they once more resigned themselves to his 'authority' and followed him in silence back towards the truck.

Harry's great strength closed them in with a bang followed by the resounding clatter as the bolts were secured.

'You'd think we've proved ourselves enough to be allowed to ride in the cab instead of being locked up in here,' moaned Rae.

'You can never be too careful,' Ronnie answered. 'It's probably best we don't know where the headquarters are. They're just being professional. I respect them for that.' Rae remained unconvinced but, having no option, prepared himself for the tiresome journey ahead.

Harry drove away from the docks and headed towards the Victorian manor house set in the deepest countryside of North Wales.

7

Charles Verdusca walked into the British Midland VIP lounge. The girl at reception looked up and smiled.

'Good afternoon, Mr Verdusca, did you have a good trip?'

'Yes thank you, my dear. I don't like Munich airport though. There's more armed guards there than passengers these days. I'll be glad to get home – always am. No delays today, I hope?' The girl checked the departure screen.

'No sir, no delays on the Guernsey flight. You'll be called in about twenty minutes.'

He went through into the almost empty lounge, sat down in a comfortable chair and opened the *Financial Times*.

Charles Verdusca was a worried man. He needed time and was not sure whether there'd be time enough. Although he tried to concentrate, the prices were not registering on his mind. He already knew the shares in almost all companies in which he held an interest had dropped yet again. There seemed little chance within the foreseeable future of a turn-around. Reluctantly he'd come to accept this as fact and had looked elsewhere for salvation.

'Would you care for a drink sir?' Verdusca lowered the newspaper.

'Thank you, Billy, I'll have a Chivas.' The steward

filled a tall glass with ice and poured the golden liquid over it. The ice crackled. Verdusca took a sip at the smooth velvet whisky.... There was just a chance he could still pull it off. The arrangements in Munich had gone well – the people had impressed him as being most professional. He'd been surprised at their quality, so different from what he'd imagined .... It was definitely a chance worth taking.

He'd always been a man of positive action and as always, before making a decision had carefully weighed up the odds. If he'd just sat back and waited he would certainly have had to face charges of criminal misappropriation. After the meeting today, he had what he considered to be a fifty-fifty chance. Even if the plan should turn into a disaster and he was found guilty of conspiracy, the likely sentence might only be a year or two more than one for misappropriation.

He took a double sip from the glass, and felt the ice cold liquid warm the stomach. He smiled; a surge of adrenalin increased his pulse; he hadn't felt so good in weeks. If Charles Verdusca was brought to his knees, he'd go down fighting. He'd been brought down before, twice in fact, yet each time had been able to restore his fortune .... All was not lost. He still held an ace up his sleeve. He smiled and sipped the last of the Chivas; his flight was now boarding.

He folded the newspaper tidily and signalled Billy for a refill. Charles Verdusca would time his walk to the departure gate to the last second. Timing had always been his strongest point.

☆   ☆   ☆

A stunningly beautiful woman climbed out of the taxi and handed the driver a Guernsey £5 note. He reached into his pocket for change. 'That's all right, George, if I want you on Monday I'll telephone. Have a nice weekend.' The driver saluted. 'Thank you, Mrs Verdusca.' He walked to the rear of the car and took a cluster of fashion bags from the boot. 'Shall I get a trolley?' She reached for her day's purchases.

'No thank you George, my husband'll be through in a minute.' She gave him a smile of such intensity he was stunned into silence.

Mary Verdusca had become a well known figure throughout the island. Her thrice-weekly trips to St Peterport aroused consummate interest. This glamorous woman provided an insight into the world of the flamboyant rich. Whether she walked through Commercial Arcade, or deigned to make the effort to include Mill Street within her itinerary, the rest of the town heard about it. Local business had been quick to learn that with Mary Verdusca as a regular customer, others were sure to follow.

Fully aware of her influence, Mary Verdusca did not abuse it. She treated everyone alike. She hadn't always been rich. She hadn't always had it easy. During the hard times she had learnt that much could be achieved by making full use of her beauty, especially when combining it with a pleasing personality. If all else failed she could revert to being as cold and ruthless as any of her husband's less savoury business associates. At thirty-six, slim, long-legged, and with blonde shoulder-length hair, she was still considered an international beauty. Nevertheless she had her worries. Although understanding little of her husband's business, she was aware of some deep and impending crisis. She sensed a real chance of losing everything she had worked and suffered for. The sacrifice of being married to Charles had been well worth the financial rewards and prestige it brought her. A few years

95

ago the thought of losing it all would not have troubled her unduly, but now at the age of thirty-six . . . ! Recently she had become aware that she needed to work at being beautiful. Gone were the days when she could throw on any old dress and still be as lovely.

Mary Verdusca walked into the airport building as the Vickers Viscount taxied in from the runway. She hated airports, only remembering the tearful goodbyes the heavy sadness of being left behind. Perhaps he had been the only man she'd ever loved. She'd said goodbye just like all the times before and had made her lonely way back to the little London flat to await his return. She had never heard from him since. It seemed a century ago.

Mary walked over to the incoming passenger gate. She waited, clutching carrier bags in both hands.

'Good afternoon, Mrs Verdusca.' She turned towards the uniformed man who walked towards her.

'Oh, hello, Henry. Take these for me will you.'

'Certainly, madam. Mr Verdusca's flight's on time for a change.' Her attention diverted as Charles came through the swing doors. For a brief moment he didn't notice them.

Charles Verdusca, a typical fifty-eight-year-old epitome of the successful businessman. He was still a good-looking man even though the excesses from countless heavy business lunches and his indulgence of Chivas Regal had thickened his physique to a portly fourteen stone. He caught sight of his wife, stubbed out his cigar and walked over. She offered her cheek and he kissed her lightly. 'Hello, darling.' He looked at his employee. 'Everything all right Henry?'

'Yes sir, can I take your briefcase?'

'Thank you.' Charles linked arms with his wife and followed through a side door which opened directly on to the tarmac.

Mary tried to keep her hair in place against the blustering wind with one hand, holding the collar of her fur coat tightly up to the neck with the other. Henry ran ahead, unfolded the aircraft steps and followed them inside.

Edging his way between the seats, he settled himself into the cockpit and donned a pair of earphones. He threw several switches. Electrical circuits whirred into activity, the instruments lit up and threw a cold shallow light into the cabin. Traffic control were called on the radio, and permission for take-off asked for and given.

The motor coughed into life, the sixty-two foot rotor turned, and built up speed. The machine lifted into the air and almost immediately was propelled forward as it gained altitude.

Eight years ago the ninety-nine-year lease of one of the small islands off the Guernsey coast had been acquired by one of Charles Verdusca's companies. Within three years the island had been transformed.

Set in the twelve acres of grassland, its only residence, a semi-derelict farmhouse, had been replaced by a six-bedroomed mansion.

When floodlit, indoor and outdoor swimming pools linked by an electrically operated glass screen acted as an approach light to the landing pad. Two tennis courts had been constructed and the grassland planted with heather and seeded with rare and colourful wild flowers. Great care had been taken by the internationally acclaimed landscape designer Anthony Paul, to retain and enhance the natural beauty of the island.

To avoid the uncertainty in rough weather of bringing building materials by small boat, Charles had looked for a helicopter, and was fortunate to find the amphibious Sirkorski S-6IR (HH-35) at a most reasonable price.

Originally brought into service by the Italian Navy in

1965, it had proved a reliable workhorse. Once building works were completed, it still proved an invaluable asset. Charles had often thought of replacing it with a smaller, more economical machine, but somehow he'd never got round to it.

☆   ☆   ☆

Within five minutes of lift-off, the irridescent floodlit pool shone like some precious jewel beneath them. Henry guided the Sirkorski gently down on to the concrete landing pad and switched off the engines. The two passengers waited for the blades to come to rest before stepping out, then hurried across the lawn.

A warm yellow light spilled from the house, as a young woman, dressed in a black tailored suit, opened the front door to receive them.

'Good evening madam... good evening sir. Did you have a successful meeting?'

'Yes thanks, Martha. Have there been any calls?'

'Several calls, sir, only one I couldn't deal with. Mr Sinclair called a few minutes ago. He asked for figures relating to the projected cash flows. I didn't know whether you would want me to give them over the phone so I told him I couldn't find the file. I hope I did the right thing sir?'

'You certainly did, Martha. Bloody fool, he should have known better... I'll take the file with me tomorrow.'

Mary Verdusca had already walked on up the stairs and disappeared into her bedroom. Charles handed Martha his coat and went into the living room.

A log fire burned in the grate. A crystal chandelier formed the centrepiece to a finely detailed corniced ceiling. A deep and springy blue-grey carpet covered the floor. Two settees and two single armchairs stood in front of the fireplace. Charles walked over to an eighteenth-century walnut cabinet and took out a bottle of Chivas and a tall crystal glass. He topped it up with ice from the concealed fridge and poured out a generous measure. Taking a long sip, he walked over to the fire and stood with his back to the warmth. He could sense the tranquillizing and therapeutic effect of the alcohol as it relaxed his jaded nerves. He sank down into the settee nearest the fire, closed his eyes and fell into a gentle sleep.

☆   ☆   ☆

Mary switched on the bedroom light, closed the door and went through into her dressing room. She slipped off her coat and placed in amongst several others hanging in the specially built wardrobe. Carefully she unwrapped her newly acquired outfits and arranged them on sturdy wood hangers among an exquisite collection of designer clothes.

Kicking off her shoes, she returned to the bedroom and studied herself in the full-length mirror. She detached the tortoiseshell hair-clip and re-adjusted her fine blond hair, pulling it provocatively over her face. She reached behind to unclip the scarlet silk dress and narrowed her shoulders; the dress fell to the floor. She stepped out of it and looked again into the mirror. Her long beautiful legs tinted black from the fine hose of her stockings highlighted the whiteness of her thighs. A black suspender belt over brief red silk knickers accentuated her natural sensuality. Her slim waist curved upwards to firm breasts cool beneath a microlight bra of delicate silk. Mary turned sideways. She touched her left nipple lingering there a second, then ran her hands down her sides into her waist. She held in her tummy, searching for some imaginary slackness; satisfied she again relaxed and turned her back to the mirror.

Placing her hands on each rounded buttock she looked over her shoulder to view her most beautiful asset. She caressed herself through the fine silk then lifted the weight of rounded flesh allowing it to fall back to its natural curve. Slightly aroused by her own sexuality, she fought the unwanted sensation, pleased by it nevertheless. If her own body could still move her, it could still move others. She forced such thoughts from her mind and walked briskly into the bathroom.

She had learnt to exist without sex, without a lover. The rare occasions Charles sought to penetrate her didn't count. He never excited her in any way or even bothered to try. She was always dry inside for him and it always hurt terribly. It had been several months since the last time. She hoped he had given up and found himself a mistress.

As the bath filled she returned to her room and sat on the edge of the bed. She undid her suspenders and peeled off the delicate hose. She removed the lace-trimmed belt and reached behind to unclip her bra. She bent forward slightly to watch her breasts support themselves. She stroked each nipple alternately with her forefinger; they stood erect, pointed and firm. Standing up she slipped off the red panties, hurried back into the bathroom, and eased herself gently down into the therapeutic warmth. She closed her eyes; all the old memories came flooding back yet again. Perhaps they would for the rest of her life. As if frightened by the thought, she slid deeper into the bath until the hot water reached her chin.

Mary rested her hands under the water on to her inner thighs and brought them together, running the fingers of both her hands into herself. Contracting her muscles she sucked hot water into the far reaches of her womb. The warmth invaded her entire body. She tensed, and stretched her legs in tight contraction. The depth of her climax convulsed her forward at the waist. The bath water surged and spilt over the edge on to the carpeted floor. She lay back gently and sighed deeply, the wistful longing soon dispelled from her mind. She thought of Charles and the awful times he was going through. A pang of guilt resolved her to help and support him in any way she could.

Half-an-hour later, dressed in jeans and an angora sweater she made her way downstairs to the kitchen. Martha was emptying a steaming saucepan of Guernsey new potatoes into a tureen.

'Dinner's almost ready, madam. I think Mr Verdusca's fallen asleep in the sitting room. If it's all right to wake him I'll bring the meal through in five minutes.'

'Thank you so much, Martha, it really is too kind of you to do all this for us whilst cook's on holiday. Anyway I'll prepare the meal for all of us tomorrow.' Mary gave the live-in employee a warm smile and went to the sitting room.

She placed two logs on the fire from the basket, then lent down and stroked her husband's forehead. He opened his eyes.

'Oh, there you are dear,' he pulled himself upright. 'I haven't been sleeping too long have I?'

'No, darling, I'm sure you must be quite exhausted. Dinner's nearly ready.'

'Damn good of Martha to look after us like this.' Charles held out his hand and she helped him up. He smoothed the creases from his jacket and followed her into the dining room.

Martha served a simple meal with an ice-cold Chablis which they sipped from delicate crystal. As usual he had no intention of discussing his trip. Their conversation hinged largely on how she had occupied her time. She had

101

learned long ago that his apparent interest saved him from having to talk himself. They finished their meal and took their glasses into the sitting room.

'I think I may have finalised a deal that can restore our credibility,' he offered.

'It's a risk but it's our only chance.'

'Can you tell me about it?'

'I think it would be better if I didn't .... You understand don't you?'

'Oh,' she smiled knowingly. 'It's another one of those sort of deals is it? You'll never learn will you, Charles?' She reached across to the coffee table, picked up the remote control and switched on the television.

Charles Verdusca realised his wife was irritated. He rose from his chair and bent to kiss her cheek.

'Good night, darling. Please excuse me but you know I can't watch that rubbish, I'm off to bed .... I shall be leaving about 8.30 in the morning so I might not see you. I should be back by six.' Mary continued to watch the screen. She nodded without looking up. Why, oh why did he always make her feel so guilty?

'Good night, darling. Have a good day tomorrow.' Her words fell on deaf ears; he had already left the room.

8

Charles came down into the kitchen for breakfast. He looked in the bread bin and cursed under his breath. 'Bloody woman wouldn't know how to look after a bloody cat.' He settled for cornflakes and a pot of strong coffee.

Henry came in: 'Good morning, sir.'

'Morning, Henry, sit down. Won't be long. Would you like a coffee?'

'No thank you, sir. I've one or two things to check out on the Sirkorski. I'll be ready when you are.'

Charles Verdusca, an intensely private man, was not one for the trivial niceties of early-morning conversation. He finished his coffee and went into the study to collect papers necessary for the day's meetings.

It was a pure spring morning; the house basked in the early-morning sunlight. He stood for a few minutes on the portico steps marvelling at the beauty of his island.

Beyond the dew covered lawns, grassland undulated down and away from the house spilling out into a small shingle cove that looked towards St Peterport. The morning ferry bound for Poole had just emerged between the pierheads. Several yachts were already in the Channel between Brechou and Sark. Seabirds circled their wake.

Charles wished he could remain here for the whole day. He sighed deeply; no matter how unsavoury, problems had to be confronted head-on.

103

He walked briskly across the lawn and climbed aboard the Sirkorski, pulling the steps in behind him. Henry fired the engines; the rotor blade gathered momentum.

The helicopter climbed to an altitude of 600 feet heading south-south east. Charles looked down to see his island in its entirety and as always felt an immense pleasure. There were the granite cliffs of the south coast with white frothy waves breaking over jagged rocks. Gulls and other seabirds spiralled in the warm air flows. The undulating grassland, speckled with different hues, meandered down to cobble-beached coves indenting the coast on the opposite side. He took particular pride in the tidy planning of the red pantiled roofs of the main house and outbuildings. The way they related to the York stone terraces, the swimming pool, tennis courts and lawns. No roads, no cars and, apart from the property, nothing to interrupt the natural pattern of nature.

Now, with the receding landfall, they followed the white rippling wake of some high-powered craft and soon caught and passed the Condor hydrofoil plying its way towards St Helier.

Within fifteen minutes of take-off, they had reached the west coast of Jersey. The emerald green of the grass oval race-track stood out sharply against the brown scrubland of Les Landes. Now the bold sweep of St Ouen's bay stretched before them. The strong surf rolled in from the Atlantic and was already dotted with keen early-morning surfers.

Henry reduced altitude and swung the aircraft in over the dunes. He guided it beyond the airport buildings and settled on to the reserved landing pad adjacent to one of the large service hangars.

After a brief exchange with tower control he switched off engines, and turned to ask for the day's schedule. Charles looked at his watch, it was 8.50.

'My wife wants picking up at twelve and bringing here for the Ladies' Variety Club luncheon. Before you do that though, take Martha over to St Peterport and get some groceries in, will you? She'll know what we're short of.' Henry jotted down the instructions on to a clipboard.

'Oh, and whilst you're in Guernsey pop into Bob Froome's and see the horses are all right. I just haven't had time to look in there lately and I do like to show some interest. Ask him the date of the first race meeting, will you? Mrs Verdusca will be ready to be picked up about 3.30 then come back for me at six. Got all that, Henry?'

'Thank you, sir. I hope you have a good day.'

'So do I, Henry .... So do I. Christ! I nearly forgot. The dogs were kept overnight at that bloody Poodle Parlour. You're supposed to pick them up this morning, aren't you?'

'Yes sir, I hadn't forgotten. I'll do that when I go for the groceries.' Henry put down the clipboard and moved over to open the door. Charles climbed out and was soon in the arrivals hall. He walked through customs, green sector; no officers were evident.

'Good morning, sir, lovely day.' A uniformed chauffeur held open the door of the dark blue Mercedes.

'How's the wife, Jack?'

'Very well, thank you, sir.'

'And all the kids? How's little Jamie?'

'Much better sir. Should be back at school on Monday.'

'Glad to hear it Jack. Sorry to bring you out on a Saturday. I shouldn't need you again though, not until 5.15 that is ... from the office.'

'Right you are, sir.'

Jack pulled away smoothly and headed for town. He turned left into Grenville Street and pulled into the kerb opposite a modern office block. He got out, opened the door for his employer and saluted.

Charles walked up the granite steps. He pushed open the heavy bronze doors and entered the carpeted reception area. A girl attended a large digital telephone exchange; she smiled and bade him good morning. He returned the greeting and walked up the staircase towards his own suite.

Sitting down at the rosewood desk, he unfolded *The Times*. Its headline caught his eye. He shook the paper open.

ARMS RAID ON IMPOUNDED TRAWLER

In the early hours of Wednesday morning an undisclosed group executed a commando-style operation on the German trawler currently impounded in St Malo.

It was said to be carrying a cargo of light weaponry bound for Iran. The communiqué issued by the French Ministry of Defence stated that a considerable amount of arms and ammunition of Eastern-bloc origin were taken. A full enquiry into the incident was immediately commissioned.

The incident raised grave concern as to the security arrangements implemented by the French Navy. No organisation has yet claimed credit for this brilliantly planned operation where the perpetrators achieved their objectives without loss of life or injury to either side.

Charles read the article once again. No one had even been hurt! This demonstrated the true professionalism of the people he was dealing with. If they could run rings around the French Navy ...! Charles felt a growing confidence. What had started as a panic measure, grown to a calculated even-money chance, now seemed to have matured into a sound investment. He felt strangely light-headed.

He walked over to the window. Beyond the town fringe he could see Grève d'Azette and the sweep of St Clement's Bay. The jagged rocks, a feature of the south-east coast, linked the grey sand to the sea. Many a low water fisherman had lost his life in those treacherous gulleys. Often so intent on their pastime, they found themselves surrounded by the incoming tide to be sucked out screaming into fast-flowing currents.

There was an element of danger in the most gentle of pursuits; it was all a matter of fate, and fate sometimes could be manipulated to one's own advantage. The bank itself had been an acquisition of fate.

The subject of an unsolicited takeover, his UK-based company, formed in 1962, became a subsidiary of a large International American-based conglomerate. He had remained chairman for six months but resigned due to disagreements over the level of redundancies the new management had demanded. He sold his remaining shares in the company over a period of months and found himself with £4.5 million in the bank and nothing to do. He had spent weeks pondering and had finally decided to sever all UK interests and move to the secure financial climate of Jersey which offered the incentive of huge savings in tax.

Applying to the Policy Advisory Committee for permission to become an island resident, he had been astounded when the application was refused. Only five applications from wealthy immigrants were to be granted that year, and his immediate reaction had been 'to hell with Jersey'.

He wasted no further time and approached the sister island of Guernsey. There he was warmly received. If he had the money to buy an open-market house, he would be most welcome.

Many local properties were viewed before he was offered a ninety-nine-year lease for the tiny island, a priceless jewel, half-a-mile off the east coast and owned by the Guernsey States. He had taken it on the spot without even mentioning it to his wife. The next day he paid one of the local fishermen to taken them across in a small boat on what he pretended to be a simple day's outing.

He would never forget her look of astonishment and sheer joy when they'd set foot on the island and he told her it was to be their home. She had run up the overgrown path towards the empty house like a young girl, wide-eyed and unbelieving. When he caught up with her she had turned towards him and flung her arms around his neck. That had been one of the few precious moments of their relationship.

With the lease secured, they rented a modest house in Guernsey for the year it took to plan, design and build their present home. Time, he thought, to find a suitable business that might absorb his interest.

His capital and expertise were much sought after and although many a proposition was offered, nothing caught his interest. After a while it had come to be believed that he was not serious in his intention, and the offers, deals and propositions dwindled. Charles became restless and frustrated. If it hadn't been for the work involved in developing the new house and beautifying the island he probably would have gone back to the mainland and be buggered with the tax. A call from the manager of a small merchant bank, however, changed everything.

He was told that the principal shareholder in the Jersey Bank of Commerce had died recently and that the family wished to sell its holdings. Within a week Charles, and his London accountant, had flown over to Jersey and concluded a deal. He had been appointed to the board and within two years had taken over as chairman.

He was now the majority shareholder, owning 25.75 per cent of the stock.

Charles's thoughts were interrupted by a knock at the door. He returned to the desk and pressed a small button in the arm of his chair. It changed from red to green.

'Good morning, Charles.' A tall, slim man in his middle thirties entered, immaculately dressed in a grey pinstripe suit. He clutched a sheaf of files tightly under his arm.

'Good morning, Andrew, are they ready for me?'

'Yes sir, shall we go in?'

'Not until you've told me what the bloody hell you mean by ringing my home asking for confidential information over the phone.' Charles was annoyed and showed it.

'I only wanted the figures so I could prepare you a recommendation, Charles, I ...'

'Recommendation my arse. You must think I'm a prickhead. Well it's you that's still wet behind the ears, sonny. If anyone overheard, it could have started a run. Just one little rumour is all that's needed and once it starts there'd be no stopping it. I'll save the fucking bank my way. I don't need any fucking recommendations either from you or those self-righteous bastards in there ....'

Charles gave Sinclair a half-smile and removed his papers from the briefcase.

'Let's go in now shall we, Andrew?'

Pushing past his subordinate, he walked from the office; Sinclair followed clutching the files to his chest with both hands.

'Good morning, gentlemen.' Charles crossed the boardroom, beaming confidence as he took the 'chair'. Sinclair sat at his right hand. The six other members already seated comprised two retired bank managers, a retired stockbroker, the President of the States Finance Committee, the chairman of the Jersey Farm Produce Association and a retired Colonel; all were over sixty-five years of age. No one looked at all happy as they mumbled a response to their chairman's greeting.

Charles shuffled his papers, looked at each man in turn and smiled. 'Gentlemen, I have called this meeting today to discuss the letter of resignation I have before me. As you must all be aware, our longest-serving member Senator Le Patrisse has serious misgivings as to our current financial status.

'I am sure he has given the matter full consideration in relation to the delicate position he holds as Jersey's President of Finance. He feels, quite rightly, that he cannot afford to have his name linked to a finance house whose actual reserves are less than those listed within our annual report and accounts filed year ending 31 December.'

Charles now addressed himself directly to the Senator.

'Sir, I am prepared to accept your resignation, but if you would do me the courtesy of hearing me out, I would beg you to reconsider.' The Senator nodded, gratified that he was being treated with the dignity and respect to which he felt justly entitled. The importance of persuading this self-righteous, pompous, yet honourable politician to retain his seat on the board was paramount. If he were allowed to relinquish his long-standing commitment to the bank, the others would surely follow and the bank would lose its credibility. Charles chose his words with care.

'First, gentlemen, allow me to present our current financial position.' He passed copies of the draft interim balance sheet around the table. 'You will see from the figures, we are in a much healthier position. The extremely grave situation that has arisen over the last few months, as you are well aware, has been caused by withdrawals exceeding deposits by increasing, and of late, substantial margins. However over the last few days we have been able to reverse this trend.'

'Oh yes, we can see that,' interrupted Alfred Dubois. 'Offering depositors increased rates of interest, one-and-a-half per cent above that of any other financial institution, is not sound business. How long can you buy money at this sort of price?'

'Long enough, Alfred.' Charles paused, and there was a general muttering around the table. He continued.

'In the short term it was the right and proper thing to do. It was imperative that we prevent a run on the bank. We could not have sustained the situation for more than another three weeks before being forced to close our doors .... Gentlemen, we have stemmed the tide. As you can see from the figures in front of you, our deposits last week totalled £635,000 against withdrawals of £15,200. A net gain of £619,800.

'We intend to offer this inflated interest for another four weeks only. We will then reduce it in line with our competitors, and in the meantime ... in the meantime, gentlemen, we intend to adjust our portfolio to rid ourselves of the bad performers and to re-invest in gilt-edged shares showing higher yields.

Our half-yearly audited accounts do not have to be filed until July, so we have until then to get ourselves back on an even keel. I have every reason to believe, and Andrew here will bear me out on this, that this will be achieved.' Charles looked around the table, challenging comment.

Alfred Dubois voiced their underlying concern.

'I think I speak for all of us, Charles. It's about this unsecured loan you deemed fit to give yourself in January. Without it none of these problems might have occurred. I mean £1.5 million is a substantial amount of cash, enough to considerably affect our liquidity. We feel that you should give us some guarantee that this money will be returned within the next few weeks. We can not consent that it be shown in our half-yearly audit as a viable asset. Neither do we consider it would be looked upon as an acceptable transaction of business by the examining authority.' Charles was ready for this criticism. He felt sure the real bone of contention had at last been brought out into the open.

'Glad you raised the matter, Alfred . . . . Yes, I agree, it is an unsecured loan, which I alone authorised on behalf of the financial investment company of which I am the beneficial owner. As you know I have just returned from Munich where I successfully concluded a transaction which will enable my company to return the money in full within the next five weeks. I might add that a proper rate of interest was included within the loan and this has been paid back into the account monthly. I respect your feelings of concern, but ask that you may accept my word that this loan will be repaid in full within the time stipulated.' Dubois, with some reluctance, muttered his acceptance. Charles continued: 'Now, Senator, I ask that you withdraw your resignation for the following reasons.

'One, your invaluable services to this board are indispensable.

'Two, if you do resign others may follow. The public will see it as a lack of confidence, start a run, and within three weeks we could be insolvent. Whether you resign or not your name would still be linked with a financial disaster.

'Three, as this loan will be repaid within five weeks and will completely restore the balance of our liquidity no such problem will arise. There is no reason therefore, for anyone to resign from this board.'

112

Charles leant back in his chair. He waited, as the Senator deliberated, hoping that his logic would achieve the desired effect.

'I consider your actions to be unacceptable, Charles. However, in the circumstances I have no alternative but to accept that you will honour your commitment. I am therefore willing to withdraw my resignation for the time being if you give an assurance that you will never seek to utilise our assets in this way again.'

'If it is the board's wish, then I give my word. I gratefully acknowledge your decision.' Charles passed the letter of resignation to the Senator and without displaying an ounce of emotion, continued with the agenda of a normal week's business.

Conducted without further controversy, the meeting was brought to a close shortly before noon.

☆   ☆   ☆

Charles felt he had achieved as much as he dared hope for. He now had five weeks to return the money he'd manipulated in an attempt to accumulate a quick profit for himself.

Acting on inside information, he had purchased a large parcel of shares in a conglomerate of listed companies. He had expected to be in and out of the market before anyone had time to notice. The stocks had risen, but thinking they would move higher he had waited too long. Prices had then plummeted due to the collapse of a proposed takeover, and the shares had never recovered. Now, with the board's acceptance of his proposals, and his own private solution to the problem already under way, things were beginning to look up. Charles took himself to his favourite restaurant for lunch and returned to the office at 2.30 to catch up on a backlog of correspondence. He worked on

113

alone and uninterrupted until 5.15.

The short journey home was smooth and trouble-free. A red setter, a labrador and a poodle bounded across the lawn to greet him.

'Hello, boys and girls. I wondered why the place seemed like a morgue yesterday. Come on then, Sally, come on.' He bent down to fondle the dogs so excited to see him home again. 'Yes, I know ... I really missed you too. There's a good girl. Just let me change out of these clothes and we'll go for a walk.' Charles felt an immense happiness. He had grown to love the dogs as he loved his home and his island. With Mary, somehow, love was not quite that simple.

☆   ☆   ☆

The following Saturday Charles treated himself to the luxury of a day off, something he'd been promising himself for weeks. The opportunity to enjoy his home, for perhaps the last time, was not to be measured against a few hours' work at the office where little more could be achieved anyway. Apart from anything else he needed space to collect his thoughts and prepare himself for the traumas that lay ahead.

He got up later than usual and took a hot bath. He felt relaxed and strangely resigned that yet another chapter of his life had come to a close.

Putting on his oldest and most comfortable clothes, he went down to breakfast. Mary held a piece of toast in one hand, a cup of coffee in the other, and was reading from a book open on the table in front of her. She looked up. 'Hello, darling, did you sleep well?' She smiled at him warmly.

'I took a long time to drop off but I must have slept really well. For the first time in weeks I don't feel at all tired. Could you pour me a coffee, please?' Charles sat down in the white cane chair opposite.

'There's coffee in the pot, darling. You're not quite the geriatric yet.' She returned her attention to the book. Charles gave a resigned sigh. 'Christ, Mary, it's not even hot. Look, I don't want to start the day off on the wrong foot . . . today of all days, but couldn't you just for once do something for me?'

'Why, darling, what's so special about today, surely it's not our anniversary already is it? My, how time flies!'

'Stop being bloody facetious and get me a fresh coffee, there's a good girl.' Marking her place in the book she snapped it shut, and flashed him a false smile.

'Charles, you make me so angry. You'll never tell me anything, will you? You never ask for help or support, you never confide in me. I know you're going through a difficult time, it's just as worrying for me you know. You didn't even bother to tell me you weren't going in today and I've made arrangements to meet Lucy for lunch.'

Charles took a piece of toast, broke it in half and buttered it lazily. She bent down and kissed his thinning hair. He took her hand and kissed it.

'I've nearly got it beat, Mary, I really have. As soon as things settle down we'll take six weeks off and do that Caribbean cruise again. You go and enjoy your lunch, I just want to walk the island with the dogs, I might even do a little fishing.'

They finished breakfast in silence. Although the rare outburst of mutual understanding had brought them closer, it was not enough to sustain the effort required to re-establish their relationship. It was so much easier, instead, to let things drift on just as they were.

9

Fifty passengers disembarked from the plane and walked across the tarmac into the arrivals hall. The four men had travelled separately, taking care to show no sign of recognition.

Two waited at the reclaim conveyor, whilst the other pair, carrying only hand baggage, walked through the customs green sector to coincide with the confusion caused by a large party of holidaymakers. The only officer on duty made no request to examine either credentials or luggage.

Safe in the knowledge that they carried no unlawful substance or contraband, they were still greatly relieved to climb into a taxi away from official scrutiny.

'Where to, sir?' asked the driver.

'Just wait a minute please, there's two others yet – a hold up with the baggage I think. We'd like to be taken into town please.'

'Certainly, sir.' The driver got out of the car and opened the boot. Tensions mounted as the minutes ticked away. The driver opened the rear door.

'The flight's just coming through now, sir.'

Ronnie waved at his companions standing in front of the exit doors. They walked over, placed their cases in the boot and got into the car.

The driver pulled away from the kerb and turned left towards St Peterport.

Franco asked if he could recommend a good place to eat.

The man beamed with pride as if the restaurant were his own. 'Whistlers, sir, you'll get the best steak you've ever had.'

The taxi dropped them outside the place, off a tiny cobbled street just above the town. The four men entered; the warmth and atmosphere was immediately apparent. A semi-circular bar jutted into the middle of the room, the red glow of an open charcoal grill its focal point. Eight or nine people sat around drinking and talking or just watching the chef cutting generous portions of steak from a butchered loin. A certain air of decadence that somehow pervaded the room in no way detracted from its appeal, indeed it enhanced an atmosphere of anticipation. Only two of the tables were presently occupied.

An attractive blonde in her late thirties approached them.

'Good evening, gentlemen. Have you booked?'

'No but we want to eat now please,' stated Hammond. He made a point of looking towards the empty tables.

'If you'd excuse me just one minute I'll check for you. I'm sure we can fit you in somehow. If you'd like to put your cases in the cloakroom over there, perhaps you'd care to take a drink at the bar?'

Rae duly obliged and, by the time he'd returned, the others had got their drinks. Franco had a red wine, Ronnie was drinking Perrier, Hammond's glass was already empty. 'What would you like?' Hammond enquired gruffly. Rae looked at Ronnie then asked the barmaid for a mineral water.

'And another large brandy,' shouted Hammond as the girl dispensed the order. The others, embarrassed into an awkward silence, watched the chef beat at the portions of steak with a wooden mallet. He then moulded them into shape with cupped hands and placed four pieces on to the grill. They sizzled and spat droplets of fat on to the hot coals. Yellow flames licked eagerly at the underside, adding their own special ingredient and further enticing the appetite.

'We can fit you in gentlemen,' the manageress diverted their attention. 'We've managed to juggle the bookings around to accommodate you. Would you like to order now before the rush starts?' She passed them each a menu and left to attend a nearby table.

Ronnie looked up at an old Victorian wall clock, 7.45. There was no need to hurry except that the longer they were in the restaurant the more opportunity there would be for drinking. He knew he could control Franco and Rae even though he no longer had the authority, but Hammond was a different story.

Ronnie had at first accepted Hammond's command without complaint, but now felt great concern. The heavy drinking had continued unabated; at the airport, on the plane, and now in here. For the operation to have any chance of success it couldn't be allowed to continue.

He had hoped the three of them could do the job together. It was not possible; this time they had need of a pilot.

Hammond's service record with the American Air Force Reconnaissance, fitted him admirably for the job. Whether his quality of leadership matched his flying ability had yet to be proved.

The woman returned to take their order. The bar was becoming overcrowded from a constant stream of pre-booked diners. Franco bought another round of drinks and a pretty waitress showed them to an oak refectory table by the curtained window. 'Couldn't have chosen a better place than this!' drawled Hammond. 'No one's likely to notice us here.' He took a sip of brandy, smacked

118

his lips, returned the glass to his mouth and gulped down the remainder. Ronnie could not contain his anxiety. 'Take it easy, Jason, we've another hour to go yet.' Hammond's expression changed in a flash. Thrusting his elbow into the middle of the table he leant across and grabbed at Ronnie's jacket. Ronnie made no effort to retaliate. He looked the man straight in the eye. Hammond released his grip, and without a word, left the table.

'Bloody hell!' exclaimed Rae. 'That was a bit over the top. The bloke's a nutter.'

'If he'd done that to me I'd have broken his arm,' added Franco.

'That would have been great, that would,' smiled Ronnie. 'Who's ever heard of a one-armed pilot.'

Tensions were soon calmed by the arrival of the food. They refused wine and cut into the succulent steak. Hammond rejoined them. No mention was made of the incident but to re-establish his authority he ordered another double brandy, downed it in one and looked around the table challenging further criticism. The three men chose to ignore this display of immaturity and finished their meal in silence.

Hammond paid the bill. Franco smiled at the manager-ess and in a sudden impulsive movement kissed her on the cheek. He held his forefinger to this thumb in a sign of satisfaction. '*Mara vilha ....*' The woman blushed and held her hand to her cheek; she returned Franco's laugh.

'Thank you, sir, I do hope you enjoyed your meal.' Smiling provocatively, she closed the door behind them.

The four men walked down the steep cobbled street until it joined the main approach road that led into town. They turned to their right and crossed to the promenade fronting the marina. The lights of the town shimmered over the still water, embracing the warm yellow light from the few inhabited yachts, moored collectively on the

119

central pontoon.

'I've never been to Guernsey before,' commented Ronnie. 'Looks like a great place. Must come back some day.' Hammond grunted and checked the time.

'Ten past nine, this guy should be here by now!'

Much to the relief of everyone, he seemed to have regained his sensibilities. They walked along the quay and scanned the boats below, searching for a signal.

'There at the bottom of the steps – see it?' Rae had spotted a light flashed in their direction. As the others looked, it flashed again.

'Come on,' said Hammond, re-asserting his authority. 'That must be him.'

They increased their pace, stopping at a flight of granite steps that led down to the water. A man, crouched at the stern of a small open boat, shone the torch at them and whispered hesitantly.

'George, is that you, George?' Hammond led the way down the narrow steps. 'Take that bloody thing out of my eyes.... Yes, we're George and you must be Simon. Everything ready for us?'

The man pulled the boat into the side and held on to the steps. Once they were aboard he let go, knelt down on the floor and lifted a trap which gave access to the propeller shaft and bilges. He removed something wrapped in a blanket and placed it on top of the small motor housing. The four men peered closely as he unfolded it with great care to reveal two sawn-off shotguns. He passed one to Ronnie; Franco reached for the other.

'I cut the barrels off myself,' said the man, gaining confidence.

'Here, there's the three boxes of cartridges and I managed to get hold of this. It's a Smith and Wesson model, a 15.38 revolver.' He held the gun lovingly in the palm of his hand, then passed it to Hammond.

'Where did you get this from?' Hammond asked. 'It can't be traced, can it?'

'Don't think so. I've had it for about a year now.'

'What about ammunition?'

'Yes, of course, I've got a box somewhere.' He rummaged around in the blanket. Hammond flicked open the gun and held it up to the faint light. The six chambers were already loaded. He snapped the gun shut, checked the safety catch and stuck the gun into his trouser belt. The sealed box of ammunition was put straight into his jacket pocket.

'You two keep the shotguns, I'll hang on to this. You'll have to do without for the time being, Rae, but it won't be for long. You ready then boy? Let's be off.'

The man untied the mooring rope and allowed the boat to drift away on the incoming tide. Once clear of other boats he threw a switch on the engine housing and cranked the starter handle.

With a puff of blue smoke the diesel motor chugged into life. The man took hold of the tiller and put the boat into forward gear. He opened up to half-throttle and pointed the bow towards the pierhead.

The water was smooth and calm, the sky clear. A full moon highlighted the wake of the small boat as it maintained its progress at a steady five knots.

Ronnie ran his hand over the smooth butt and along the twin stub of blue-black steel. He attracted Rae's attention and passed it to him.

'You take this, Rae. I couldn't bring myself to use a murderous thing like this. Until I get my own gun back I'd rather take my chances without one.'

He turned to the man at the tiller: 'How long will it take us?'

'It's over there ... see the lights?' The shape of the house was just visible, lit by a shimmering blue light. A second later it was gone.

The helmsman turned to port to negotiate an open passage between two outcrops of rock. He leant forward and reduced the engine back to half-throttle. When the offending rocks had receded below the water line, he turned to starboard and soon the dark shape of a granite jetty loomed before them.

The little craft edged its way forward. 'Two of you get in the stern here with me,' said the man. The rise and fall on the heaving swell was considerable and both Ronnie and Franco held tightly on to the gunwale as they scrambled aft.

With great skill, the helmsman manoeuvred the stern of the boat up to the jetty and on his command the two men timed their leap at the height of the flood. The manoeuvre was repeated for the other two. As soon as they were safely ashore the man opened the throttle and, with a final wave, slid away into darkness.

10

Mary decided that as soon as she got home, she'd make a concerted effort to be nice. It was ironic; the one Saturday Charles decided to stay home, she was having a good time with her friends. She knew very well in her heart of hearts that he preferred to be alone. Nevertheless she determined to try again.

Henry showed no irritation when she arrived back at the airport forty minutes late, and she offered no apology. Nothing was said during the short flight until he offered his hand to help her out. She thanked him and asked that he tell Martha there was no need to prepare dinner.

'Enjoy a nice quiet evening together in that cosy little apartment of yours. Charles doesn't require you tomorrow, does he?'

'No, madam. He said we could have the day to ourselves ... I'll carry the shopping in for you, madam.'

'No, silly,' she laughed. 'Give it here.' He passed her the three plastic bags and watched as she walked away from him across the lawn. Was there a hint of seductiveness in the way she moved those hips, or did he just imagine it? Henry often wondered about Mary Verdusca. There was something about her he could not quite comprehend.

The dogs bounded up and around her excitedly. She put the shopping on to the kitchen table and gave them each a chocolate drop.

'Now you lot, out of my way – come on.' She walked through into the utility room and let them out.

'Charles, I'm home.' She called out, expecting him to be in the study. He came out of his bedroom and walked down the stairs towards her.

'Hello, darling. Did you have a good lunch?'

'Smashing,' she answered. 'Lucy sends her love. Did you enjoy your day?' He put his arm around her waist.

'Marvellous ... just what I needed. Thank you.' They walked together into the sitting room, where the fire was already lit. He went to the drinks cabinet and made her a Bacardi and Coke, with ice and fresh lime.

Much to her surprise and without any prompting, he began to talk of the problems facing the bank and how the situation had deteriorated over the last few months. She listened attentively, appreciating his candour and when he told her of the 'property' deal he'd concluded in Munich and how it should solve their predicament, she went over and kissed him on the lips.

'You are so clever, Charles, I just wish you'd confide in me more. I have got a brain you know.'

'I do know, dear. It's just I get so involved in what I'm doing, my mind never stops; it's always two jumps ahead. I know it sounds stupid but I make myself believe I can't afford the time to talk unless there is a positive reason to.'

'The positive reason for you to talk to me, Charles, is the saving of our marriage.'

He caught hold of her hand and looked into her eyes. 'You're entirely right and I know I'm at fault. I'll try in future, I promise.'

If Charles' candid resumé of his financial difficulties was a revelation; his willingness over the dinner table to contribute to the conversation astounded her. He seemed to need reassurance and support, something she had never seen in him before. It worried her a little and she wondered whether the major problems yet to be resolved would, after all, restore his financial credibility.

After dinner he sat by the fire whilst she cleared away the dishes and let in the dogs. He looked up from his newspaper as they followed her back into the room. 'Darling, if you want the television on I don't mind.'

'I don't know what's got into you tonight, Charles. Thank you, but I'd like to read.'

The dogs settled on the rug to blink and stare into the fire. Mary, feeling more content than she could remember, lay back into the cushions and opened her book.

A gentle growl from the poodle distracted her. The other dogs became agitated. Charles put down his paper.

'What is it, Sally? What can you hear?' The three dogs were already on their feet. The poodle cocked her head to one side, she growled and gave a piercing bark. The other two joined in and ran to the door, hackles raised.

'What do you think's worrying them?' Mary asked nervously.

'It's probably Concorde or one of those French jets going over,' said Charles as he looked at his watch. 'It's usually about this time.'

'I don't remember it disturbing the dogs before . . . . She stood up and walked towards the door. 'Be quiet, for goodness sake.'

They barked incessantly, and when she opened the front door they dashed out in a frenzy. She started to follow them, but they'd already disappeared beyond the escarpment.

Peering across the moonlit lawns she saw nothing untoward. She shrugged her shoulders and went back inside.

Someone else pushed the door shut from behind. She froze; a cold sensation of fear ran through her entire body.

She willed herself the courage to turn around, but a

hand closed over her mouth, an arm encircled her waist and she was swung round with her assailant still behind her. She saw someone else by the sitting room door holding a sawn-off shotgun. He kicked open the door and she was thrust forward into the room. Charles sprang to his feet; she was half-carried, half-thrown across the room and into one of the chairs. The other man pushed Charles roughly back into his seat. Still no one spoke. For the first time she could see the man who'd grabbed her. There was something about him ... the way he stood, the same ... her attention was diverted as another person entered the room. He waved a pistol aggressively towards them. She looked towards Charles; he gave her a pathetic smile. She felt sick.

Not really understanding why, she glared at him angrily, then looked away to speak to the man who had grabbed her.

'What do you want from us? You won't find any money here.'

'You'll find out soon enough.' Hammond butted in before anyone else had time to answer. 'Just keep your mouth shut until ...' There was a movement at the door. Hammond swung towards the sound. He lowered the gun as Henry and Martha were thrust into the room, a shotgun pressed hard against his shoulder.

'You two sit down there.' Hammond waved the pistol at their faces. 'And I don't want a word out of any of you, unless you're spoken to.' Martha started to cry; Henry put his arm around her.

'No one will be harmed,' continued Hammond, 'as long as you do as you're told. You' – he waved the gun at Henry – 'Come with us .... Yes, you.' Henry kissed Martha on the cheek and stood up nervously as Hammond addressed Franco and Rae. 'We should be back by ....' He checked the time, 'By one.' He looked poin-

126

tedly from one woman to the other and smirked: 'And behave yourselves.' He shoved Henry in front of him.

Ronnie glanced towards the blonde woman who looked him straight in the eye. He winked to offer her some re-assurance, but she immediately averted her gaze. He turned away and followed Hammond outside.

The three men climbed into the helicopter and Henry was ordered into the co-pilot's seat. A minute later the machine lifted from the ground.

Hammond held steady then swung to port and set course for St Malo at an altitude of 300 feet. Twenty minutes later when the lights of the town came into view he turned to starboard and followed the dimly lit motor-way.

They climbed to a height of 500 feet and hovered, scanning the dark expanse of land beneath.

'There, Hammond, there they are!' Ronnie leant over and pointed away to their left where the raked-out embers of a spent bonfire glowed in the darkness. Hammond eased to starboard and reduced height.

Eight successive flashes from a powerful torch con-vinced him that it was safe, and with speed and great skill he settled the Sirkorski down on to the grass. He switched off and shouted at Ronnie as the noise abated.

'Get out and organise the loading. I'll look after things here. If we need to get away quickly I'll be ready.' Ronnie grunted acceptance, climbed over and opened the door. Two men appeared from the darkness.

'*Ronnie, c'est vous?*'

'Serge – great to see you. Everything OK?'

'*Oui d'accord.*'

'Back the van up, quickly as you can.'

Serge opened the rear doors and with the driver's help passed up the guns. Ronnie wiped the sweat away from his eyes as he stowed away the last box of ammunition.

'*C'est tout?*' he asked.

'*Pas tout*,' said Serge, and he handed up the three .22 pistols and the remaining grenades.

'Thanks mate,' Ronnie spoke gratefully. 'When this is all over I'll come back and visit you someday.'

'All loaded,' he shouted towards the cockpit at the top of his voice. 'Let's get the hell out of here.'

The helicopter lurched into the air as he struggled to his seat, and within seconds he had dozed off.

Awakened as if by instinct, he looked down to see the shimmering blue light of the swimming pool; the Sirkorski touched down just after one.

Ronnie collected the three Hush Puppies and followed the others towards the house. The dogs ran across the lawn barking until Hammond kicked out at the poodle, catching it a vicious blow. The dog somersaulted and ran away on three legs, yelping loudly; the other two stood off growling.

Apart from the illuminated pool, the house was in darkness; Franco stood at the open door, the shotgun held across his chest. He peered through faint light towards the approaching men.

'Thank God – did everything go all right?'

'Everything went like a dream,' Ronnie answered. 'Serge sends his regards. Here, I thought you'd like to have this back.' He handed Franco the pistol and followed him into the sitting room.

The fire still burned brightly. Charles sat alone in the corner, the two women together on the settee. The remnants of a hastily prepared meal littered the marble coffee table. Martha, red-eyed and tearful, showed obvious relief at Henry's return.

'Where's Rae?' Hammond asked.

'Upstairs asleep.' Franco answered curtly. Hammond re-adjusted his pistol between belt and trousers and sat on

128

the arm of the settee. He reached for the telephone and dialled. There was a pause – everyone in the room listened intently as he spoke.

'This is George. Is Archibald there? Yes, its "sky-train". This is the message. The message is: The consignment arrived on schedule and was found to be in perfect order, no problems. Thank you.' He replaced the receiver then, holding the instrument to the full extent of its cable, he yanked it fiercely from the wall.

'Franco, go through every room of the house and do the same. We have no further need of telephones – and send Rae down here. I'd like a rest myself.' Franco gave a half-smile of resignation and left the room.

Hammond turned his attention to Ronnie. 'Go with the woman and get us some coffee and something to eat,' he said.

To save Martha further distress, Mary quickly stood up and made her way through to the kitchen, her mind in turmoil.

Still in a state of shock from the intrusion of her privacy, she felt weak and numb. She knew she must try to communicate with this man but found difficulty in forcing the first word. She busied herself making the sandwiches.

'What . . . what are you doing here?' she asked almost in a whisper. 'What do you expect to gain from all this?' Ronnie leaned against the draining board, watching her.

'All I can say is the less you know about what's going on the safer it'll be for all of you.' Ronnie spoke kindly. 'Just do as you're told and I'll see no harm comes to any of you.'

'Would the name Kenneth Brownlowe mean anything to you?' she asked, looking him full in the face. Ronnie felt the shock thunder through his body. He fought to control his voice.

'No it doesn't, why do you ask?'

129

She explained how he reminded her of an ex-boyfriend, who'd gone away on a business trip, never to be seen or heard of again.

Ronnie wanted to explain, but couldn't. Once she knew that Kenneth had been his twin brother, his own identity would be blown.

He remembered Ken telling him about this woman, a Mary Cartwright, and of how much he thought of her.

Ronnie had been on service abroad when he first learned of Ken's sudden and violent death and it was not until seven months later when back in London that he finally traced the flat. It had been empty, and no trace could he find of the girl, Mary Cartwright.

Ronnie looked at her with renewed interest. How many years ago would that have been. Twelve, thirteen years ago? She was stunning even now, but then his brother too had been dashingly handsome.

Mary picked up the tray and paused at the door. She looked back at him.

'What's your surname?'

'I can't tell you that.'

'You must be related to Ken. I'm sure of it. When all this is over perhaps you could write and tell me about him . . . . It's not that I expect anything, you understand, I just have to know what happened.'

Ronnie reached out and touched her shoulder: 'I'm really sorry I can't help you, I'm afraid I haven't got a brother.' Mary sighed, and continued through to the sitting room. She placed the tray on the table, and sat down next to Martha.

Everyone took coffee except Hammond who'd discovered the Chivas. He held a half-filled glass in one hand and the bottle in the other. He drank greedily. 'It's going to be a long night,' he slurred. 'Everyone's to stay down here; me and Rae'll take first watch. The rest of you get some sleep.' No one wished to argue. Franco curled up on the floor, Ronnie settled into the armchair. He looked at Mary sitting opposite, head laid back, eyes closed. Her beautiful long legs rested diagonally to one side, her skirt had risen just above the knee. Ronnie fought to clear his mind of her and pushed himself deeper into the chair. He closed his eyes and tried to sleep.

☆   ☆   ☆

Within the dream, Mary Cartwright's cries for help echoed through his brain. He woke up startled, instinctively alert, and resisted the impulse to take immediate, unthinking action.

The coffee table had been pulled away from between the chairs and Hammond lay sprawled in front of the two women. He held the empty bottle of Chivas in his left hand and with the other, was attempting to prise open Mary's legs with the barrel of the revolver. She resisted with all her strength, pleading for someone to help her.

Franco appeared to be sleeping through the commotion whilst Rae, although sickened by what he saw, remained confused and at a loss what to do.

Mary was hit a sharp blow across the knees with the revolver. She lifted her legs in reflex action, showing black suspenders and a flash of white thigh. Hammond forced her legs apart and pulled her forward to the edge of the settee. He held her there gazing mesmerized at the scanty knickers that had ridden up into her. He seemed transfixed. Martha fainted.

'For God's sake leave her alone,' Ronnie said, trying to keep his voice calm.

'Unless you want to fuck it just stay out of it sonny,' drawled Hammond. 'Here, have a look at this pussy. Did you ever see anything more beautiful?' He moved to

131

bring his face between her thighs. Ronnie calculated the time it would take to cover the ten or twelve feet distance – too long for sudden impulsive action.

'Come on, Jason, be fair ... let's have a look in.'

Easing himself gently out of the chair, he covered half the distance slowly and casually. Hammond took his face from between the woman's thighs and turned towards him, eyes glazed.

'You fucking wait your turn; you had your chance.'

Sensing danger, he released his hold and swung the revolver towards his assailant who lunged towards him. An ear-splitting crack rent the room as the first round was fired at Ronnie's chest followed by another at point-blank range.

A small black hole appeared in Hammond's forehead; his head snapped back. Fragments of bone and blood flew out at great force from the back of his head, covering Martha and half the settee.

The impetus of Ronnie's lunge carried him over the top of Hammond and sent him crashing into the mêlée. Mary screamed and screamed again. The smell of cordite and traces of blue smoke hung heavy about the room. For a second, it might have been a year, everything was still, silent; no one moved.

Ronnie, not yet aware of the extent of his injury, eased himself away from his entanglement with Mary, sat down on the floor, and felt his chest and stomach with both hands. Franco stood up, returned the Hush Puppy to its holster and walked over to kneel down by his friend. His eyes filled with tears.

'Are you hit bad?' he asked gently. Ronnie got slowly to his feet.

'I can't believe it but I think I'm OK.' He ran his hands down his front and over his thighs looking for some injury.

'How could he miss at that range?'

Rae walked across the room and eased the gun away from Hammond's clenched hand. He examined it carefully, breaking open the gun and shaking out the remaining four cartridges. He picked them up from the floor. His face broke into one of his rare smiles.

'It's a bloody replica.' He opened his hand, revealing four blank cartridges.

'That stupid fisherman gave him a replica.'

'He said it was a Smith and Wesson model 15,' said Ronnie, shaking his head in disbelief. 'He probably thought we would have understood it to be a replica.'

'Can't say I'm sorry.' Ronnie turned to Franco. 'Thanks mate, that was some shot of yours. It's nice to know who one's friends are. Now we'd better clear up this mess.'

Mary had eased herself away from the gory spectacle. She sat on the rug in front of the fire, staring into the embers, her face a blank.

Charles stood with his back to the room. He looked out across the lawns and fought to control his shaking limbs.

Henry sat in one of the armchairs and seemed unable to speak. Ronnie quickly realised he was in a state of shock and tried to reassure him as the dead man was lifted clear of Martha and placed on the floor behind the settee.

'It's OK, she'll be OK. Look, before she comes round we should clean her up a bit. Can you fetch her something clean to wear?'

Henry tried to stand up but his knees seemed to buckle and he fell back into the chair.

'Rae, help him find a dressing gown or something.' Ronnie turned to Franco. 'Get some soap and a bowl of hot water from the kitchen, quick as you can.' A few minutes later Henry had eased off the blood-stained dress and put his wife into a white towelling robe. He settled her into a more comfortable position and bathed her clean. He stroked her hair and soon she started to regain consciousness. She opened her eyes, looked up at him and smiled. Franco discreetly carried the bowl of blooded water to the kitchen and by the time he returned Martha had fully recovered. Charles shuffled across the room.

'Could I have a word ... alone?' he asked.

'If you must,' answered Ronnie impatiently. He looked towards Mary, concerned with the way she was acting. He set two logs on to the fire and gently brushed his hand against her cheek as he followed on into the study.

Charles walked behind the desk and sat down. 'This sort of thing was not meant to happen,' he said, holding his hand to his forehead. 'Didn't they explain my involvement?'

'What do you mean, involvement? Nothing was ever said ...' Ronnie paused for a moment, '... except for the immediate job ahead.'

As if freeing himself from some awesome responsibility, Charles started to explain his own participation and how he'd been promised and assured that no member of the household would be mistreated or harmed.

Ronnie listened in amazement, as specific details of the raid on St Malo were revealed, confirming beyond doubt an implicit involvement. When pressed for the ultimate objective the man leaned forward over the desk, composure and confidence restored.

'I don't think I should divulge any additional information,' he said. 'You have your orders and should act on them. No need of a responsibility you may not be able to handle.'

'That's good of you,' replied Ronnie condescendingly. 'There is however a big problem: we have just shot our pilot.'

'Leave that to me,' Charles smiled reassuringly. 'My

134

man will co-operate, I'll see to that. In the meantime I'd appreciate you keeping our little secret.' Ronnie reluctantly agreed and felt revulsion for a man, who for financial gain would risk the violation of his wife and employees.

They returned to the sitting room and Charles made straight for his wife. He put his arms through hers and, whispering words of comfort, lifted her to her feet. A look of scorn spread over her face which quickly turned to anger.

'Don't ... you ... touch ... me ... ever again.' Charles reeled from the force of her words. She continued. 'If we ever get out of this mess in one piece and at the moment I don't care much one way or the other, I never want to see you again.' She pushed at him roughly and shot a defiant look towards Ronnie.

'I would now like,' she said flashing an obviously false smile, 'to go to the loo.'

There was an embarrassed silence as Ronnie wondered whether he should instruct one of the men to accompany her, or allow her the privilege of going alone? Mary made much of his dilemma and stood in provocative pose awaiting his decision.

'That's all right,' he said tentatively. 'You go ahead, but if you're not back here in ten minutes we'll come and get you.'

Switching off her smile, she gave a toss of her head and walked out of the room.

Ronnie focused his attention on Martha who'd completely recovered her senses.

'Have you got a deep freeze, the chest type?' he asked.

'Yes, there's two of them in the utility room,' she replied, puzzled by his question.

'Then I suggest you hide your eyes,' Ronnie turned to Franco.

'Get rid of the bastard, it's the best place for him.'

As the dead man was carried from the room, Henry's new role was explained to him.

'Don't consider us to be in anyway a soft touch,' Ronnie concluded. 'One wrong move and there'll be trouble for all of you. If you co-operate I guarantee you my protection.'

'Look,' said Henry, 'all I ever wanted is a quiet life – that's why we came to work for Mr Verdusca. I'm sure we all appreciate the way you risked your life to help madam and because of that I am prepared to trust you.' He paused and looked across to his employer; Charles nodded approval. 'Under the circumstances,' Henry added, 'I'll co-operate any way I can.'

'Glad you see it that way,' said Ronnie, 'and now we seem to have reached an understanding, I'd advise you to get some sleep. I'm afraid we have a long wait ahead of us.'

Ronnie instructed Franco to take first watch and went upstairs to find where Mary had got to. The second door he tried revealed a room that could only be hers, stamped as it was with her own provocative elegance.

He called out, closed the door behind him, and moved across the deep pile towards the kingsized bed. Multi-coloured cushions were arranged at the cane headboard and silk underwear had been thrown casually on to the exquisite hand-crocheted bedspread. Ronnie felt an impulse to touch the cool black silk and to smell her body scent that might linger there. He turned towards the bathroom door; she stood wrapped in a scarlet robe watching him.

For some reason he felt foolish and awkward, like some small boy caught doing wrong.

'Are you all right?' was the only thing he could think to say. She smiled nicely and walked up to him, untying her belt as she did so. The robe fell open to reveal her nudity.

Ronnie took in the pure beauty of her breasts, the whiteness of her skin. She pressed herself against him and placed her arms around his neck. She looked up at him, her blonde hair cascaded over her shoulders.

'Fuck me, please,' she spoke with a false sweetness. 'Fuck me, kiss me, do things to me,' she pulled Ronnie towards the bed. She jumped up on to it, threw open her gown and cupped her hands under each breast thrusting them invitingly towards him.

'Come on, I'm hot for it, that bastard's made me crazy for it.' Her eyes were staring, she was high on sex. Ronnie wanted to touch her, to taste her, to smell her, but not like this, he would not take advantage. It wasn't him she wanted but a need to purge her body of the previous violations forced upon her.

Abandoned to unashamed wantonness, her hands stroked at her stomach and thighs, caressing, touching, teasing. She brought two fingers of her left hand either side of her vagina and pulled the flesh up tight towards her. The index finger of her right hand moved to her clitoris, her head tossed from side to side. Ronnie turned away, cries of ecstasy and pain followed him into the bathroom.

He closed the door, locked it, and ran the cold tap. He bent down and immersed his head in cold water holding his breath for several seconds.

Sitting on the edge of the bath he dried the surplus water from his hair with the towel. He unlocked the door and placed his hand on the latch. He paused, and taking a deep breath opened it.

Mary lay face down on the bed, still and quiet. He knelt by her side. She turned and looked at him, her eyes filled with tears. He stroked her hair; she started to sob.

Burying her face deep into the bedclothes she cried out

137

her shame until emotion slowly subsided. Finally she sat up, leant back against the headboard and pulled her robe tightly around her.

'Please forgive me,' she whispered, 'I just can't understand what happened to me.' Ronnie raised himself up to sit on the edge of the bed.

'Perhaps it was nature's way of preserving your sanity,' he offered.

'It's kind of you to be so generous.' She smiled with genuine affection and explained how she and Charles had grown apart, consequently living virtually without sexual contact.

'I suppose that horrible man triggered off my pent up frustration ... I don't know.' She placed a hand on Ronnie's arm, lay back and closed her eyes. 'I must thank you for not taking advantage of me and for your great understanding ... I think I'd like to sleep now.'

Ronnie pulled back the covers and she eased herself into bed. He covered here over, bent down and kissed her forehead. Curled up like a little girl, she was already asleep.

11

The grand opening of the United Services Christian Association's first conference was scheduled for the following day, and the Dean of Jersey had been asked to officiate.

He had made some effort to research the Association's history and it was not until he received a printed leaflet setting out its worthy aims and causes that he had agreed to offer the blessing and to lead the morning prayer.

Ten mini-buses had already been delivered and parked in a neat row in front of the hotel. The hire car operator had been delighted to offer a most competitive rate and was grateful to the Jersey tourism committee who made such great effort to promote and encourage out of season business such as this.

Delegates began arriving in the early morning and continued to arrive throughout the day. They had travelled in small groups either by ferry or variously aboard the many scheduled air services which operated into Jersey daily.

On arrival, they retired directly to their twin-bedded rooms, and there they stayed. Few knew the companion with whom they shared, and greetings varied between warmth and suspicion, confidence and embarrassment. As the day dragged on tensions and a general restlessness increased. Room service was on constant call, watches were frequently checked.

By evening all one hundred delegates had been accounted for, so many similar faces, so many unlikely characters. Suspicions might well be aroused amongst the private guests if they were seen together. Questions might well be asked.

Hidden away in their rooms they waited. Most were well used to it, a prerequisite of their 'profession'. A long period of inactivity was usually the forerunner to some explosive action, and most had their own method of coping with boredom.

Some smoked, some drank, several dozed and others simply waited, thinking of past lovers, of wives, girlfriends or family. Each man in his own way sought to pass the time until the moment it would all start, the rendezvous, at 0300 hours.

☆　☆　☆

With stealth and silence they flowed down the broad sweeping staircase. The night porter was quickly despatched, bound and gagged and laid out behind the reception desk.

They continued to file outside and collected in predetermined groups under the floodlit palm trees bordering the large forecourt. No one spoke, or had a need to; everything had been well rehearsed.

Moving off down the sloping drive at two-minute intervals, they marched the short distance turning into the driveway of Government House and passed its uninhabited guardhouse. Here they regrouped on the lawns, crouching or kneeling low within the shadows of tall trees and surrounding shrubs.

Four specialists closed on the Edwardian brick mansion. They placed a suction pad against one of the windows and etched deeply into the glass with a diamond-edged cutter. The pad was pressed forward sharply, then with the piece of glass attached, eased out gently. A hand, thrust through the aperture, unfastened the catch and pulled open the window. The four men climbed through; someone flashed a torch – they were in the dining room.

Once in the hall they split, two men moved to the rear of the house to secure the staff, the others climbed the elegant staircase to the first floor landing. They had full knowledge of the layout and made directly for the Lieutenant Governor's bedroom.

Faint moonlight lit the white counterpane covering the sleeping form in the nearest bed. One of the men crept close, took a knife from his belt and signalled to his companion. The light was switched on; both sleeping forms stirred. One groaned at the other for the disturbance, then, sensing something wrong, sat up with a gasp of astonishment. The woman in the adjoining bed pulled the covers over her eyes and screamed.

The Governor and his wife moved with calm and dignity and did as they were told. Brought downstairs into the drawing room they found their maid and manservant already under guard.

One of the men opened the front door and the ten section leaders entered the house. Within minutes each and every room had been checked. Every telephone, intercom and computer terminal ripped out or disconnected. Satisfied that the house was secured, they returned outside. Four small beacon fires one at each corner of the lawn burned brightly into the night sky.

The rhythmic beat of a helicopter could be heard in the distance, approaching from the north-east. Not the most natural and direct route from its point of departure but certainly on a bearing that would attract the least possible attention.

It zoomed in low over the trees to make an expert and

141

speedy touchdown. The engines cut immediately, and the alarming din quickly subsided.

Curtains were pulled aside in the drawing room; light spilled out across the lawn as the four guards took it in turns to peer out. Little could be distinguished amidst the fleeting shadows that danced at random across the darkened green.

Ronnie ordered Henry and Charles out of the Sirkorski and instructed Franco to issue the arms and ammunition to the 'troops', then, taking four of the machine pistols with loaded magazines, he escorted his two 'hostages' towards the house. The three men entered the hall where they were taken without fuss into the drawing room.

The Governor and his wife sat together on a settee, their two servants stood nervously behind. Ronnie noticed the guards appeared awkward and self-conscious.

They took the offered guns eagerly; once properly armed, confidence and stature were quickly restored. Ronnie wished them luck and, leaving Henry and Charles in their care, returned to the helicopter. Securing the door from the inside he settled down into one of the comfortable seats, and with Franco already asleep, prepared himself for another long wait.

GROUPS 1 & 2. MISSION: POLICE HEAD-QUARTERS 0430 HOURS

Sections 1 and 2 moved out of the shadows and into the two waiting mini-buses. The twenty men were driven down St Saviour's Hill and into Rouge Bouillon. Three or four hundred yards on they turned right into a private crescent and pulled up under cover of several tall elm trees.

Immediately opposite stood a large forecourt shared by the police and fire service and partially lit from the overspill issuing from both reception areas. No sign of life or movement was evident.

The section leader walked boldly across the road; his men in contrast dispersed silently into the night.

Clasping his jacket tightly to his chest he pushed open the aluminium entrance door and walked up to the unattended desk. The duty sergeant came out from a small room behind. 'Good evening, sir,' he spoke genially 'and what can I do for you this early in the morning?'

The section leader stood back a pace and threw open his jacket revealing the machine pistol slung over his shoulder. He thrust it menacingly at the bewildered policeman.

'Come away from behind that desk.' The sergeant obeyed and within seconds ten men had rushed past him, continuing through the swing doors into the operations room.

Six uniformed officers jumped to their feet in alarm. A policewoman, wide-eyed in astonishment, remained seated at the radio communications desk. She turned back to the transmitter and leant towards the microphone. As she opened her mouth to speak something hit her on the nape of the neck. There was a sharp crack as bone shattered, her head collapsed to one side and blood trickled from the corner of her mouth.

The second wave had by now entered the reception area. One man was left to cover the police sergeant whilst others ran upstairs to restrain anyone else that might still be in the building.

The section leader, well satisfied with the way things were going, followed through into the operations room.

'Who's in charge here?' he asked.

'I am,' a young police corporal answered.

'Well, son, if you don't want to get hurt like your lady friend here, do just as I say.' Catching hold of his arm, he

143

thrust the officer towards the radio desk and kicked viciously at the seat. The dead girl slumped from her chair into an unnatural and twisted position on the floor. The policeman was pushed into the vacated seat. 'Now put a call out to foot patrol, squad cars, and motorbikes. Get them back in here one at a time, no flashing lights, no sirens; just keep things cool. One wrong word and one of your mates gets it. Do you understand?' The policeman nodded acquiescently.

Instructing one of his men to monitor the transmissions, the five remaining policemen were hustled to the rear of the building where they were held for the few minutes it took to locate the keys. A couple of drunks jeered and shouted abuse as the police were joined by several others and pushed unceremoniously into one of the adjoining cells. The entire building within minutes had been cleared of all personnel except for the sergeant in reception and the young officer at communications.

Police officers on patrol duty started to arrive and as they walked unsuspectingly into reception they were greeted with the barrel of a machine pistol and frog-marched down to the cells.

The next shift was not due to clock on until 0800 hours, two-and-a-half hours hence, more than adequate for the occupying forces of groups 1 and 2 to complete their mission.

Section leader Group 2 took four men to the mini-bus and drove the short distance to Vallée des Vaux, and the home of the Chief of Police. Together with his family, the protesting official was taken to Government House and held there for the duration, along with the others.

The mini-bus returned the men, accompanied by Commander Teal, Major Jones, Captain Sobbard and the German, to the police station which was to become headquarters and where the patrol cars could be utilised

144

as a radio contact to all other points of command.

Meanwhile it had been a simple task to clear the adjoining fire station where the night shift was similarly rounded up and secured in the now crowded cells.

GROUP 3. MISSION: CHANNEL TELEVISION 0615 HOURS.

A mini-bus followed the patrol car into the forecourt of Channel Television, not a half mile distant from police headquarters to the west, and Government House to the east.

Two men in police uniform got out of the white Escort as five others, each concealing a gun under a loose jacket or thrust uncomfortably down the inside of his trousers, disembarked from the bus.

The 'policemen' pushed open the front doors and led the way in. At such an early hour, the reception area was unattended.

Dispersing his men through the building, the group leader walked up a short flight of stairs to the viewing room. From there he could see the controllers at work below him, relaying the national network of TV AM.

He allowed things to continue undisturbed for the moment and returned to reception; only three other night shift workers had been found throughout the entire building.

The empty studios were lit only by the emergency lighting, until someone threw the switches. The dazzling arc-lights froze the faces of the two controllers into shock. An instant later they jumped from their seats, mouthing indignation through the glass screen of the soundproof booth. The door opened behind them and they turned to be confronted by a gun waved menacingly towards them.

145

The braver or more stupid of the controllers pushed his chair aside and, protesting profusely, moved towards the intruder. In sudden action, the butt of a pistol arched downwards. Staggering backwards, the man collapsed into his chair. He put a hand to his blooded face and wondered what to do with the three-inch piece of flesh hanging loosely from the wound.

The group leader walked into the booth and produced a bandage from his pack. He did his best to patch the wound as he issued instructions.

'I want you to do exactly as you are told. In a few minutes, I shall order you to switch over for a live broadcast from the studio.'

'But we haven't a cameraman,' stammered the controller.

'You will have,' snapped the reply.

Fifteen minutes later, at precisely 6.45, the Bailiff of Jersey Sir Henry Le Selleur and his wife Lady Margaret were brought in by mini-bus, shortly followed by a patrol car carrying a bewildered and dishevelled George Wheatman, the CTV cameraman.

Hustled into the studios, he was surprised to see the Bailiff at the newsreader's desk studying a script.

Wheatman quickly realised, as had the Bailiff, that innocent lives were at stake and this was not the time for irrational heroics. Both wisely decided to co-operate.

The group leader instructed the technicians to proceed and called down to the studio by microphone.

'Are you ready?' The Bailiff looked into the autocue. Wheatman signalled the camera was rolling.

'Then – action.' The green light on the wall above the newsdesk turned to red. The Bailiff cleared his throat.

'People of Jersey . . . it is my duty as your representative to advise you of a serious and potentially dangerous

146

occurrence that could affect us all.

'Just over an hour ago the French authorities reported news of a serious accident within the nuclear power plant at Cap de la Hague on the coast of Normandy. Leakage of radioactive dust has polluted the atomosphere and the meteorological office forecasts that the cloud will pass over the island in three hours' time. We are told that the leakage has now been contained.

'I implore you not to panic. Shut yourselves in your homes and seal all doors and windows. Fill all baths, basins and containers immediately for use as drinking water. Please do not use your telephone. It will be essential that all local, inter-island, and UK lines are kept open for emergency service calls. We have every reason to believe, however, that the immediate threat will disperse within twenty-four hours.

'I am advised that if these precautions are followed responsibly, no harm will befall you. Under no circumstances are you to venture out of your homes until further notice.

'This announcement will be broadcast every fifteen minutes. I thank you and may God protect us all.' The Bailiff looked up towards the control booth. The light behind him changed back to green.

'That was very moving, Sir Henry,' the group leader's voice echoed around the studio. 'If you'd like to come out, we'll take you to Government House.'

The announcement had been recorded on video and audio tapes and would be relayed automatically over the local network every fifteen minutes until such time as it was removed.

An alternating siren started to wail its ominous warning to the far reaches of the island. Several loud reports shook the town as rockets exploded over the harbour. Both were signals of nuclear disaster.

GROUP 4. MISSION: RADIO JERSEY & BBC TRANSMISSION STATION 0630 HOURS.

Having driven up Queen's Road, past Sion and Haute Croix, the mini-bus came to the tee-junction at Les Platons. It turned right and followed the road that ran along the north coast high above the rocks and sea; a 300 foot aerial pinpointed its destination.

The driver turned left off the road into a gravelled forecourt and stopped tidily in front of a flat-roofed single-storey building. A cold, pale light shone from the windows; the time was 0655 hours.

Ten men disembarked and skirted the premises; the panelled entrance door opened easily and quietly. Technicians monitoring the start of BBC breakfast television turned towards the intruders; looks of astonishment quickly turned to fear.

Hands thrust high in a compulsive act of submission were instantly brought forward in vain attempt to protect their bodies. The barrel pointing at them spat blue smoke and fire in three short bursts. One of the technicians stared in bewilderment, first at his own broken hands, and then at his friend who lay in convulsions on the floor. A look of compassion crossed his face, he attempted to speak but, sinking to his knees, retched and vomited a trickle of blood. From deep inside his body a hoarse gurgling pre-empted a gush of blood from the mouth as he collapsed choking. Several of the men averted their eyes, sickened by the needless violence; others appeared little concerned as the perpetrator ordered them out of the room.

Standing back a few paces and holding rapid-fire mode, he blasted off the remaining rounds into the electrical circuitry and equipment. The noise was deafening. Bullets ricocheted around the room, electrical sparks

148

buzzed and hissed in short circuit. A second magazine was emptied into the console screens and monitoring equipment. Several small fires had already broken out.

☆ ☆ ☆

The people of Jersey who were already up and watching BBC news and weather tried in vain to adjust their sets. Some little time later they switched over to Channel TV. The picture was clear and bright.

☆ ☆ ☆

No one had spoken during the seven-minute drive to St Helier, most men searching their conscience at being party to the brutality previously enacted.

Just two hundred yards on past the police station they turned right into the car park of a modern office building. A man in police uniform got out of a parked patrol car and handed over an audio tape.

The group leader thanked him, slipped the tape into his inner pocket and asked how things were going. The 'policeman', without smiling, nodded and followed the ten men into the building. He climbed the stairs behind them to the fourth-floor landing at his own leisurely pace.

Pushing open the glazed doors he walked into the reception area and looked through the glass panel to the one engineer on duty being held at gunpoint. Beyond, he could see through to the studio where a Radio Jersey presenter was being thumped back and forth against the glazed screen, finally to be pushed back into his seat in a state of sheer terror.

The man, visibly shaking, put on earphones and flicked a switch. His unsteady voice carried through into reception.

149

'THIS IS RADIO JERSEY. WE REGRET TO INFORM YOU THAT WE ARE NOW UNDER CONTROL OF THE CIVIL EMERGENCY DEPARTMENT. WE ADVISE YOU TO STAY TUNED TO RADIO JERSEY OR TO CHANNEL TV WHERE OFFICIAL ANNOUNCEMENTS WILL BE MADE BY THE BAILIFF OF JERSEY EVERY FIFTEEN MINUTES THROUGHOUT THE DAY. STAND BY FOR HIS MESSAGE, RECORDED JUST OVER ONE HOUR AGO.'

There was a short pause as the presenter inserted the Bailiff's taped message.

The siren repeated its alternating whine; another three rockets echoed successive explosions over the town – alien sounds, disturbing the hearts and minds of those old enough to remember still the nightmare of enemy occupation.

The 'patrolman' turned casually away and returned downstairs to the white Escort. Sitting sideways in the driver's seat, he leaned over and picked up the microphone.

'This is Champagne Charlie calling base. Are you receiving me?'

The clear acknowledgement returned almost immediately. He again pressed the transmitting button.

'Group 4. Mission 1 and 2 successfully accomplished, over and out.'

GROUPS 5 & 6. MISSION:
JERSEY AIRPORT 0630 HOURS.

Twenty men disembarked in front of the airport building. Group 5 went straight through into the ground-floor offices and rounded up the early morning shift.

Hustled gently into main reception they were told that

the island was in a state of civil emergency and that they were to go home and put on Channel Television where everything would be explained.

The whole operation was handled in a low-key manner. Some of the staff started to ask questions, but when a uniformed 'officer' asked them to leave the vicinity of the airport immediately, his authority was readily accepted.

☆　☆　☆

Simultaneous to Group 5's rush through the building, Group 6 made their long run up three floors before climbing the spiral staircase to flight control.

The early-morning aircraft that brought in the daily papers had landed at 0600 hours; it had been tracked and plotted by the three duty controllers. Their concentration would not have been further taxed until the next scheduled flight which was due on screen in fifty-five minutes.

Startled by the intrusion, the controllers were given scant explanation and told that no plane was to be landed at Jersey airport for the next twenty-four hours.

This preposterous instruction was immediately challenged. 'We can't possibly refuse to accept them,' remonstrated the senior man.

'I am afraid you will have to,' the group leader showed great patience and restraint. 'The runway will shortly be rendered inoperative. You will remain on duty and disperse all approaching aircraft to alternative airports. You will inform them that there has been a major accident and the runway is temporarily out of service. Is that clear?'

Showing the first signs of aggression, he waved the MAS 16 machine pistol at the three men. 'If you'd care to look outside you will see that what I ask you to do is wise and sensible.'

151

The controllers watched in awe as the aircraft, a Boeing 737, was towed across the grass perimeter and parked in the centre of the single concrete landing strip.

Four cars drove into view at great speed and headed in pairs to points equidistant between the plane and both ends. Here they were parked and abandoned; the runway had now been rendered unusable to all fixed-wing aircraft, large or small.

The men watching the scene unfold below them leapt back in alarm as the control tower trembled and the glass panels shook and rattled. The shock wave was closely followed by the muffled sound of an explosion and within seconds dense black smoke engulfed the aircraft. Future reports to all scheduled services could now be confirmed visually from the air.

The uniformed 'officer' returned to the patrol car and radioed to base. His message was received and understood. Groups 5 & 6, mission accomplished.

☆   ☆   ☆

GROUPS 7, 8, 9 & 10. THE TAKE 0700 HOURS.

Teal, Jones, Sobbard and Mueber drove off in patrol cars to their separate destinations, each closely followed by a mini-bus carrying Groups 7, 8, 9 and 10. The roads were deserted, an eerie silence pervaded the crisp early-morning air.

Commander Teal studied his map and directed the uniformed driver through the small country lanes. The Commander was relaxed enough to take in the beauty of the surrounding countryside. The lush meadow grass, covered by a heavy dew, shimmered in the sun. He wound down the window and breathed in deeply. The air was as fresh as toothpaste.

152

The car turned off the road into a short driveway and stopped in front of a granite-fronted house. The mini-bus remained at the front gates and discharged its ten occupants. The men were tired and stretched their aching limbs.

Commander Teal held his finger on the bell push. Chimes rang his impatience through the hall and around the house. An upstairs door banged shut, lights were switched on. Someone trod heavily down the stairs; the front door opened.

A man of indistinguishable age looked at them bleary-eyed. He wore a dressing gown and half his face was covered in shaving foam.

'What the ...?' He noticed the 'police officer' standing behind the 'gentleman'. 'Is anything wrong?' he asked, slowly wiping his face with the back of his hand.

'Pretty serious I'm afraid, sir,' Commander Teal spoke. 'You haven't heard anything on the TV or the radio then?' The bank manager shook his head. 'Well sir, we've apprehended three men who'd entered the bank in the early hours. We think they attempted to make a money transfer through your computer system. They also entered the vaults.' The manager looked aghast. He opened wide the door and invited them in.

'Impossible,' he said. 'They wouldn't know what password to use. Everything goes through London.'

'That may be the case, sir,' answered Teal, 'but we urgently need your transfer operator, also the major key holder. We'll need to check everything to establish whether anything's been taken. Unfortunately there were others involved who got away, and we've no way of knowing how long they were in there.' There was a pause; the manager tried to organise his thoughts.

'Yes, of course. Look, I'll give you the address of my under-manager, he'll have the details of all our employees.' He wrote the address on a pad next to the phone. 'I'll call him if you like,' he added.

'That won't be necessary, sir.' Commander Teal picked up the piece of paper. 'Perhaps you should come with us.'

'Yes, of course.' The manager started towards the stairs. 'Can I get dressed?'

'Please be quick,' answered Teal. 'We've no time to lose.'

As they moved off in the patrol car, the mini-bus pulled in close behind. The manager peered nervously through the rear window. 'Are they with us?' he asked.

'Just a precaution, sir,' answered Teal. 'They're from Special Branch.'

'Well I never,' the manager shook his head. 'I never even knew we had a Special Branch.'

'That's why they're special, sir.' The Commander turned around and smiled.

It took nine minutes to reach the modest detached house. Teal got out of the car and seconded two men into the back seat, one either side of the manager.

'Look here!' he leant over to wind down the window. 'What's going on?' One of the men grabbed hold of his arm.

'Just you keep quiet, Shylock, and we'll let you keep your balls.' The man, now terrified, sank back into the seat and shut his eyes.

Commander Teal rang the bell and pushed at the door sharply to reveal a man in his early thirties holding a large roll of Sellotape.

'Sorry about that, sir,' said Teal. 'We have your manager in the car and he wants you to accompany us to the bank with your keys.'

'For Christ's sake! Haven't you heard about the disaster?' The man's voice was close to hysteria.

154

'I shouldn't worry about that, sir,' the Commander smiled reassuringly. 'The wind's changed direction and the radiation's heading back over France.' The man's face lit up; he called upstairs. 'It's all right, Jean. It's going to be all right.' 'Come on now, sir, we've a small problem at the bank and we need the operator of your money transfer system. I believe you have her address.'

'No need,' answered the young manager, now only too anxious to oblige.

'I can tell you everything you need to know. It was me who originally trained the girls to use it.' The Commander waited as the man ran upstairs to reassure his wife.

'You've got the patience of a saint, sir.' The 'police officer' looked at his superior with renewed respect.

'No need for physical persuasion,' answered the Commander. 'Whenever possible our aims should be achieved by friendly means. Wouldn't you agree?'

'I'm not sure all your employees quite see it that way, sir.'

The under-manager reappeared and followed the two men to the car. He paused, realising suddenly that something was wrong. He bent down and peered inside. 'Are you all right, sir?'

Before he received an answer the Commander's boot caught him a stinging blow on the base of his spine. He stumbled forward, sprawling half in, half out. The door closed hard against his legs and was opened again to be slammed shut. Pulling his legs in quickly, he saved himself a second bout of searing pain. He clawed his way to a sitting position and stammered an apology.

'I would suggest, Stephens, that you do exactly as these men say.' The manager had been listening to the exchange of messages over the intercom and had not been slow to realise the enormity of the situation. Commander

155

Teal looked over his shoulder from the front seat. 'If you do exactly as you are told, no harm will come to either of you or your families.' The car was driven away from the house towards the town. Commander Teal continued.

'We hold all key positions throughout the island. We have your Bailiff, the Lieutenant Governor, the Chief of Police, their wives and children. If we need to, we can play the hostage game but that's not what we're here for. It's up to you – co-operate and by this evening we can all go home.'

'And what of the nuclear disaster?' asked Stephens, still rubbing his shins. 'There's no nuclear disaster,' Teal smiled his reassurance, then turned to the driver. 'Come on, son, remember you're a "policeman", no need to keep to the speed limit.'

☆ ☆ ☆

The car pulled into Library Place and stopped outside the Midland Bank. Commander Teal was pleased to see one of the other cars and a mini-bus already parked a little way down on the opposite side. Both vehicles were empty and stood adjacent to the main entrance to Barclays.

The four main clearing banks were situated within one hundred yards of each other. A police car and a mini-bus, a principal and ten armed mercenaries per bank. The logistics were predetermined. Four managers, four key-holders and where necessary four computer transfer operators. The plan of robbing each was the same. The vast wealth of Jersey was about to be tapped.

The under-manager opened the side door and was then made to switch off the alarm systems.

The Commander and his allotted group filed into the main banking hall; each man carried a bundle of hessian sacks. 'Your staff normally arrive just before nine,' said

156

the Commander. Stephens nodded his confirmation. Teal looked at his watch; it was nearly 8.40. He called over to his group leader.

'Place a man at each door. The rest of you come down with us.'

The two bank officials led the way to a central lobby and through a steel-plated door which had been locked and bolted. The under-manager flicked on six brass light switches and continued down the stairs to the concrete floor below.

The entire basement was partitioned by stout iron grilles to form room-sized metal cages not unlike cells. The atmosphere created a general uneasiness amongst the men.

'I'll tell you what I want,' clipped Teal, 'and you' – Stephens looked up at him wide eyed – 'you open things up for us.' He pushed the under-manager roughly.

'One wrong step and I'll . . .' He gently patted the man on the shoulder, his face changed instantly from impatience to tolerance. 'But there won't be need for that,' he smiled. Stephens' face was creased with fear. 'First of all,' continued Teal, 'your foreign currencies.'

Stephens fumbled with his keys and unlocked one of the iron gates. Teal followed him inside and watched as the under-manager consulted his notebook for the combination to the safe. He turned the dial to the left and then spun it expertly the opposite way, searching through a sequence of numbers towards eight individual selections. He stood back a pace and spun a large wheel set within the centre of the seven foot door. There was a loud clunk as the bolts withdrew, Stephens eased open the door and Commander Teal stepped forward. The interior of the safe was arranged in shelves, each shelf holding a sliding tray, each tray a particular currency.

'You men,' the Commander looked back over his

shoulder, 'bring those sacks over here.' They walked forward one at a time as the Commander emptied French francs, Italian lire, Portuguese escudos, American dollars and German marks into the sacks which were then carried upstairs and stacked against the counters of the main banking hall.

Commander Teal now concentrated on United Kingdom currency including Scottish and Isle of Man denominations. No effort was made to remove the Jersey notes, which in such amounts would prove conspicuous. The Commander looked at his watch; it was almost 9.20. He ordered the under-manager to accompany him upstairs. Stephens looked concerned. 'For Christ's sake, man, get a move one,' said Teal, not unkindly, 'we're not going to hurt you.' He rechecked his watch as they climbed the stairs. 'This money transfer system, it's called Swift, isn't it?'

'Yes, sir.' Stephens walked ahead with little enthusiasm.

'Then hurry, for God's sake, get a move on.' Teal pushed the man in the back, causing him to stumble against the door which opened into the computer room. Stephens felt under a desk and switched on the power to a computer and line printer. He took out his notebook and with clumsy fingers fumbled through it, attempting to find a particular page. Teal spoke whilst looking at his watch.

'In exactly four minutes' time I want you to make a transfer. Are you ready to proceed?' Stephens nodded. 'Yes sir, fire away ... I mean yes I'm re' re' ready.'

'You will transfer £5 million sterling to the Bank of Versailles, Rue Charles de Gaulle, Paris.'

Stephens took a gold fountain pen from his inner pocket and wrote the information on a blank pad in front of him. The Commander continued: 'The account number

158

into which the money is to be transferred is . . .' He read from a small printed business card, '03204340. The account is held in the name of J.B. Fernandes.' Stephens jotted down the details.

'From which account is the money to be transferred?' Teal shook his head in disbelief. 'From the Midland Bank, you stupid clot. Now get on with it.'

Stephens keyed the current password into the computer and gained access to the Swift software package. Within three minutes the transaction was completed. 'They'll acknowledge acceptance of the transfer by printout,' Stephens looked up with satisfaction, 'it takes a little while.'

Commander Teal returned to the banking hall and asked for the front doors to be opened. He peered cautiously outside. Apart from three pairs of empty vehicles parked at each of the other banks, the streets were deserted. He closed the doors and ordered them relocked.

He noticed the men who'd been consigned to cover the entrances looking towards him and sensed they seeked reassurance. The Commander was a natural leader. He understood the responsibilities of command and the psychology of getting the most from his men. He walked to the centre of the hall, where they could all see him. 'Things couldn't be going better for us.' He swept his arm towards the bulging sacks of money. 'I could never have dreamt it could be so easy.' Seeing the relief in the men's faces, he added a word of caution. 'So far so good, but to get away scot-free we mustn't relax for one second. You chaps have done a grand job, keep it up.' Teal turned to the under-manager and ordered him back downstairs.

The six guards lounging against the iron grilles sprang to attention as their Commander reappeared.

'Just two more things, Stephens.' He signalled the men to pick up the few remaining sacks. 'I want all your

American stocks.'

'Do you mean bearer certificates?' asked the senior manager, speaking for the first time.

'If that's what you call them, I think they're also known as coupons.'

'Bearer certificates,' confirmed the manager. 'You'll find them in the trust boxes over here.' Another gate was unlocked to reveal black metal boxes stacked from floor to ceiling. Each had a code number written on it. The manager went straight to boxes A36 and A37 and removed twelve certificates from one and nine from the other. Teal took them and totalled up the combined value to $2.8 million. He thrust them nonchalantly into the open sack and, stretching his neck, tried to ease the tension from his shoulders. 'Thank you, manager, that saved us a lot of time.' Commander Teal relaxed his taut muscles; for a moment he felt a little dizzy. He breathed in deeply. The musty damp air did little to help clear his head.

'Just one more bit of help and then we can leave you – travellers cheques.'

Stephens spoke out before his superior had a chance to answer. 'Over here, sir.'

He led the way to the far end of the basement, unlocked the gate and set about opening another safe. He stepped back and spun the wheel; the bolts withdrew with a healthy clang.

Travellers cheques stacked on open shelves were scooped into the remaining sacks and carried upstairs. The two bank officials, realising their usefulness was at an end, grew more nervous by the minute.

Stephens handed over his keys as instructed; his eyes pleaded for compassion. The Commander walked out of the cage and turned to stop Stephens from following. 'You stay where you are.' He placed a hand against the man's chest. 'Put the other one in with him.'

The guards jostled the senior manager forward. Teal pushed him inside, slammed the gate and locked it. Stephens stood dejectedly holding on to the bars with both hands. Teal ordered everyone else upstairs.

'We'll leave a message that you're down here, but I'm afraid you're going to have a long wait.' Stephens gave a little whimper and nodded, relief showing in his face. The Commander, without another word, turned on heel and followed his men up to the main banking hall where he unlocked the doors and looked out. Seeing a second mini-bus with driver at the wheel parked behind their own, the Commander opened wide the entrance doors and ordered the sacks loaded. Soon done, the men climbed into their own mini-bus and were driven off at speed with the other following close behind.

Teal closed and bolted the bank doors from inside. He started to walk back through the building but froze in his tracks. His hand, in reflex action, grabbed at the butt of the holstered pistol.

The whirring of high-tech machinery continued for another few seconds, stopping as suddenly as it had started. Moving stealthily towards the sound realisation dawned. The Commander straightened up and relaxed. He walked across to the line printer, tore off the message and read the bottom line.

' *Transfer £5,000,000 sterling exchanged as 48,250,000 French francs and credited to account No 03204340 confirmed.* '

The Commander smiled, folded the paper and put it into his jacket pocket.

He locked the side door to Vine Street behind him and walked around the corner to the waiting patrol car. 'Government House if you please, officer.' Commander Teal noticed with satisfaction that he was the first to have completed.

161

All sacks containing UK currencies were emptied on to the expansive ballroom floor to be counted into one hundred shares of £25,000.

As the other groups followed in, a growing number of men watched fascinated from the open doors.

Commander Teal barked a command; men parted to make way as the four principals walked into the room. Teal stopped and addressed them.

'You chaps get off to the kitchens. I've arranged food and hot coffee for you.' The four officers were soon left to watch the vast amounts of money first being sorted into some kind of order.

'I reckon it'll take at least three or four hours at this rate,' commented the Major. 'If you don't mind I think I'll go and have a lie down.' The Commander looked at his watch; it was 11.45. 'There's nothing much more we can do until it gets dark. I think I'll do the same.'

Sobbard volunteered to stay and supervise the counting.

'Good idea ... thank you, Sobbard.' The Commander noticed Mueber seemed reluctant to leave; he put his arm around the German's shoulder and turned him away from the proceedings. 'Give yourself a break, Reinhard,' he smiled. 'Relax, no one's going to steal it.' Mueber shrugged his shoulders and started towards the door. The Commander restrained the Major, allowing the German to continue on his own.

'Carry on then, Captain, there's a good chap.' Commander Teal turned away and with the Major at his shoulder walked stiffly out of the room.

12

The glow from a match lit up the cabin, Franco coughed from the seat behind. Ronnie woke up stiff and cold, his clothes still damp with perspiration after the physical effort of the unloading. He sat up and pulled at his shirt, easing the fabric away from his skin, then with a conscious shiver, he pulled his jacket tightly around him.

Franco started to snore gently. Ronnie leaned over into the aisle and stretched for the cigarette still held between his friend's fingers. He put it to his own lips and inhaled deeply just the once before stubbing it out. His head spun, he'd not smoked for three years and wasn't used to it. He lay back into the seat and shut his eyes; the sensation passed, his mind settled and he began once more to consider his position.

There had been opportunity in Guernsey when contact could have been made with the Department. For a second he'd hovered by the phone but somehow he'd lacked the motivation. And then again with Hammond out of the way it would have been so easy to fly to Guernsey and scupper the whole operation. At the time this course of action had occurred to him but never with serious intent.

The facts of the matter had to be faced. The pace and professionalism of this highly organised outfit had seduced him with the excitement he craved. On a personal level he valued the relationship built up with Franco and to a lesser degree with Rae. Until such time as they were guaranteed safely away, Ronnie decided he'd make no move to play the informer. After all he'd only been put here as an observer – to serve the purposes of those who would simply treat him as a pawn to be sacrificed, to be discarded should it suit their purposes.

His presence had already served its purpose in protecting Mary. He would help any innocent party who might be unnecessarily threatened. No more should be expected of him. They had only themselves to blame for throwing him into a situation without previous psychological assessment. Things had changed since his service days. He had changed. They had seen fit to cause that change. And what of his family? Somehow he would have to justify his silence at some time in the future, in order to resume a normal life. A normal life! He'd buy another house, perhaps somewhere by the sea. Francine would come back to him and the kids. Christ, he missed his girls. The love he had for his children was the most wondrous thing. Ronnie was capable of great love, he knew it. Sometimes he had difficulty in expressing it. Francine had understood, once, but now she was gone. Ronnie started to feel emotional . . .

He touched her soft golden hair and held it to his face, he breathed in the sweet fresh smell. He held her away from him and looked into her face; that beautifully shaped mouth, those few little freckles she was so conscious of. She bent her head down on to his shoulder, blushing.

Ronnie drifted into a light sleep; he thought he'd dreamt of nothing.

☆   ☆   ☆

Suddenly awake, he stretched and yawned, it was bright daylight. He checked his watch, 11.42. He moved down the aisle and shook Franco gently.

164

'Come on, let's go up to the house for a coffee and something to eat.' Franco looked up with a broad grin and pushed himself out of the seat. The two men entered the hall just as Commander Teal and Ashley Jones walked through the double doors.

'Good morning, Brown,' said the Commander jovially, 'I must congratulate you on a marvellous job.'

'Thank you, sir. Everything's gone according to plan, has it?'

'Extremely well, Brown. Things couldn't have worked better for us.' 'We have to refuel, sir,' Ronnie reminded him. 'Is the airport secured?' 'Yes, Brown, thank you. Take the pilot – he's in the sitting room with the others. Before you go make sure you use the police radio to say you're coming. Do you think the old machine's going to stand up to it?'

'I would think so, sir.'

'Carry on then, Brown, there's a good chap.' The Commander walked across the hall and started up the stairs. 'And, Brown,' he added as an afterthought 'go and help yourselves to refreshments from the kitchen ... and thank you for saving the young lady. I'll have no truck with mindless behaviour like that nor with unnecessary brutality. I commend you both for your action.'

Ronnie was surprised that the Commander had been so well briefed. He turned away and followed Franco towards the appetizing smell of fried bacon.

The two men enjoyed their late breakfast in the crowded kitchen amidst a buzz of excited conversation. Half-an-hour or so later they made their way to the sitting room.

Sleeping forms were stretched out on the floor, others curled up in chairs. Guards standing at each window, another at the door, queried their entry. Ronnie explained their need of the pilot and without waiting for authority walked across to where the man dozed.

'Come on, mate,' said Ronnie pleasantly as Henry's eyes blinked open. 'We have to refuel the Sirkorski.' Henry smoothed out the creases in his jacket. He brushed at the lapels with his fingers fastidiously, then patted his trousers into shape. Grooming completed and without comment, he followed them out of the room.

☆   ☆   ☆

Henry started the engines and, moving off in a westerly direction, took the machine to 400 feet. Ronnie looked below and felt the cold sensation of fear. The roads were deserted: no traffic, no people; it was if a nuclear holocaust had already taken its toll. He averted his eyes until they were over the airport and settled on to the hardstanding. Within seconds a British Petroleum tanker had pulled alongside.

Henry climbed out to supervise as Ronnie and Franco looked towards the runway. Black smoke swirled from a stricken Boeing, a major fire had virtually burnt itself out. Ronnie walked to the other side of the Sirkorski.

'I assume we sabotaged that aircraft to block the runway? I hope no one was in it at the time.' The man still keeping his eyes on the gauges at the side of the tanker shouted above the noise of the pumps.

'That's right, mate. I towed her across myself. Me mates chucked a couple of grenades into her.' He turned, frowning. 'Went off like a bomb it did. Planes shouldn't burn like that; really puts me off flying – straight up!'

Ronnie smiled back at him then, shouting to Franco, caught hold of Henry's arm and pulled him good naturedly towards the airport buildings.

They made their way through into the departures hall and, before sitting down, took papers, cigarettes and confectionery from the airport shop which had been abandoned in such a rush.

Henry started to read *The Daily Telegraph*, Ronnie reached out and gently pushed the paper aside. He talked as if to a friend. 'Henry, I'm afraid we've involved you very much in all this and we're extremely grateful for your co-operation.'

'You're only getting my co-operation because you've got my wife and Mrs Verdusca.' Henry answered with a disarming degree of honesty: 'I'm not *that* involved,' he added.

'You realise that as soon as the light goes, you're going to have to make four crossings to the south coast, in the dark, without navigational aids and at a height of no more than 300 feet.' Concern clouded the pilot's face.

'But that's over ten hours' flying time. I'm not going to be able to cope with such narrow margins of safety. I'm knackered already, let alone coping without sleep for another night.'

'That's why I'm telling you now,' answered Ronnie. 'There's no two ways about it, you've got to do it; there's no one else.'

'Bloody hell!' exclaimed Henry, almost in a whisper.

'One thing I can promise,' Ronnie added. 'Do this for us and you'll be back with your wife, safe and sound, by tomorrow morning.' For a moment Henry looked pensive, then, realising there was no alternative, he walked over to one of the bench seats and lay down.

'Do you think he can do it?' Franco asked.

'He's going to have to ... I didn't dare tell him we've got to pick Rae up as well.'

Franco looked worried. 'I didn't like leaving him behind. Do you think he's all right?'

'You don't believe I'd leave you in the house with two women, do you? Of course he's all right.' Ronnie picked up Henry's discarded *Telegraph* and tried to put all thoughts of Rae from his mind.

13

A man in his late twenties pressed the bell to the side door of the Banque Nationale, just off La Rue Charles de Gaulle, Paris. Four heavily built 'gentlemen' stood two paces behind. A fifth sat waiting in the driver's seat of a Renault van parked in an area reserved specially for transfers of cash.

Immaculately dressed and well groomed, the young man positioned himself in front of the spyglass. He heard the bolts being pulled; a middle-aged bank official smiled recognition.

'Ah, Monsieur Fernandes, you are always on time.' The bank clerk spoke English, coloured by a thick accent. 'We have not yet finished counting, but please do come in.' The door was held open as Fernandes stepped inside followed by the four large men, each carrying a metal trunk.

☆   ☆   ☆

Over the last four weeks Fernandes had formed a special relationship with Banque Nationale. For a large fee they had agreed to process a weekly money transfer into French francs which would be collected later the same day.

Early on a Monday morning the transfer would be effected through the international computer system

169

known as Swift, transfers that Charles Verdusca had seen fit to originate from his own bank.

To disguise its origin it was first processed through a numbered account in Switzerland before being sent on to Paris where it would arrive just before noon. This allowed the bank three hours to process the amount into francs, ready for collection by the young Spaniard at 2.30.

Loaded into the van it would then be driven just 400 yards away to a small independent finance house of German origin.

The money was again counted and unbeknown to either institution, transferred back into the same Jersey account it had left some six hours previously.

Today would be different, no longer the charade. This time the amount would be doubled. This time the transfer had originated from a main clearing bank. This time the money would not be returned.

☆   ☆   ☆

The clerk escorted the five men into the manager's office. Four tellers were just finishing the count; the manager got to his feet and with hand outstretched sought to shake hands across the desk.

'Mr Fernandes, how good to see you again.' He spoke in perfect English. 'I regret that this is to be the last we see of you for a little time.'

'Thank you, Monsieur Rabat, for your courtesy,' Fernandes answered in a quiet and cultured voice. 'I hope we will be in a position to repeat our arrangement during the autumn months.'

'We will be delighted to assist your corporation at any time,' beamed the manager. He turned to his senior cashier. '*Êtes-vous fini, Henri?*'

'*Oui, Monsieur Rabat, nous sommes fini.*' The manager

170

gestured grandly with the open palm of his hand. 'Is it OK,' he smiled broadly, 'please you take.' Fernandes nodded politely and watched his assistants place the money into the four metal trunks. The lids were closed and then locked with a single master key.

'I am recommending to my senior directors that we transfer our major trading accounts into your bank.' Fernandes spoke with great authority. 'Thank you for your help and efficiency.'

'*Vous êtes très gentil*,' said the manager. Fernandes closed the exchange with a smile, then followed his men as they carried the money out to the van.

Traffic seemed much worse than usual and the drive to the finance company Allemand took nearly twenty minutes. Fernandes was nervous and uneasy; he had come to dread these short Monday journeys. If the contents of the van were ever leaked there was little doubt they could be hit and taken with ease. It was a calculated risk, and each time he considered it fortunate to arrive without incident.

Now, faced with the dilemma of where to park, he gesticulated in despair and ordered his driver to pull up in the centre of the narrow street.

The five men jumped out, quickly unloaded the trunks on to the road and banged on the side of the van; the driver pipped the horn and drove off.

Fernandes pushed the bell with some impatience, beads of sweat on his forehead. If it had been planned they could hardly have looked more conspicuous or at that very moment been more vulnerable.

It seemed an interminable age, but by the time the door opened, Fernandes had regained his self-control and appeared calm and self-assured. He shook the director's hand.

'This will be the last deposit we ask you to process,' he said. 'You've been so kind to afford us the use of your

171

excellent facilities.'

'You are most welcome,' answered the director. 'We shall be pleased to assist you at any time. I am sorry this will be your last transaction.'

'You do realise,' – Fernandes handed across a printed card – 'this time the money is to be transferred to the Cayman Islands; The Royal Standard Bank of Cayman, the name of the account and account number is there on the card.' The director looked at his watch. 'We will be able to effect the transfer this afternoon. Do you wish to remain while my staff do the counting?'

'I'm afraid I have another appointment,' answered Fernandes. 'I will leave everything in your capable hands.' He bent down, unlocked the trunks and handed over the key.

'The Bank of Cayman were informed some days ago to expect the transfer today. It settles a liability of capital repayment with accrued interest on an international loan, granted to our company for exploration and development costs. It is imperative to the standing of our company that this is honoured.' He shook hands warmly. 'Of course, you will deduct your fees from the capital.'

The man smiled: 'If that is your wish, thank you, monsieur.' Fernandes nodded to his assistants that the meeting was terminated; he made to leave, then turned towards the director and, as if an afterthought, he added: 'I am recommending to my board that we transfer all our financial services through your good office. We will be in touch within the next few weeks to discuss our requirements.'

'You are most kind,' beamed the director. 'I look forward to meeting you again.'

Fernandes turned on his heel and closely followed by his assistants made his way out of the building into the street. Here the five men separated, each to take his predetermined route away to anonymity. Fernandes heaved a sigh of relief. He had never felt easy in the company of these men; their physical presence unnerved him.

Walking a few yards, he turned into the main avenue and entered the first street café he came to. He moved between tables and chairs, sat down under the glass dome next to the pavement and removed a small black cheroot from a cigar case. He lit up and inhaled the rich flavoured smoke, exhaling long and hard as if breathing out the tensions built up over the last few weeks. He played with the gold Dupont lighter, stretched his legs out under the table and contented himself for a few minutes watching passers-by and the busy traffic beyond. A waiter with a long white apron tied at the waist, and looking as if he'd stepped out of the 1920s, interrupted the daydream.

Fernandes tapped fingers on the table in subconscious release of nervous energy until the coffee and treble Cognac was served. He started to feel pleased with life. He was safe. All that was left to do now was to collect his bonus. He felt confident it would be honoured; all previous commitments and assurances had been met to the letter. He wondered what it had all been about.

Apart from a few minor misrepresentations, he had not acted illegally, merely represented others. He would not presume to question their private business and it was necessary for him to take the occasional risk.

Fernandes placed a fifty franc note on the dish; he lit another cigar and made his way out into the busy street where his attention was drawn to a young girl standing in the entrance to the Metro. A large battered suitcase stood at her feet; she looked lost and bemused.

With captivating smile Fernandes engaged her in conversation and within minutes had picked up her suitcase and hailed a cab.

She clambered into the taxi showing finely shaped legs. She struggled into the back seat and the outline of her knickers through a skin-tight skirt left little to the imagination. His eyes penetrated to the spotless white panties that had ridden up between those faultless rounded buttocks.

Fernandes placed the suitcase inside and climbed alongside her. He leant forward and whispered instructions to the driver and, turning, caught her looking at him. She blushed and hung her head. Fernandes smiled and touched her hand. The street value of this one could prove priceless.

14

It had been a long day, but it would be a longer night. The first group had already arrived from police headquarters; it was 6.26 and time to make a move.

Ronnie gently shook the pilot awake. 'Time to go.' Henry looked up, dazed and disorientated. 'We take off in fifteen minutes,' said Ronnie. 'Get yourself together. It's time we got this show on the road.'

Ronnie gave instructions for the men to assemble in the main reception area where a further sixteen, made up from those holding the airport, already waited. Each man clutched an identical sports bag bulging with his own personal bounty.

The two group leaders supervised a detail to load the first quota of ten sacks of loot into the helicopter and then proceeded to embark the twenty-six men.

Ronnie waited until the area had been cleared, then spoke to Franco: 'Look, mate, this is going to be a real pain in the arse.' He placed a hand on the Portuguese's shoulder. 'No reason for both of us to go. I'll do this trip and you do the next.'

'What about Rae?'

'We'll pick him up on the last trip out. We'll be back from this one around nine o'clock. Confirm with base that the next twenty-six are here ready and waiting by 8.30. It's imperative we achieve a quick turn-around.'

Restricted by the Sirkorski's payload of twenty-five

men plus crew of three, four journeys during the hours of darkness would be required to get everyone off the island. It was an achievable operation provided no serious delays were encountered and Henry possessed the necessary ability and stamina.

Franco hadn't moved; he didn't seem to know what to do with himself. 'Don't worry about Rae,' Ronnie sensed his friend's concern. 'He knows we won't let him down.' Franco smiled and nodded. 'Good luck, eh!'

'See you at nine o'clock.' Ronnie hurried out to the hardstanding. He broke into a trot; the rotor blade of the Sirkorski had already started to turn on the starter motor, it coughed into rapid motion, willing hands stretched out to pull him aboard.

Henry passed over a set of earphones and switched to internal communication. 'You said the south coast.' Henry kept his eyes glued to the altimeter. 'Whereabouts on the south coast? I need to take a bearing.'

'The same bearing you fly Verdusca twice a week,' answered Ronnie, 'Herne airport.'

'Christ, that's a relief,' answered Henry. 'You've just taken a load of my mind – no problem. You're not putting down on the airport surely?'

'No, cross the most westerly tip of the Isle of Wight and then head due north for ten kilometres, leaving Lymington to the east. Our rendezvous is just seven kilometres on west of Brokenhurst – Wilverley Plain.' Henry nodded. 'You know it?'

'I know it.' Ronnie could sense the man's relief.

'Good lad. We can expect a marker somewhere within its three square miles. They'll light a fire for us, I shouldn't wonder.' He looked out of the starboard window to the floodlit structure of the nuclear power station at Cap de la Hague. Fascinated, he continued to stare at this awesome place until slowly it disappeared from sight.

176

Somehow it remained etched in his mind until the distant glow of city lights captured his attention.

'That's Bournemouth in the distance.' Henry spoke for the first time since his flight instructions. 'I'm bearing off twenty-two degrees east to pass over the Needles in about four minutes. Just now we're over the Isle of Wight, Freshwater and Yarmouth, there to your right.'

Henry changed course and headed due north. They crossed the small stretch of water, left Lymington to starboard then eased away a few points west. 'May I gain altitude to locate the marker?'

'Make it a quick one, Henry.'

The Sirkorski surged upwards, all eyes scanned the expanse below. 'Bear off a little more to the left,' said Ronnie, his concern quickly turning to elation. 'There, down there at eleven o'clock, see those red lights.' Henry immediately reduced height and within two minutes hovered above the markers. Successive flashes from a powerful torch beamed upwards. 'That's it, Henry, take us down, quick as you can.'

The Sirkorski settled on to the springy turf, the men quickly disembarked. Ronnie scrambled through to the open door and peered into the gloom.

'Christ, it's you Harry. Never thought I'd be pleased to see you again.' Harry grunted a reply and asked if there was any 'luggage'.

'Ten sacks,' Ronnie answered, 'I'll chuck them out to you.' Harry called for assistance and the heavy sacks were dragged to the door and lowered down to outstretched hands; the job was completed in minutes. Ronnie shouted into the darkness.

'With any luck we'll be back in just over two hours' time. See you! OK, Henry, move, move, move.'

The Sirkorski surged up and away, its turbulence beating down the grass and surrounding bracken. Men

177

bent low and turned their backs against the rush of cold air. Within seconds it had passed, and within minutes the rhythmic sound had disappeared into the night sky.

Harry counted the sacks in as they were stacked into the external feed compartments of an old sheep transporter. He padlocked the doors then, with the men already loaded aboard, he closed the ramp.

A few miles up the A35, the lorry pulled into a lay-by, and the men transferred to a coach parked in darkness nearby.

As if by magic the engine sprang to life and Harry watched as it pulled out into the road and headed off in the general direction of Southampton.

☆   ☆   ☆

At eight minutes past nine o'clock, they picked up the runway lights of Jersey airport. Henry swung the helicopter across to the hardstanding and settled it down without fuss or ceremony. He switched off the engines and removed the headphones.

'I must have a coffee and freshen myself up,' he said. 'How long have I got?'

'I can give you ten minutes, Henry, not a second longer.' Having said it, Ronnie immediately felt he had been overgenerous. He followed the pilot out and saw Franco standing in front of the men already assembled.

Within a few minutes all twenty-six were seated with eleven bulging sacks stacked along the aisle. Ronnie briefed Franco what to expect and what to look out for.

'We're running about fifteen minutes behind schedule, every minute you can save is precious.' He re-checked his watch for the umpteenth time. 'Here comes Henry now. See you, hopefully about 11.45.'

Franco waved from the door as he closed it and Ronnie

178

could see him scrambling into the co-pilot's seat as the helicopter rose up and banked away to the north.

15

Rae had watched from the window with some misgivings as the helicopter took off. Once alone he felt vulnerable.

He had grown fond of both men, accepting Ronnie's natural leadership and the warm comradeship and generosity from the Portuguese. He felt that between the three of them nothing was impossible, nothing unachievable, but now they'd gone and he was on his own. Somehow no matter how things started he always ended up alone. In his heart of hearts he knew that unless things went drastically wrong, they would never purposely desert him yet he still wondered whether he'd ever see them again.

A woman's voice broke his train of thought. 'Don't worry,' she said. 'My husband will get them back.' Martha spoke in a gentle reassuring voice. 'The biggest mistake would be to underestimate him.' Rae appreciated her kindness. He drew the curtains and shut the doubts from his mind. 'They'll come back for me,' he said confidently. He walked over to the fire. 'You mustn't worry too much either. You'll soon have your husbands back safe and sound.'

'I don't want mine back, thank you very much,' said Mary.

Rae was somewhat taken aback by the venom in her voice. 'I never want to see the man again – ever.'

'Why, Mary, why ever not?' asked Martha, showing genuine surprise. 'How can you say such a thing?' Rae now wished he'd kept quiet; he bent down and placed a log on the fire.

'God how naïve you are, Martha,' continued Mary scornfully. 'You really think the sun shines out of that man's arse don't you?' Martha, tight-lipped, sat down. Rae thought it opportune to suggest they try to get some sleep. 'You can either bed down in here or share a room upstairs,' he said. Mary instantly made the decision for them. 'I'm sorry, Martha, I didn't mean to be so nasty. We'll go up to my room.'

Locking the bedroom door, Rae pocketed the key. He returned to the living room, switched off the lights and stretched out on the settee. The flickering shadows from the fire soon eased away the tensions; he closed his eyes.

✩   ✩   ✩

The fire was out but the room was still warm. He squinted to look at his watch and went into the kitchen; it was already 8.45. Over a large mug of coffee and several pieces of toast, Rae tried to calculate when he could expect the return of his friends and eventually came to the conclusion that, if no serious problems were encountered, it should be somewhere between two and three o'clock that night.

Clearing the dishes on to the draining board, he made his way upstairs to see if the girls were awake.

✩   ✩   ✩

Lucy Petworth considered herself fortunate to have Mary Verdusca as a friend. Since their meeting just fourteen months ago, so many good things had come about. Apart from being caught up in Mary's own social whirl, she now received a constant stream of invitations from people

181

hoping for an introduction.

Lucy realised only too well the reasons behind this sudden acceptance into Guernsey society, but rather than be upset, she was determined to make the most of it. Her newly acquired popularity had already helped her estate agent husband; the business which had struggled previously was now transformed. They had much to thank Mary Verdusca for.

Lucy in no way considered herself to be outshone by her friend, she was complementary. Bright, pert and natural, two years younger, dark and pretty – the friendship was a genuine one.

She walked from her nineteenth-century terraced house that overlooked the harbour, and crossed the narrow cobbled street.

Skipping down the granite steps leading to the Pollet, she window-shopped along the High Street, turned into Commercial Arcade and entered the old bakery.

She waited a few minutes, then ordered coffee. It was so unlike Mary to be late; perhaps she'd mixed up the arrangements. Perhaps they'd meant to meet up in the restaurant instead?

Lucy paid the bill and walked down the steps across to the promenade fronting the marina.

She climbed the little winding staircase that creaked and groaned at her every step and pushed open the door into the main dining room. A huge window gave panoramic views of the marina. Sunlight streamed in across the century-old cedar flooring. A smell of wax polish mingled with a salty smell from a large table display of a fresh shellfish laid out on a bed of moist seaweed. Animated conversation in French from the two occupied tables added to the overall character and charm of the room.

The *maître* greeted her warmly and offered to take her jacket. 'Mrs Verdusca hasn't arrived yet, has she?' asked

182

Lucy.

'No madam,' he answered with the hint of an Italian accent. 'Her secretary booked the table for . . .' He looked at his diary, '. . . 12.30, madam. Would you care for an aperitif whilst you wait?'

'Just a glass of white wine please – dry.' Lucy felt a growing concern. It was so unlike Mary; if she had been delayed she would surely have called the restaurant.

Dialling the number, she held the receiver away from her ear, not understanding.

Shaking it, she hung up, waited a second and re-dialled. The alien unobtainable signal rang through her brain. She had always loathed that sound. It conjured up memories of unpaid bills, disconnection and hopelessness. She replaced the receiver and returned to her table.

Lucy took a sip of wine and looked beyond the harbour towards the small group of islands. They looked so peaceful, so beautiful set against the blue sky and sweeping cotton wool cloud. The waiter claimed her attention: 'Would you care to order madam?'

'No thank you, Maurice, I was supposed to meet Mrs Verdusca. If you don't mind I'll see if I can find out what's happened to her.'

She collected her jacket and returned to the promenade. 'She wasn't being silly, there must be something terribly wrong. Positive action was called for, even if it was just for her own peace of mind. Now determined, she hurried the few yards to the police station and waited her turn whilst the sergeant gave directions to a French couple looking for the Victor Hugo Museum.

'Good afternoon, madam, what can I do for you?' Lucy blushed. She felt a little stupid and embarrassed, feeling sure he'd treat her like a schoolgirl who'd lost her friend. She paused a second, trying to make sense of her concern, then took a deep breath.

'I was supposed to meet Mrs Verdusca at 11.30 this morning. She hasn't rung me and hasn't turned up. It's very unlike her. I've tried to ring and the number is unobtainable. I'm worried that something is terribly wrong.'

'Is that Mrs Verdusca from L'Ancresse Island, madam?'

'Yes, it is.'

'Can I have your name and address please, madam?'

'For goodness sake,' she felt unable to control her frustration. 'What's my name got to do with it? It's Mrs Verdusca I'm worried about ... Lucy Petworth, 26 Havelet Street, St Peterport.'

'Thank you,' the sergeant wrote the details in his day book. 'Shall we try the number again?' She wrote it down for him. He dialled, waited a second then held the receiver towards her. 'Unobtainable, madam. I'll telephone the airport. They'll be aware if the helicopter's taken them off someplace.' He looked up the number, dialled and was put through to flight control.

'The last contact was on Saturday. They were surprised themselves. It seems Mr Verdusca would not have gone into work today.'

'Then there must be something wrong.' Lucy now realised she had acted wisely.

'Charles would never miss going to the office; it's all he ever cares about.'

'I think you may have good reason to be concerned, madam. Just to be on the safe side we'll send the patrol boat over with a couple of men.

'Thank you, officer. You've been most helpful.' Lucy wondered whether she dare ask: 'Do you think I could go with them?' He saw no reason why not.

'If you'd like to take a seat, Mrs Petworth, I need to make my report and get this thing organised.'

'Thank you, thank you.' Lucy suddenly felt quite weak. Sitting down on one of the upright chairs she shut her eyes and offered a silent prayer that her friend was safe and that it was all some ghastly misunderstanding.

☆   ☆   ☆

It took over an hour to obtain full authorisation. Both crew members were off duty, needing to be called in, and by the time they brought the sturdy little craft from its moorings it was almost three o'clock.

The boat was held into the side as Lucy and two uniformed officers climbed aboard then, easing away from the quay, they headed slowly for open water.

Lucy was questioned in detail by the senior officer. She told him all she knew, but could find no logical reason for her concern. She felt a pang of guilt when she found herself hoping that something really was wrong, that she would not be found completely stupid, wasting the precious time, money and the resources of the Guernsey police.

She felt ashamed, better she were humiliated than some awful disaster involving her dear friend.

☆   ☆   ☆

The two police officers climbed up on to the jetty and each stretched down to offer her a hand. She grabbed hold and was swung up and on to the slippery causeway, her feet shot from under her.

Throwing her arms around the two men she regained her balance and was immediately aware of the physical contact between them. There was a brief moment of embarrassment until the senior man reached down and took a loud hailer from one of the crew.

'Hang on here for us, Jack,' he said, straightening up. 'Shouldn't be too long.'

'We'll take a turn around the bay,' answered the helmsman. 'The swell's too heavy to tie up here. Give us a shout when you're ready.'

Lucy declined any further help and picked her way gingerly up the slippery causeway.

Within five minutes they'd climbed the narrow winding path and the seven granite steps that brought them out on to the lower lawn.

'There's no helicopter, miss. I think you'd better stay behind just in case.'

They walked on a little more cautiously to the top lawn. Lucy followed someway behind. Fifty yards from the house, the senior constable lifted the loud hailer to his lips. 'Mrs Verdusca... Mrs Verdusca, this is the Guernsey police. Are you there? Is anybody there? Will you come out please?'

He lowered the hailer and scrutinized the building, searching for any movement. He repeated the call; there was still no response. They walked forward a few yards and then, simultaneously catching movement of the front door, they stopped short. A woman appeared and started to walk towards them.

'Mrs Verdusca?'

'Yes officer, can I help you?' she answered smiling.

'We were asked to come over to check you were all right. Is everything in order madam?'

'Yes, thank you, I think we have a fault with our telephone. It's most kind of you to take the trouble, I'm sorry you've been inconvenienced.' The two officers seemed relieved until Lucy ran past them towards her friend. A look of fear spread over Mary's face and she backed away.

'For God's sake, Lucy, get out of here.' Lucy stopped in

186

her tracks, shocked. Before she had time to recover, Mary had turned away and was running towards the front door. The policeman called after her but she rushed into the house, slamming the door behind her.

✿   ✿   ✿

Hearing the loud hailer, Rae had jumped from his seat to switch off the television. The startled females sat bolt upright. For a moment he dithered; he turned and appealed to the women.

'I can't let them take me – please realise that.' He picked up the machine pistol from the settee.

'What do you want me to do?' asked Mary.

'Go out on to the front porch and tell them everything's all right.' Rae gave instructions calmly and quietly. 'You know I'm not goint to hurt you but I can't vouch for the safety of this lady's husband if there is trouble. Try your best to get rid of them without making them suspicious.' Mary walked across into the hall. Rae followed, hustling Martha in front of him.

As Mary opened the front door, he took Martha upstairs into one of the front bedrooms. He got her to stand in one of the windows and squatted down at the side of the other.

He could see Mary facing two uniformed policemen. Some way behind stood a young woman who started to run forward. Mary shouted something then ran back out of sight. Rae heard the front door slam.

The woman started to walk away from the house, looking back over her shoulder every few steps. The policemen were now in an earnest discussion and after a few seconds started to moved forwards.

Rae opened the windows, just enough to permit free movement of the muzzle. He released the safety catch and taking careful aim fired three single shots at the large

187

terracotta flowerpot to one side of the advancing men. The pot shattered, fragmenting at their feet.

Instinctively they turned away, crouching and shielding the back of their heads. They quickly realised the hopelessness of their position and straightened, slowly raising their hands into the air.

Rae was faced with a dilemma. If he wanted to stop them leaving the island, there was no way he could get down to the front door by the time they scarpered. Even if he could, it would prove an impossible task coping with them on his own and, anyway, they'd soon be missed and reinforcements would be sent.

For a second Rae knew he should kill the two men from where he stood. He opened the windows wide. 'There's ten of us in here!' he shouted aggressively. The policemen looked up; he remained half hidden behind the net curtains.

'We have the two women and if you act sensibly no harm will come to them.'

'What is it you want from this?' called the senior man, having recovered his dignity. 'What are your demands?'

'Our demand is a very simple one: just piss off, leave us alone, and no one'll get hurt.'

As if to reinforce the point, Rae switched the pistol to rapid fire and rattled off a few rounds over their heads. No further persuasion was needed. Catching hold of the young woman, they beat a hasty retreat to the lower lawn and disappeared from view.

Martha sat down on the edge of the bed, her head in her hands. 'Don't fret, love,' comforted Rae. 'It'll all turn out OK, you see.' He turned towards the movement at the door. 'Thank you for trying, Mrs Verdusca.'

'What's going to happen now?' Mary asked as she tried to console Martha. 'They'll radio back and report our presence here.'

Rae thought for a moment. 'They'll expect to find the police armed and ready to be shipped over by the time they get in.'

'But you won't have a chance against so many,' said Mary, genuinely concerned.

'What they will find,' Rae smiled, 'is their administration in total confusion. It'll take them several hours to work out some sort of plan. They won't be seriously equipped to cope with a situation like this. Remember, they think they're dealing with ten of us – seriously. I don't think we'll see anything of them until late tonight.'

Rae closed the windows and, locking the girls in, went downstairs and secured every window and door. He loaded a tray with biscuits, cake, chocolate, and a carton of orange juice and carried it back to the bedroom. 'It's going to be a long wait, girls, but at least we've got the telly – switch it on if you want.'

The afternoon film was drawing to a romantic climax; a few minutes later, a news flash.

Rumours of a nuclear disaster at Cap de la Hague were strenuously denied but it was confirmed that all TV, radio and telephone communications had been lost with Jersey. This was put down to problems of a technical nature.

The two women looked at Rae for reassurance. 'Don't worry,' he said. 'The nuclear thing is just a ruse to get people to stay indoors. It confirms that everything is going according to plan.'

Pulling aside the net curtain, he looked out over the emerald-green lawns to the sea beyond. The St Peterport skyline merged with the deepening blue sky and white cumulus cloud. Several small boats were milling around the pierhead and he fancied that one of them might be the patrol boat scurrying back to brief the local constabulary.

☆   ☆   ☆

189

Rae first spotted heads, bobbing up over the escarpment. In the failing light he strained his eyes to count about a dozen. It was going to be extremely difficult covering both the front and back of the house by himself, but a few shots at a well-chosen time from one of the rear windows might help to suggest he was not alone. Hopefully, the police would prefer to tackle the siege by protracted negotiation rather than any immediate offensive action.

Rae felt his chances of holding out for twenty-four hours at the very least were relatively good and decided to do nothing until the police made further contact.

The television had been turned off and now an unnatural silence pervaded the entire house.

'This is the Guersey police.' The words spoken through a loud hailer reverberated against the stone walls, giving an inhuman resonance to the voice. 'We have you surrounded. Come out with your hands up and no one will get hurt.'

A powerful beam of light trained on the front door then settled at each window in turn. Rae moved out of sight and, locking the girls in, darted into one of the back rooms, knelt by the window and fired four single shots into the darkness. Then, returning to the front bedroom, he moved over to the window and, cupping hands to mouth, shouted: 'We have hostages here, they have not been harmed. We wish you to convey to the authorities that for their safe return we require the modest sum of £500,000 in foreign currencies, and guaranteed safe conduct.'

Rae took another deep breath: 'We are willing to make a deadline of five o'clock tomorrow, when, if our needs have not been met, we will execute one of the women.' He hoped the police would be convinced with the seriousness of the situation and that the women would understand it to be a bluff.

He stared into the darkness, and was suddenly blinded

190

by the searchlight. 'We shall relay your terms to our committee but we will need time to secure these demands – please be patient.' Rae rattled off a quick burst of fire into the general direction of the searchlight. It was quickly turned off or perhaps hit. A heavy silence returned, the smell of cordite filled the room.

Rae felt strong feelings of nostalgia. That wondrous smell carried him back in time. A small boy standing besides a bonfire lighting fireworks with his parents in those happy days before they'd split. He'd loved his father to this day, but had not seen him since.

A few years ago his mother had produced an address somewhere in Perth, and he had made great efforts to find the old man. It had been a starting point and three months had been spent covering the length and breadth of Australia.

He hadn't found his father but he'd enjoyed the big country and probably would have stayed on if he hadn't run into trouble.

Rae thought back to those raucous wondrous days, and then again to his father. Memories of everyday family life flooded back. He longed to be part of a close-knit family again . . . .

In some strange way, the bond formed over the last couple of weeks with Franco and Ronnie had helped. But it was also why he felt so alone now.

Rae prayed silently that they would come back and not abandon him.

16

Henry switched off, removed his earphones and slumped forward on to the controls. Ronnie put an arm around him. 'Well done, mate, just one more trip.' Henry leaned back and rubbed his eyes. 'Bloody nightmare, this,' he smiled weakly and with some effort eased his way out of the Sirkorski.

The last contingent of men were already assembled, anxiously waiting their departure. Ronnie found Franco in the canteen, standing with Commander Teal, Jones and Sobbard. 'We're ready to move out if you guys are,' said Ronnie, trying to instil some enthusiasm into his voice.

'Mueber is just supervising containment of the officials we brought up from Government House,' said Teal. 'We're locking them in the hangar storeroom with the rest of the airport staff.'

'What about the people from the TV and radio stations?' asked Ronnie, making no attempt to disguise his concern.

'We sent them all home,' Ashley Jones smiled reassuringly, 'and then destroyed all their equipment. The police and fire people are still locked up, so we should have ample time before anyone can get organised to come looking for us.'

Ronnie checked his watch; it was 2.28. 'Can we get moving, gentlemen? We haven't too much time.'

The Commander looked amused. 'Quite right, Brown, let's be off then.'

Mueber with his detachment of five men were last to board and everyone waited for the pilot with increasing impatience.

A spontaneous cheer went up as Henry pulled himself through the hatchway and took his seat at the controls beside Commander Teal. Ronnie picked his way forward between the booty that littered the aisle to confirm that the objective was to pick up Rae. He had some difficulty talking over the noise but to his relief the Commander nodded. Teal put on the headphones and relayed the revised flight plan to the pilot. The Sirkorski lifted off and set course for L'Ancresse Island, everyone ignorant of the fact that it was now besieged.

As the approach was made, their suspicions were aroused; the pool lights were not on and the house was in complete darkness. Ronnie considered the possibility of a power cut, but suddenly the pool's irridescent light shone towards them. Ronnie thought it strange that Rae was unprepared; first suspicions were soon confirmed.

A powerful searchlight caught the Sirkorski in beam, for an instant blinding the pilot. The helicopter banked suddenly, then held steady. Ronnie saw what might have been several flashes of gunfire, confirmed a fraction of a second later by the clank of tearing metal as one or two rounds caught the fuselage. Commander Teal shouted Henry out of his daze, gesticulating for him to gain altitude.

The Sirkorski swung up and away. Ronnie wanted desperately to go back and make an attempt to pick up his friend. The passengers were confused, not realising what had happened. Franco stood up to look over the rows of heads towards Ronnie, his glance questioning, pleading that they take some action. Ronnie signalled him to stay

193

calm, but felt sick in the stomach.

Clambering forward to the cockpit he pulled the head-phones away from Henry, to speak to Commander Teal.

'You've got to put me down on the island, sir. It's the very least you can do.'

'We can't,' answered Teal. 'It would be suicide to land there. We'd be a sitting target.'

'We don't have to land near the house, Commander,' answered Ronnie, a trace of desperation creeping into his voice. 'The pilot lives there, he must know a suitable landing point some way away. It would only take a few minutes to make the drop – ask him.' Ronnie replaced the pods over Henry's ears and waited anxiously for the Commander's decision. Henry thought for a moment, then nodded.

'We'll try one approach,' said Teal. 'If we don't draw their fire we'll make the touchdown. This man will then fly us on to the mainland and as long as your partner is willing to take the risk they can come back for you.' Ronnie breathed a sigh of relief and, as Henry banked the Sirkorski in a bold sweep of 180 degrees, he struggled back to shout the revised plan to Franco who shook his head. 'I go, my friend, not you. It is I who can see in the dark. It is I who am the hunter, not you.'

Ronnie considered the suggestion – it did make sense. Although he had no qualms about going himself, the Portuguese was the better man for the job. He nodded agreement and passed over a MAS16 and four magazines.

Franco clipped a powerful flashlight to his thick leather belt that already carried the holstered Hush Puppy. 'Get Rae to a relatively safe part of the island,' instructed Ronnie. 'When you hear us, and when you think the time is right, flash us three times. We'll come straight in for you.'

Ronnie followed him to the door and was about to

194

shake his hand when they felt the bump as the helicopter hit the ground hard. Ronnie overbalanced and in the instant it took him to recover, Franco had already disappeared into the darkness. There had been no time to wish him luck, and before the hatch was secured they were already airborne, speeding away without a shot being fired.

17

Assuming that the helicopter would have given away his position, Franco darted away to the right. He crouched within an outcrop of rock until the rush of air and turbulence subsided. A feeling of isolation overwhelmed him as the rhythmic beat of the Sirkorski faded into the distance. Even so, the fact that no shots had been fired inspired confidence.

He took a knife from his boot and dug into the coarse grass, scratching at the dark soil beneath and raking up a small loose pile. He replaced the knife, undid the zip of his fly and urinated. He kneaded the wet earth with both hands and, when satisfied with its consistency, spread it over his face and forehead, finally rubbing the residue over the back of his hands. The caked mud was highly uncomfortable, but provided a makeshift camouflage.

Slinging the machine pistol more securely on to his shoulder and re-adjusting the four spare magazines that had slipped into an awkward position inside his jacket, he started his move.

A bush here, a rock, small indentations, and several young trees provided good natural cover, until finally he crept up behind the hedge that bordered the vegetable gardens. He froze, voices filtered through the dense privet.

Franco backed off, placing his weight down gradually at each step. It only needed the snap of one twig, the rattle of one stone, and all might well be lost.

He'd learnt his craft in the hills back home hunting mountain goat and seldom was the time he'd returned without the means for a feastday roast. Goat was more difficult to hunt than man, but not as dangerous. He would take no chances; other people's lives were at stake as well as his own.

Moving back a suitable distance, he skirted the privet until once more he reached open ground where he stretched out and wormed his way slowly forward towards the house.

All the subliminal instincts supposedly long lost to man were at his command; only three men guarded the rear, if there had been more he would have smelt them.

In his present frame of mind, when the need arose, he would kill instinctively. He could not play with time and reason. He would act on reflex and once he struck, it was with the knowledge there'd be no second chance.

Feeling the soft earth of a cultivated garden beneath him he realised he must be close. He crossed the smooth damp grass of the rear lawn, and two minutes later lowered himself from the dry stone wall to the yard below.

☆　☆　☆

Rae's heart leapt as he heard the approaching helicopter. He locked the girls in and darted downstairs.

He switched on the pool lights only to hear shots ring out over the increasing roar of the Sirkorski. Hurriedly switching them off again, he dashed back upstairs, and let off several rounds in the general direction of the gunfire.

He could now hear the helicopter overhead, then, to his utter dismay and despair, he judged it to be gaining altitude. The sound that a few minutes previously had brought hope and joy to his heart disappeared into the distance.

'What's happening?' queried Mary from the darkness.

'I think we've been ... shhh! ... listen! Can you hear something?'

Rae could hardly believe the sound was returning; he held his breath.

It was a helicopter but the closer it got, the more he worried it might be some other machine bringing reinforcements.

The aircraft gave a wide berth to the house and swung off somewhere behind it.

The sound had almost disappeared again, but Rae's experience told him that this time it had made a touchdown. A second later the increased tempo signified a liftoff. Once more it swung up and away towards some other destination; this time no shots were fired.

Rae struggled to visualise what might be going on. Either the helicopter had dropped someone off – maybe Franco or Ronnie, or it had landed a contingent of armed forces. He thought the possibilities through. The machine had not been on the ground long enough to offload more than one or two men.

'I've got to go downstairs again, girls. I don't think I've been abandoned after all. Wait here please.' Taking no chances he again locked them in, made his way to the kitchen and peered out into the darkness. Whoever had got off the helicopter, if working under cover, would take some time to reach the house. He withdrew into the shadows and waited patiently.

The tense atmosphere of silence was broken by a faint scratching which seemed to come from the windows of the next room. Rae wondered what to do. How could he distinguish friend from foe without giving himself away? He crouched below the window line and moved stealthily across the kitchen and through the open door into the utility room.

Flattening his back against the width of the wall units, he focused attention towards the second window. Someone outside was trying to insert an instrument between the two sashes in an attempt to release the catch.

Rae stretched out on the floor and pulled himself along the polished surface, keeping tight against the sink units out of sight of the windows. He slid through the open archway into the rear lobby, eased himself to his feet, moved over to the outside door and slowly turned the key. He opened it a fraction and could just distinguish a dark form at the window. Taking the Hush Puppy from the holster, he removed the safety catch.

His heart beat fast and hard. He took a deep breath to steady himself, prepared to speak and stopped short. He thought for a second longer – there was nothing else for it. 'Ronnie...' Rae could see the figure freeze. 'Ronnie... Franco... it's me, Rae.' The figure very slowly turned towards him. Rae could just distinguish the six-inch blade of a hunting knife. 'Thank God it's you – it's you, Franco.' The form moved towards him like a shadow.

Closing the door silently and re-locking it, Rae turned towards the visitor. Franco returned the knife to his boot and stood up. The whites of his eyes shone from his darkened face; Rae saw the flash of white teeth. 'Christ, am I glad to see you,' he exclaimed. The two men embraced warmly. 'What the fuck's happening?'

'We had a full load on board,' whispered Franco. 'Unaware of any problem we made the approach, came under fire and Teal made us back off.' Rae led the way upstairs.

'It's going to be touch and go whether we can ge out of here before daylight,' he said, 'but it's great to see you – thanks, mate.'

He unlocked the bedroom door. 'It's all right, ladies, we've got a visitor.' Franco moved over to the window to

199

assess the deployment of the opposition. 'We've got to keep them where they are for another couple of hours at the most,' he said. 'Have you made contact?' Rae explained what he'd asked for and the deadline he'd given. 'OK,' Franco said, satisfied. 'We stay here for another hour and then we'll move out. I'll take you through the back to the other side of the island; hopefully they won't realise we've gone until it's too late.

'How's my husband?' Martha asked.

'He's doing really well, senhora. It won't be long before you see him again.'

Rae decided to take the initiative and asked Franco to go into the back room. 'When you hear me rattle off a few rounds, do the same across the rear yard. If they were beginning to think otherwise, it'll confirm there's at least more than one of us here.'

Rae knelt down by the window, checked the gun was set on rapid fire and blasted off several rounds in a wide arc. Franco's contribution could be heard from the rear.

When the sounds of gunfire ceased, he cupped his hands and shouted towards the policemen who cowered behind the escarpment out of sight.

'You have under two hours to meet our demands.' Rae turned towards the women. 'Could you shout out to them please, pretend you're both terrified.' 'What do you mean "pretend"? I am terrified,' answered Mary. 'If it'll help to get Henry back safely .... What do you want me to say?'

Mary spoke out loudly, pleading that no action be taken without prior negotiation. A minute later the reply came back over the loud hailer. 'We are attempting to meet all your demands. We would ask that you extend your deadline.' Rae made no immediate answer, surmising that if he had been part of a group, time would be required for a decision.

Cupping his hands once more he shouted that the deadline could be extended to 1900 hours the following evening. The police, thinking they had achieved first success in a war of attrition, readily accepted, and in doing so gave away a remarkable concession.

Franco returned carrying a tin of black boot polish and a couple of large navy sweaters. The two women put them on, and allowed him to blacken their faces as he explained to Martha that she would be soon reunited with her husband aboard the helicopter.

Rae slung the machine pistol over his shoulder and held open the door.

'If we get any trouble use the Hush Puppy,' whispered Franco. 'We don't want to give away our intentions. Use the MAS16 only as a last resort. Now, follow me.'

He led the way out by the back door and off to the left. First the retaining wall to the rear lawn and then the privet provided adequate cover until they moved into open ground and distanced themselves from those who guarded the rear. He now changed direction, leading the two women across the springy turf, with Rae following behind.

Having good reason to think they had crossed without incident, a loud report shattered their illusion. A white flare broke the night sky and froze the surrounding landscape into surrealism. Instinctively, the two men dropped to the ground, but the women remained upright and looked towards the pretty firework sizzling its way back to earth on the end of its parachute. 'Down!' spat Franco angrily. 'For God's sake, get down.' The two women knelt gently on to the grass. Rae pushed Martha from behind and held her flat against the turf. Now realising what was expected, Mary did likewise.

'Do you think they saw us?' Rae asked.

'We won't know for a while,' answered Franco. 'If they

201

did, they'll surely come after us.'

Lying low, waiting for the security of darkness to return, each had time to contemplate in his or her own way. Time to think, time to worry, time for fear, and when Franco again got to his feet to move off, they did so in an altered state of mind. To the women recent events had been almost a game; now the danger was for real.

They walked on in silence; the desire to communicate had gone. That feeling of closeness and commitment had for the moment disappeared, each now concerned solely with self-preservation.

It took another seven minutes to reach the outcrop of rock where Franco had originally hidden; it proved ideal for their present needs.

Just a few yards from the proposed touchdown area, it gave enough cover from advancing forces and an open field of vision on all sides.

Rae and Franco took up positions as far apart as the cover permitted. The two women lay huddled together in the centre, each now glad of the thick sweaters protecting them against the chill and damp of the night air.

Peering into the darkness beyond, it was easy to mistake natural images for human forms. The moon broke through the heavy cloud and for the few seconds it restored some confidence, revealing no sign of movement.

Rae put down the MAS16 and rubbed his hands vigorously. He whispered to the women, joking about the cold in an attempt to raise their spirits. Franco scolded him to silence.

At first they heard nothing and then a faint sound. It might have been a stone kicked forward, it might have been a rifle knocked against rock. It was enough, enough to raise the senses to screaming pitch.

Other sounds now reached them – surreptitious sounds they were not meant to hear: muffled whispers of command, the movement of boot through grass. Rae struggled with his own instincts to take the initiative.

A loud report heralded another flare, its trajectory formed a perfect arc between those who had despatched it from the entrenchment to their own advancing party.

The foolishness of this action was immediately apparent. Whereas the hunted were lying low, concealed by natural terrain, the hunters were caught on open ground, silhouetted against the skyline. There were five of them and before they had time to fully understand their predicament Franco let off a burst of rapid fire. Instinctively they threw themselves to the ground.

With a blood-curdling scream Franco ran towards the terrified men firing from the hip. The flare fell to earth from its low trajectory and, in its dying light, Rae could see two men scramble to their feet and start to run away. Both pitched forward as if hit by a sledge hammer. Franco carried on running, now zig-zagging his way towards the remaining men. One lay motionless, one seemed to be writhing in agony. The fifth tried frantically to sight his rifle on the relentless charge. The rattle of machine-gun fire and Franco's continuous battle cry brought a chill of its own, deep into Rae's gut. Before the outcome was resolved, the flare extinguished. Darkness and uncertainty returned.

The shooting had stopped; the shouting had stopped; the moaning and gasps from the wounded man continued. Rae was unsure whether or not to go to Franco's aid. He heard a gasp and a long drawn-out gurgling moan. A second later, almost too suddenly, it had stopped. An awesome silence took its place; violence and atrocity hung heavy in the air. Rae had never experienced a similar sensation in all his life. He shuddered and called out in a hoarse whisper.

To his great relief Franco returned, carrying five

Heckler and Koch G3 SG/1 rifles.

'Thank God you're all right', said Rae. 'That was a bit impulsive, wasn't it? Do you think that was really necessary?'

'The Virgin Mary granted us a miracle.' Franco's voice seemed different. 'What else could have caused them to act so foolishly? If I had not acted then I would have been the greater fool.' Rae felt in no mind to contest such logic, and took one of the rifles; he looked through the Zeiss/Orion starlight scope. 'Christ! These are fantastic,' he spoke with some enthusiasm. 'I can see everything. With equipment like this we can pick them off a mile away and with our own superior firepower close-range, we shouldn't have too much trouble in holding them off – provided Ronnie makes it on time. How much longer do you think they'll be?'

Franco made no effort to answer, putting Rae's immature enthusiasm down to nerves, and anyway right now he didn't feel like talking. He didn't need to be told he'd acted impulsively. Not really understanding it himself, he knew only that when threatened, he changed into something else, a dangerous vicious animal.

Whenever possible he had always tried to avoid physical confrontation; sometimes when threatened it became unavoidable, and sometimes in terms of self-preservation it was necessary. Nevertheless, he didn't like himself for it. Franco felt remorse, his action might well have saved their lives and probably their freedom, but at what cost? He offered a silent prayer and made his confession.

Having to some extent purged his guilt he concentrated once more on the task ahead, and scanned the terrain through the starlight scope, searching for any movement beyond.

Suddenly his attention was distracted. He looked away from the limited arc of the telescopic sight. Lights were

204

being switched on and off in the house; someone was making a search of each individual room. 'They're in the house,' Rae whispered the obvious. 'Now they've discovered we've moved out they'll concentrate on our position here.'

'They'll be pretty cautious about it,' added Franco. 'They must have realised that the others have copped it.' He returned his attention to the night scope and waited for the inevitable.

Watching the men spread across the open ground and begin their slow advance, Franco told Rae to hold his fire. 'Remember you've only got five rounds in each magazine.' He settled himself into a more secure position. 'Take your time and only fire when you have one of them steady in your sights.' Rae swallowed hard. He trained his attention on one particular man and, with finger taking up the first trigger pressure, was about to fire when he heard the crack from Franco's rifle. Distracted, he removed his eye from the scope in time to see the tracer bullet speed its way towards its quarry. He heard the other man swear.

'What's wrong, did you miss?'

'I don't know, bloody tracer bullet, given our position away.' Rae returned his attention to the night sight and tried to pick up another target. Suddenly a streamer of light shot to one side of him, passing through a small clump of bushes. The sound of the charge reached them a fraction later.

'Stay where you are,' whispered Franco. 'I'm going to take up another position to draw their fire away from here. For the moment, hold everything.'

Once again, Rae was able to pick out advancing men but now each moved in turn, running a few yards before diving into the grass for cover. He heard Franco fire off another round, but had no way of knowing whether it found its target; it had not been a tracer bullet. Possibly they were simply loaded as the first and last rounds of the magazine.

Several shots were loosed off in return. Two or three tracers sped by harmlessly, one hundred metres or so away to the left. For the moment the opposing forces had not pinpointed the rocky outcrop, but still 300 or 400 metres distant, they were gradually closing. In just a few minutes the cover would become obvious; the situation was fast becoming critical.

Rae was aware of being hot and clammy despite the chill of the heavy dew; he was becomingly increasingly worried. Suddenly and only for an instant, he caught a familiar sound. It was his imagination! He could hear nothing but the movement of the sea against the jagged rocks some way behind them.

Close by another shot rang out; the tracer sped away, this time to end up in some man's chest, the burning phosphorous searing flesh from the bone into which the bullet lodged.

Metal clinked against stone. Rae's heart leapt, he spun towards the sound and breathed a sigh of relief as Franco whispered from the darkness.

'When the helicopter lands, take the two women and run for it. I'll cover you from here.'

Carried on the back of an irregular breeze blowing in from the channel, Rae could just hear what might have been the rhythmic beat of the Sirkorski. Seconds later it was unmistakable.

☆   ☆   ☆

Giving landfall a wide berth, the helicopter swung in from the sea, keeping low. Franco flashed the torch three times and without appearing to hover it came in fast, settling straight down on to the turf to their left.

The rattle of machine-gun fire spurred Rae into action. He shouted at the women to stand up, grabbed their hands and urged them into the hundred metre dash to safety.

Someone also provided covering fire from the door of the helicopter. Rae could hear the rattle of the MAS16 in counterpoint to the beat of the rotor. He could see the red-and-blue explosive fire at the end of the gun. He ran on, encouraging the two women who were trying desperately to keep up.

Fifty metres to go – he stumbled and fell. Martha tripped over the top of him; he tried to get up, but somehow the legs wouldn't work. Not understanding why, he tried again. He screamed at the girls to leave him; needing little encouragement they ran on.

Rae started to lean forward to examine his legs but a strange grinding at the base of his spine caused him to stop. For a second he felt light-headed, thought he might faint and decided he should lie still until the sensation passed. Perhaps it was the excitement, the lack of sleep, the tension. He cursed himself for such weakness.

The moon broke cloud, Franco swore under his breath but continued to make a steady retreat, backing off and firing in random bursts; suddenly he saw Rae. Horrified he knelt down to examine him.

Rae had a half-smile on his face, his eyes were closed, no injury was visible. Franco pushed him on to his side and felt a warm sticky substance soaking through the torn clothes at the base of the spine; it seemed to be thicker than blood. He eased the wounded man into a more comfortable position, fired a long burst and made a final dash for the Sirkorski. Ronnie reached down and hauled him aboard.

'Where's Rae?' he shouted at the top of his voice as the

Sirkorski began its lift-off. 'Put this fucking thing back on the ground or I'll blow your fucking head off.' They felt the bump as Henry reluctantly obeyed. Ronnie returned his attention to Franco: 'Where is he?'

'He's hit bad, I thought it best not to move him.' Tears ran down Franco's cheeks.

'Is he alive?' asked Ronnie. Franco genuinely didn't know.

'Cover me, I'm going to get him.'

Ronnie jumped down and sprinted across the heath. He correctly supposed that all attention would be focused on the helicopter and that it was unlikely his own progress would be detected. Seeing the dark form on the ground to his right, he moved towards it.

Rae looked up and smiled, but didn't speak. 'OK, old mate, we'll soon have you safe and sound. I hope this won't hurt too much.' Ronnie knelt down, took hold of one arm and slipped his other between the wounded man's legs. He eased him over his shoulders and ran with faltering steps towards the helicopter.

Franco leaned down and hauled Rae aboard. Ronnie waited a second until the hatchway was cleared, and was about to vault up, when, with a slapping sound his jacket tore open and he felt a sharp sting of pain. He grabbed Franco's outstretched hand and pulled himself up into the cabin.

Shouting at Henry to get the machine off the ground, he secured the hatch as the Sirkorski rose and banked violently away to the left. Ronnie fell across the two seated women, he grimaced an apology and clutched at his side as he pulled himself to his feet. He wiped the blood from his hand and made his way up front.

Taking the spare set of headphones, he sat down in the co-pilot's seat. 'We can't risk landing in daylight so we haven't time to make the south coast.They'll already be out looking for us. Head for the French coast, just west of Dinard. Have you got a life raft aboard?' Henry nodded. 'Put us down in the water about two kilometres from the coast.'

Ronnie allowed no time for his instruction to be queried or challenged. He took off the headphones and made his way back into the cabin.

Rae was stretched out in the aisle with Franco knelt down stroking his forehead. 'How is he?' Ronnie asked. Franco looked up and shook his head; Rae was conscious but had a strange look about him.

'Can you hear me, Rae – it's Ronnie.' Rae smiled and tried to lift his hand but the effort was too great. 'You just rest, old mate, we'll get you to a hospital in no time.' Ronnie pulled Franco aside. 'I'd give ourselves up if I thought it would save him, but it would make no difference, I'm afraid he's dying.'

'How long's he got?'

'Minutes, I should think.' Ronnie moved aside and sat in an aisle seat. Franco knelt down once more and in his own way offered the stricken man the last rites.

✡   ✡   ✡

Rae could hear Franco's reassuring voice when, to his surprise, it changed in tone. Carried back in time he smiled, it was his father talking. He remembered now, of course, he was lying in his little room with a fever. He'd had these terrible dreams. Dad was stroking his forehead.

Feelings of deep love welled up inside him, there was no one who could ever measure up to Dad. He was always there when needed. Rae felt loved and cared for. He heard his father ask if he could hear him – a funny question. He tried to lift his arms for a cuddle but gave up, the covers were tucked in too tight. He smiled his love instead, to the man who knelt over him. His father moved away from the bedside. Rae felt warm, comfortable and secure. 'Night, Dad,' he whispered, 'see you in the morning.' The light went out and he drifted off into the most beautiful dream.

'He's dead.' Franco stood up and sobbed uncontrollably.

18

Ronnie noticed a faint lightening of the sky to the east; he instructed the pilot to reduce altitude. The Sirkorski sped on at maximum speed, now only fifty feet above the smooth water.

Henry was well acquainted with the Dinard coast. He and Martha had spent several holidays in the area, one of their favourite places being the sand dunes and semi-deserted beaches of St Lunaire. He described its situation to Ronnie; it seemed ideal.

Reducing forward momentum, the Sirkorski settled its two large floats on to the sea; peace and quietness returned as it rocked with the gentle swell.

Henry moved to the rear of the cabin, dragged out the life raft, and with Ronnie's help and keeping tight hold of the painter, slid it through the open hatchway. As it hit the water it began to inflate.

Franco lowered himself into the raft as Ronnie returned to the cockpit with the pilot.

'What I'm going to tell you now,' he said, 'please treat with strictest confidence. It's more than my life is worth if the "Spaniard" out there should find out.' Ronnie explained his involvement as an agent of the British Government. Henry and the women listened on, astonished. 'I consider the part you have played in all this,' added Ronnie, 'to be exemplary, and I don't expect you to accept my word alone.' He reached down for the cellular phone clipped between the two seats and punched in the code. The number clicked its way through to connection. 'Ladybird Fashions, can I help you?'

'This is field officer 36, my code is ASCII.'

'One moment, sir ...'

'Hello is that you, 36? Arthur here. Where the hell have you been?'

'Busy, Arthur, busy.' Ronnie flashed a quick smile. 'Look, as you no doubt have already guessed I've been involved in the Jersey job. The helicopter that escaped from L'Ancresse Island is about to be returned to Guernsey by the hostage pilot with the two women – all unharmed. Please see they are not interrogated by the Guernsey police. I suggest someone from the Department leave immediately and meet them there for screening. They are all innocent of involvement or collusion. I need a few more days. See that I don't get pressured. I will report back to you when I have completed my enquiries – over and out.'

Ronnie switched off, not allowing the opportunity for further discussion. He addressed himself to Henry. 'Wait until daylight, then make your own way back to Guernsey airport. I can only ask you not to disclose where you put us down either to the Guernsey police or to the official ... who will come to question you.'

'I don't know whether I've enough fuel to get back,' said Henry.

'Well, get as close as you can and put down on the sea. You shouldn't have any problem, everyone'll be on the lookout for you.' Ronnie leant down to remove the headphones and unclipped the cellular phone.

'I'm sorry, but as a precaution I can't risk you making contact and allowing them to get a fix on our position.' Henry nodded and they shook hands.

'Thank you, Henry, for a stalwart effort.'

212

Collecting two holdalls he dropped the radio equipment into the sea and threw the bags into the raft. A hand touched his shoulder.

'Take me with you.' He turned to see Mary, her eyes pleaded. 'Please, please, Ronnie.'

'What the hell for?' he asked, truly amazed at her request.

'I've nothing to go back for,' she replied. 'I can see you're hurt, I might be able to help in some way.' He thought for a moment, and asked Franco for an opinion.

The Portuguese shrugged his shoulders.

'If you're sure that's what you want,' said Ronnie, 'go and tell Henry you're coming of your own free will, and Mary ...'

She turned, the pleasure and excitement showed in her face.

'Yes?'

'Make sure Henry understands that he shouldn't leave until it's light. If he goes too soon likely as not someone'll take a shot at him.'

Franco held the dinghy close as Ronnie climbed aboard, and explained what he had told the pilot. 'I just hope they don't tell anyone where we are.' Ronnie started unstrapping the paddles.

'Can you trust them?'

'I don't know, but without their radio we should have enough breathing space to get away and knowing you're so desperate to get to Portugal ... I told them you were Spanish.' Franco smiled broadly, and pulled the dinghy in close as Mary lowered herself down.

Ronnie studied his compass for a moment then handed it to her. 'Can you read one of these?' She nodded. 'Then keep us on a heading due east and you'll have earned your keep.'

Placing a paddle into the water he took a pull; Franco

did likewise and after a little manoeuvring they found a rhythm.

They seemed to be moving through heavy mist. Somewhere in the distance a fog horn sounded its eerie and intermittent moan, a marker buoy whistled its warning on each rise and fall of the swell.

A searing pain pierced Ronnie's side at each pull; he felt weak and sick. For a time he managed to ignore it but it was now becoming unbearable. He asked Mary to change places with him and, handing her the paddle and muttering an apology to Franco, he sat in the bow and guided them back on course.

Their progress slowed and, as the sky lightened by the minute, the mist grew more obvious.

In one way concealment was welcome; yet with the approaching dawn it would have been preferable to see where they were headed. So much at present depended on Henry's accuracy in navigation.

They paddled on, the mist was becoming white and patchy. Suddenly the water stretched out before them and in the pale light, with the sun still to break the horizon, they saw an open beach some half-mile distant.

Ronnie picked up a third paddle and assisted from the bow; the bank of mist was now behind them and they could hear the surf breaking on the beach.

Mary clung to the sides as they were picked up and carried forward by the waves. The two men struggled to keep the raft from being caught broadside-on until Franco jumped overboard and, in up to his waist, guided them in from the stern.

Ronnie stepped into the shallows and walked painfully and stiffly out of the sea. Franco lifted Mary into his arms and waded over to the dry sand before placing her gently on her feet.

The two men pulled the raft clear of the water and

removed their bags.

'We can't risk it being found, we'll have to bury it,' Ronnie said. 'Can we carry it up to the sand dunes?' Franco took the hunting knife from his boot and without a word slashed into the rubber. The air rushed and hissed, the previously rigid form collapsed into a shapeless mass. The Portuguese folded it over then cut it into four and, stacking the pieces together, placed them over the crook of his arm and strode up the beach.

Ronnie declined Mary's offer of support. He leant over to his left in an attempt to ease the throbbing pain and followed on wearily some way behind.

By the time he reached the others the remains of the life raft had already been concealed. He tried to catch his breath, and curled up and rested beside Mary. For a few precious moments they remained in silence staring out to sea; a warm fringe of pink tinting the horizon heralded the approaching sunrise. Suddenly the sound of the Sirkorski's engines wafted through the mist only to fade away again into the far distance.

Ronnie felt decidedly depressed; it was growing lighter by the minute, he forced himself to sit upright.

About seventy metres to the right was a bungalow, its windows shuttered. To the left the dunes continued the whole sweep of the bay. A few houses nestled within the distant headland but otherwise the area was deserted. The sound of a heavy vehicle moving at speed indicated a road someway behind them.

'We've got to get into Dinard and find a hotel,' said Ronnie. 'We'll rest up a while, change into some clean clothes and find out whether we can get seats on a plane for Paris.'

'We're going to Paris?' Franco showed surprise.

'First we've got to get into Dinard – I need some attention.'

'My God, you were hit,' Franco looked amazed. 'I'm sorry, Ronnie, I never realised – let me look at it now.'

'No, this isn't the place,' Ronnie brushed his friend away. 'Go scout round that house, see if you can find us some transport.' Franco nodded and started off.

'And, Franco,' he stopped and turned to face them. 'Wipe that bloody muck off your face will you? You not only smell like a goat, you look like a monkey.' Ronnie turned his attention to Mary. 'You've still got a smear on the side of your face ... here.' He leaned across to wipe it clean, grimaced and clutched his side. She moved closer and put her arms around him. He let her hold him as if he were a young child, and indulged himself with the comfort it brought.

☆   ☆   ☆

'The house is empty, but there's a car in the garage and I've managed to get it started.' Franco was beaming with pleasure.

'Our luck's still holding,' Ronnie showed relief. 'Must be a weekend holiday home. Well done, mate.' He stood up painfully. 'How the hell did you get it started, are you a mechanic as well?'

Franco smiled: 'I was very clever – the keys were under the seat.'

Ronnie allowed himself a chuckle. Perhaps things were not quite as bad after all.

The Deux Chevaux was backed out of the garage, and in a short time they had reached the little town of St Lunaire where they stopped at a *boulangerie* and picked up a bagful of hot croissants. A few kilometres on they reached Dinard, and parked in the square.

The overnight ferry was not due in St Malo until 6.30 and if it were to be presumed they'd travelled with it, it was still too early to book into a hotel. They crossed the square and entered a small café. For several minutes they sat in silence over hot coffee and brandy, each reflecting on the traumas of the night, and of how they had managed to survive it.

Ronnie pushed his untouched glass across the table. 'It would increase my pulse and the bleeding,' he offered apologetically and explained it was time to go. Franco's attention had wandered; Ronnie caught hold of his arm.

'Mary and I will book into that hotel on the corner, Hotel Madeleine.' He drained his coffee. 'Follow in about fifteen minutes. As soon as you've booked in, find our room. I need you to fix me up.'

Left to his own devices, Franco sipped at the second brandy. It was good to be alone for a few minutes. The warmth from the alcohol gave some relief from the chill of his wet clothes. He rubbed his legs and stamped his feet under the table, then moved over to the bar for another.

Pushing open the mahogany and brass doors, he walked up to reception and stood tight against the counter to conceal his wet clothes. He noticed the pink registration card lying on the desk behind and by leaning over was able to distinguish Ronnie's room number.

Soon he was in the safety of his own room where he immediately ran a hot bath. He took off his wet trousers and rubbed at his legs with a warm towel. Feeling the circulation return, he placed his damp clothes over the heated rail and, lowering himself down into the hot water, breathed a huge sigh of relief.

☆   ☆   ☆

Ronnie dropped the holdall on to the polished wood floor, and took off his bloodstained jacket. Mary sat down on the edge of the large Victorian double bed; she seemed

217

uneasy and embarrassed.

'I'm going to have a lie down until Franco comes,' he said. 'Why don't you have a nice hot bath.'

'Can't I do something for you? Can I bandage your side?' She showed a genuine concern. 'We could tear up one of the towels.'

'Just leave me ... please,' he said, a little impatiently. 'Franco understands what needs to be done, thanks all the same.' She smiled, kissed him lightly on the cheek and disappeared into the bathroom, closing the door behind her. Taking off his trousers, Ronnie undid the remaining buttons of his shirt and pulled it painfully over his head. He was almost afraid to look at his injured side. The blood had congealed from the waist down, almost to his knee; it looked terrible. He tried to bend over to examine the wound more closely but the pain was too great. He moved over to the mirror and probed gently with his fingers.

Although most of the general bleeding had stopped, a deep furrow in the fleshy part of the waist still oozed dark blood. The bullet had passed clean through. From experience Ronnie realised the wound was not serious, provided it could be kept clean.

He took a towel from his bag, laid it over the bedspread and eased himself on to one side of it. He wrapped what remained around his injured side, then tried to relax.

The bedroom was so very French with its heavy cornice ceiling, faded wallpaper, heavy mahogany Breton wardrobe and two high double-opening windows. The atmosphere of the room brought back memories of his honeymoon.

He wondered what Francine would make of his present situation, booked into a double bedroom with this beautiful woman. He had to admit he was attracted, but then he'd been attracted to women before; it meant nothing. He closed his eyes just for the minute.

☆ ☆ ☆

When he awoke the room spun in circles, and he felt nauseous. He could hear a voice, from some far-off place. 'Ronnie . . . it's me, Franco.' Focusing, he saw the Portuguese standing over him, Mary at his side. She had a towel wrapped around her hair and looked like something out of a glossy magazine. He blinked, tried to sit up, and winced with pain. 'Sorry Franco,' he smiled weakly and grunted as the towel, stuck to the dried blood, was pulled away.

Franco probed at the flesh with his fingers, and looked up smiling as Ronnie jumped with pain. 'You are very lucky my friend – very lucky.' He turned to Mary and asked her to go downstairs for a bottle of gin and a jug of ice. Whilst she was gone he took a linen hand towel from the shelf and soaked it in hot water. He squeezed out the surplus and started to dab gently around the torn flesh, working away from the wound until the skin appeared undamaged. He rinsed the towel under the tap, soaked it in clean hot water then removed the dried blood from the surrounding areas. Once clean, he studied the wound carefully. 'Another inch to the right and you'd have been in real trouble,' he observed. 'Even so it needs sewing up.'

'Bloody hell!' Ronnie gritted his teeth, lay down on the bed and tried to prepare himself mentally for the ordeal.

Mary returned with the gin and emptied half the ice on to a clean hand towel to make an ice-pack. She placed it gently down on to the wound and held it there. Ronnie shut his eyes as the frost bit into his inner flesh. 'The ice will help,' said Franco, 'but this is going to hurt all the same.' He undid his thick leather belt. 'Here, bite on this.' Ronnie couldn't restrain a chuckle.

'You've been seeing too many old TV movies.' Franco didn't see the funny side. 'You bite on this. We don't

219

want the hotel to call the police when they think you're being murdered.' Ronnie accepted the point, and took the soft leather between his teeth.

Franco unscrewed the cap and poured a generous measure of gin on to the gaping flesh. Ronnie grunted, every muscle stretched taut against the sudden pain. Franco poured another hefty measure over and around the wound. He grabbed the ice-pack and pressed it down hard. 'Here, hold this.' Mary held it firm. Beads of sweat covered Ronnie's forehead, the force with which he bit the leather, contorted his face. She turned away.

Franco held a curved upholstery needle threaded with white twine and, crimping the wound together with his left hand, held the needle into position at the extremity of the injury. He paused willing himself to be dexterous; for the sake of his friend it needed to be done in one continuous and speedy action.

Clenching his teeth, he punched the needle into the flesh and pulled it through.

Mary was amazed at the speed he worked; it was as if he'd done it all his life. Within seconds he'd completed twenty-four stitches and had tied the last one with a double knot. He reached into his pocket for the scissors, cut the thread off short and replaced the ice-pack to the closely knit wound. He gently eased the belt from Ronnie's mouth. 'I have done a good job for you my friend. It's what you English say when you go dancing? Sew, sew, prick, prick, sew.'

Ronnie was unable to contain his mirth. 'You silly bugger,' he gasped, 'it's slow, slow, quick, quick, slow.'

'Oh,' said Franco, 'I see.' He smiled inwardly. 'Stay where you are. I'm going to prepare a bandage for you.'

Cutting a pillowcase into three-inch widths, he tied the ends together and rolled it into one continuous strip. He folded the remaining piece into a neat wad, doused it with

220

gin and placed the saturated material against the wound, binding it securely into place with the makeshift bandage. He helped Ronnie into bed and pulled the covers over him. 'Now you sleep.'

Franco turned to Mary: 'He must rest. I will come to your room at one o'clock. Depending on how he is, we will make our decision.'

When he had gone she pulled the curtains, stripped down to her pants and got into bed. The mattress was soft and she inadvertently rolled up close. She tried to move away but after two attempts gave up, pleased to nestle close to his warmth. She thought she should say something, but realised he must already be asleep. Pouting her soft lips against his smooth skin, she kissed him lightly on the shoulder, then, nestling deep into the pillow, she closed her eyes and drifted off into a sumptuous sleep.

☆　☆　☆

Franco crossed the room and pulled the curtains; the sun shone on to the bed and across the two sleeping forms. Ronnie with a growth of beard looked grey and ill, his companion by contrast seemed to glow with health and vitality. Her blonde hair tousled over the pillow and across Ronnie's shoulder.

Franco smiled and wished it were he she lay beside but, dismissing such thoughts, he walked over and gently shook his friend awake. 'How do you feel?' Ronnie tried to disentangle himself. 'Bloody awful,' he replied, 'but that's because you've just woken me.' He pushed himself up. Mary breathed deeply and turned over on her side.

'Call reception to get you the airport, we want three seats Dinard to Paris,' Ronnie seized the initiative. 'Once there, you can fly on to Portugal and we'll go to London.'

Within minutes Franco was through to Dinard airport,

221

and in fluent French he asked for flight times and availability.

'They've got three seats on the four o'clock flight,' he said. 'We're to pick up our tickets an hour-and-a-half before departure.' Ronnie looked at his watch. 'Christ that'll be 2.30. We'll have to get a move on.' He stood up gingerly, a circular stain of blood the size of a 10p piece coloured the bandage.

'Doesn't seem to have bled that much,' he said. 'Help me to dress will you?' Franco took the holdall, pulled out a crumpled pair of jeans and the grey sweater, and replaced them with the bloodstained towels and garments.

Ronnie leant across to wake the girl. She opened her eyes, blinked and pulled the covers up to her chin. 'We're going downstairs to settle the bill. Come down as soon as you're ready,' he said.

'Where are we going?' she asked.

'Paris.'

'But I've nothing to wear.' She immediately felt silly. 'I mean my clothes are filthy, I've got no make-up. Couldn't I slip out and buy something?' Ronnie pulled out four 500 franc notes. 'You do that,' he said. 'Me and Franco will go straight to the airport. Get whatever you need and then take a cab.' He passed her the money. 'Make sure you're there by 3.30. We'll settle the bill on the way out; I'll make some excuse about not staying.'

'Thank you,' she said. 'See you later then.'

The two men waited at the desk. A middle-aged women came out of the office and listened to their explanation. She raised an eyebrow but made no comment; the bill was made out and they were charged for the night, without reduction. Ronnie wanted to argue, but under the circumstances thought better of it.

'Bloody old cow probably thought we'd booked it for

222

an orgy.' Ronnie's anger turned to amusement. 'Poor old Mary. They'll all be waiting at the bottom of the stairs to gawp. They probably think she's a whore.'

'Never liked the French much,' said Franco. 'Look there's a taxi.'

Walking into the spacious departures hall the two men scanned the line of desks for their flight number. Almost simultaneously they saw the sign PARIS hanging from the canopy of TRANSPORT AÉRIEN TRANS RÉGIONAL. They walked over and waited in front of the unattended desk. Ronnie looked around the semi-deserted building. 'Not very busy, is it?' He felt decidedly conspicuous. 'Bit risky hanging around here too long. Go round the back, see if you can find someone.'

A minute later Franco returned with a young girl; they were laughing together as if they'd known each other for years. She went behind the desk and took three tickets from a drawer. 'All ready for you, sir,' she spoke in perfect English. 'I just need to have your names.'

'Green and Rodrigues.' Ronnie used the names on their false passports. 'And Miss...' He pretended a coughing fit seeking time to recall Mary's surname, and decided he hadn't forgotten it – he didn't know it. He apologised. 'Miss Schoefield,' he used Rae's alias.

Ronnie paid for the tickets and started to walk away; Franco hung back. The girl wrote something on a card, she laughed and handed it to him. Franco leant over and kissed her on the cheek; she put her hand to the kiss mark and blushed.

'When do you think you're ever going to get the chance of meeting her again?' said Ronnie, shaking his head.

'I'm a rich man now,' he answered. 'I told her I'd send her a ticket to Faro; I might take an apartment in the Algarve for a few weeks.'

'Girl must be mad,' Ronnie smiled. 'Come on, let's get

something to eat.' They sat at a table by the window. Ronnie could feel the warmth of the sun through the glass and turned to remove his jacket. Checking his watch, he worried about Mary. There was still plenty of time but he wondered whether she'd turn up, wanting her to – desperately.

He forced such immature thought from his mind and prepared to enjoy his first proper meal in days.

19

Ronnie looked up from his coffee; his heart jumped. With a spring in her step she walked towards them; she looked a million dollars.

'Hope you approve my outfit,' she laughed. 'Things are a little expensive over here.' She placed a carrier bag beside the chair, and sat down. 'I don't think I'll have time to eat will I?' she looked at the menu. 'I think I'll just have a sandwich.' A few minutes later the flight was called.

Grabbing their hand baggage they joined the other passengers waiting to board.

Franco's newly acquired friend stood at the foot of the steps; he bent to whisper something into her ear. A tell-tale blush spread over the girl's face as Ronnie with some annoyance pushed him on into the aircraft.

The plane pulled on to the runway. It paused for a moment, increased power and surged forward. Ronnie lowered the backrest and eased his throbbing side. He didn't want to talk.

He tried to collect his thoughts, but felt a growing awareness of the woman sitting opposite. The more he wanted her, the more he wanted to see Francine. Why was everything so converse; why must he feel so tortured. He loved his wife and kids, that was beyond doubt; everything else had to be secondary. First he'd see Franco safely on his way and then try to resolve the issue of wife and family. Perhaps he could take them on holiday. Franco could book them a villa somewhere on the Algarve. He'd ask him to do that a little later when he felt stronger. Right now he just needed to rest.

☆ ☆ ☆

There being no passport control for domestic arrivals, they walked straight through into the main terminal complex where they followed the overhead signs towards reservations.

Franco asked at the Air Portugal desk for the next available flight to Lisbon. The girl checked her computer and confirmed availability on flight AP 716 departing 1900 hours. Ronnie paid in francs and put the change into his trouser pocket. He looked up at the digital clock behind the desk; it read 17.20.

'We'll go to British Airways and see what's available to Heathrow,' he said. 'There's just one big problem and I don't know what to do about it.'

'What problem?' asked Franco. 'I didn't think we had any.'

'Mary hasn't got a passport,' Ronnie shook his head. 'I never stopped to think.'

Franco thought for a moment, and unzipped his holdall. Fumbling through the crumpled clothes, he withdrew a British passport. 'It's Rae's,' he said. 'I took it off him before we left.'

Ronnie flipped through the pages. 'A few discreet alterations, and as long as they don't look at it too closely, we may get away with it. It's certainly worth a try.'

The two remaining seats on BA flight 580 departing at 20.15 were booked for Heathrow. Ronnie confided with Mary.

'In all the excitement, we forgot your passport.' She

looked aghast. 'It's all right,' he said, 'we've got Rae's. We'll just have to doctor it up a little, but we need a photograph.'

'I saw a photo-booth by the main entrance doors,' she said.

Ronnie fumbled in his pocket and handed her two ten franc coins. 'If we're not here when you get back, wait for us.' He opened the passport at the first page. 'We need a pen and black ink.' He continued to study the document. 'And some glue . . . let's find the shops.'

The two men made their way upstairs to the shopping complex and bought what was required. Ronnie looked around for the nearest cloakroom.

'I'm going to lock myself away in one of the loos,' he caught hold of Franco's arm. 'Fetch Mary and bring the photos in to me. Cough three times so I know it's you.'

Ronnie checked the seat was clean, sat down, and placed his purchases on to the tiled floor between his feet. He re-examined the passport for a few moments then filled the pen, testing it on the back of his hand until the ink ran free. Satisfied, he opened the first page, held it securely against the top of his right thigh, and added a bold S to MR, turning it into 'MRS Jackson Schoefield.' Ronnie lifted the passport to face level and blew the ink dry. Turning over the page, he read Rae's place of birth, London; date of birth, 13 May 1950, height, 1.75 m. No change was needed.

He took a razor blade from its pack, and started to cut just deep enough to penetrate the cellophane covering around the photograph. He peeled it away, removed the photo, and carefully scratched away the residue. Satisfied with his work, he picked up the bits and pieces, returned them to his pocket, and waited for Franco's signal.

Making a careful study of the four pictures, he cut off the prettiest and smeared some of the transparent glue on

227

to the back, pressing it down firmly on to the passport. He then took the small square of cut cellophane, added touches of glue around its edges and placed it over the top, marrying up the pink wavy lines of the official seal with the lines that ran up the side of the page. He waited for the glue to dry, pressing down firmly between thumb and forefinger.

Holding the passport at arm's length, he decided it would pass casual inspection.

'You'd better start wondering why your father called you Jackson.' He handed Mary the passport; she opened it and stared in amazement. She looked up and grinned. 'My mother always wanted a boy. She gave me her family surname as a Christian name, Jackson.'

'That's my girl,' said Ronnie, 'but if you're stopped please don't look to me for help. I shall totally ignore you. Now let's have a drink, shall we?'

'Pity about old Rae,' said Franco when they were sat at the bar. 'We were so near getting away with it.'

Ronnie gave a deep sigh. 'If ever I have to get involved again, God forbid, then I hope it's with you,' he said.

Franco nodded in agreement. 'If ever you want me, contact Ginja's Bar, Praça Rossio, Lisbon. My friend, the old man, he will know where I am. Ha! He knows everyone.' Picking up his glass, Franco took a deep swig of lager.

'I might do that, mate.' Ronnie wrote down his own London address on a beer mat. 'When I get things sorted out back home, I might come over for a holiday.'

He had made no mention of the wife and kids, and immediately felt guilty. 'Perhaps we can arrange to share a villa, with a pool. My kids would love that.' Franco greeted the idea with enthusiasm, and was about to describe the beauties of the Algarve when the flight was called.

Draining his glass, he took Mary's hand; his eyes twinkled, she leant forward and kissed him lightly on the cheek.

'Come on,' Ronnie said. 'We may as well go through with him.'

He slipped the ticket and boarding card inside Mary's passport, snapped it shut and passed it back to her. 'When you go through, hand it over with the tickets still inside – it might disturb his concentration, and give him one of your special smiles.' Mary blushed, she stood up close and put her arms around him. For a second he responded, then held her away.

'It'll be all right. Go on now, let's get it over with.'

She opened the passport for a security guard to check her boarding card and joined the queue.

With only two other people now in front of her she waited in trepidation and tried desperately to calm her nerves. The official seemed to take an age examining the passport of the person in front of her. Suddenly, she realised it was her turn.

'Oh sorry,' she blurted, her face lighting up with what she considered to be her special smile. She looked the man straight in the eye, and he handed back the passport, without opening it. She looked over her shoulder to catch sight of Ronnie.

Continuing through security and baggage check, she found Franco already waiting; a minute later Ronnie joined them. 'He never even looked at it,' she said excitedly. Ronnie steered her towards an empty seat and walked Franco to the departure gate.

'Well, old friend, this is it,' he offered his hand. Franco pulled him close and hugged him. 'Please, you come and visit my country, yes?' The two men separated, Franco with tears in his eyes. 'Get of now, you silly old bugger,' said Ronnie. 'I'll see you soon.' Franco moved towards the gate. He turned and waved. Ronnie felt a great sadness, he lifted his arm in acknowledgement. In a second his friend had gone.

✩   ✩   ✩

'You two are very close,' she said. 'I suppose you've known each other for ages.'

'About two weeks actually... feels like a lifetime.' Mary sensed his need for private thought. She kept quiet, even though she desperately wanted to know his plans and whether she might dare believe herself included. Biding her time, she waited patiently for the right opportunity.

'I want you to do me a great favour.' Ronnie spoke as if his thoughts were far away. 'I want you to help me reach my wife and kids. I might not be strong enough to make it on my own.' She felt a stab of disappointment, but realised nothing could be gained by being petulant. Better to show her pleasure at the chance of his company. The longer they were together, the more opportunity she'd have of keeping him.

'Where is your family now?' she asked.

'About two-and-a-half hours' drive from Edinburgh.' Ronnie became more animated. 'It'll be too late to make the connecting flight this evening. Probably just as well, I think I need to rest.'

She could see he was in pain. 'You need to have proper attention,' she said. 'Why can't you have it looked at as soon as we get to London?'

'Because if I do,' he said, hate showing in his face, 'those bastards will be around my bedside within the hour. I know I'm gonna have to submit my report some time, but I've got to sort myself out first. Can you understand that?' She nodded, and looked up at the monitor. 'Our flight's being called now,' she said, and slipping her arm affectionately through his, helped him to his feet.

☆   ☆   ☆

The 747 taxied over to its predetermined station and shut down its engines. Passengers jumped to their feet and in a flurry of activity retrieved baggage and belongings from the storage cabinets above the seats. Ronnie restrained Mary from joining the mayhem, and in their own good time made their way into the airport building.

Ronnie, worried that immigration might have been alerted, told her to walk on ahead.

'When you go through passport control, do exactly as you did last time,' he added. She gave his arm a squeeze and hurried on.

At the end of the link corridor, she saw the two immigration officers standing at the entrance to the concourse. They seemed relaxed and even casual in their observation. She had always wondered what and whom these men might be looking for. The very thought that they might be looking out for her brought a strange sensation. She passed by without attracting any apparent interest and joined the queue at passport control. This time she felt more at ease. Even if she were challenged, this was her own country, and there was nothing that couldn't be sorted out given time.

She placed the passport on the desk, and smiled warmly. The young man removed the tickets, flicked through the pages, glanced at her photograph, looked her in the eye, smiled broadly and returned it with the tickets into her hand.

She thanked him sweetly and walked on into the baggage reclaim area and waited.

'No problems.' It was both question and statement. She shook her head and linked arms.

'Just wait here a minute,' Ronnie detached himself. 'Before we go through customs I've got to do something I should have done before we reached Paris.' He took the carrier bag and holdall and walked to the gents' cloakroom. He entered a cubicle and locked the door. Removing Mary's belongings from the carrier bag, he replaced them with the bloodstained towels and clothes. Then using the string handles, he tied the bag securely and repacked her things into the holdall.

Luggage was just coming through from Düsseldorf, the flight preceding their own, the conveyor was almost full. Ronnie pushed his way through to the front of the crowd and dropped the carrier bag discreetly between two pieces of luggage. He pretended to reclaim his own holdall and, easing his way back to Mary, walked with her through customs.

'Excuse me, sir, madam.' Ronnie breathed a sigh of frustration.

'Do you understand that this is the green sector?'

'Yes officer.'

'Have you any duty-free allowances?' Ronnie turned to Mary, she shook her head. 'No, we haven't.'

'Is that all the baggage you have, sir?'

'Yes, I'm afraid it is. Our cases were mislaid in Paris.'

'Do you live in this country?'

'Yes, we do.'

'May I examine your bag, please?' The man unzipped the holdall and lifted out the clothes, shoes and underwear. He felt around the bottom of the bag, and finding nothing untoward, replaced them. He zipped up the bag.

'I do hope the loss of your luggage hasn't spoilt your trip, madam.' Mary smiled warmly.

'You may proceed, thank you.' Ronnie picked up the

bag and they walked through the automatic doors into the arrivals hall.

'We made it!' Ronnie squeezed her to him. 'I've just got to change my francs, then we'll pick up the courtesy coach to the hotel.'

The short walk to room 432 was completed in silence. Ronnie inserted the card into the slot; the pinpoint light turned from red to green. 'I hope you don't mind me booking a double room,' he asked, a little self-consciously, 'but right now I could do with your company.' He opened the door, switched on the lights and placed the bag on the luggage rack; it was a twin-bedded room.

Ronnie sank down on to the nearest and reached for the room service menu. 'Do you want the bathroom first, or shall I?' he asked. 'When we've cleaned up, I'll order something to eat.'

'That'll be nice,' she said. 'You go in first if you like. Do you need any help with your bandages?'

'Thanks,' he said. 'You can help me off with this for a start.'

Easing the woollen sweater over his head, she removed his soiled tee-shirt. She knelt down, untied the knot and gently unwound the bandage. He peeled the folded linen away from the wound, grimacing with pain as it pulled against dried puss that stuck it to his skin. 'Doesn't look too good, does it?' he said. Mary felt sick and gave a weak smile.

'If I need any help I'll give a shout.' Ronnie went into the bathroom and closed the door. He ran a shallow bath, stepped into the hot water and lowered himself carefully on to his right side, taking care not to immerse his wound. He shut his eyes and tried to relax. For a moment the heat seemed to regenerate some of his lost energy; seconds later he had an overwhelming desire to sleep. He opened his eyes wide, blinked and shook his head. It was neither the time to let go, nor the place.

He pulled himself up to sit on the edge and, with his feet still in the water, bathed the wound clean; it looked raw and inflamed. The stitches had stretched tight against the swelling on either side and dug deep into the flesh, whilst the surrounding skin had an unhealthy tinge. From previous experience he judged a maximum of thirty-six hours before proper medical treatment would become a necessity.

Ronnie pulled the plug, a grey scum settled around the waterline. He gave a deep sigh and cleaned the bath down, then, wrapping a towel around his midriff, he washed out his pants, tee-shirt and socks.

'Are you all right?' Mary asked as he shuffled into the bedroom. Pulling the covers aside, he climbed into bed and handed her the menu.

'What do you want to eat?' he asked. She settled for à simple omelette and went to take her bath. Ronnie dialled room service and placed the order. Using the remote control, he put on the television and flicked through the channels. Something familiar caught his eye, he turned up the volume. Charles Verdusca was being interviewed.

'... if she's out there somewhere and can hear this I want her to know that I understand she's being held against her will and that I love her and pray that she is returned to me safe and sound.'

'Bollocks,' muttered Ronnie. The interviewer pressed home his coup de grâce.

'But it is our understanding, Mr Verdusca, that she left with the perpetrators of this hideous crime of her own free will.'

Verdusca threw his hands up above his desk.

'I ask you, do you really believe that? How can you possibly believe such a thing?'

The camera turned back to the newscaster.

'We hope to bring you more details of this devastating outrage as soon as they are made known to us. As far as we can determine,

234

three civilians, one Jersey policewoman and six Guernsey police officers are known to have been killed. The perpetrators have removed several million pounds from the Jersey banks and at this present time have escaped capture. This is Jeremy Baker, extended News at Ten, St Helier, Jersey.'

Ronnie switched it off. He lay back on to the soft pillow and tried to absorb the enormity of the crime enacted. Ten people's lives had been lost and that bastard Verdusca, acting as if it were he who were outraged. Any man willing to endanger his own family was not worthy of consideration. Verdusca's involvement was the one solid fact he would be pleased to offer the Department.

Ronnie had already decided on the amount of information he would impart in the inevitable debriefing. He would appear co-operative and helpful, but he would divulge only what he wished. Charles Verdusca would be his major let-out. Offer them one positive lead and whether or not the other ringleaders were eventually traced it would be up to them. A knock at the door interrupted his thoughts.

Wrapping himself with a towel, he opened the door to a smart young lady who laid out their beautifully presented supper on the table.

Mary came out of the bathroom wearing her tracksuit bottom and a white towel tied around her bust. Without make-up she simply radiated health and vitality. 'This is nice,' she said. 'How do you feel now?'

'At the moment, a lot better.' He picked up the spoon and served himself from the vegetable dish. 'I'll feel even better when I've eaten this lot.'

'Where did you go to school?' she asked, following a train of thought which equated good table manners with education.

'I went to boarding school when I was thirteen,' he answered. 'Seaford College, it's near Petworth in West

235

Sussex. I went to Sandhurst from there and got a commission. That was just the start of my troubles. I suppose my streak of independence showed so I was later seconded into the SAS. The remainder of my career, if you could call it that, is classified.'

Mary realised he would divulge no more and steered the conversation to her own life, her childhood, the school she had loved so much, and her brush with fame as one of Britain's top photographic models.

As she talked of herself, she realised that the question burning inside her had to be asked. He might have had good reason previously to steer away from the truth but now the adventure was all but over, with no further need to obscure his true identity, the answer might not be the same. Mary continued her story into the period of her relationship with Ken. '... and having said goodbye to him at the airport, for the umpteenth time, I never saw him again.' She finished speaking and looked at him closely, searching for any reaction.

Looking her straight in the eye, he reached across the table and rested his hand on hers. 'Ken was my twin brother.' The colour drained from her face. She thought she might faint and gripped the table with both hands. 'I was abroad at the time,' Ronnie continued. 'When I eventually got back to London, I came looking for you, but you'd moved. There was no forwarding address.'

'What do you mean at the time?' she whispered, hardly daring to listen.

'The only thing I knew then,' Ronnie chose his words carefully, 'was that Ken was missing, presumed dead. It took me years to finally get at the truth.' He took a sip of the iced water to give her time to gather herself. 'Ken was working for the British Government on some covert operation in Greece. Apparently his support team made a major cock-up and he got caught. The British Govern-

236

ment denied all knowledge of involvement and he was subsequently executed.

'Ken couldn't have told you where he was going all those times he left you. I only know he loved you very much. He told me so, many times. Perhaps you can understand now why I hate those two-faced bastards so much.'

Tears were running down her cheeks; Ronnie reached over and ran his fingers across her forehead. She looked up at him and tried unsuccessfully to hold back the surge of deep emotion; she began to sob uncontrollably. He went over to her. She stood up and threw her arms around his neck.

He held her close, kissing her sweet-smelling hair; her tears ran wet against his chest. He felt a growing sexual awareness, now beyond his control. For the moment she had given herself totally into his protection. It was a primitive situation drawing from him a basic instinct. He felt his erection hard against her and made to move away, but she followed his movement as if finding strength and security in his aroused masculinity.

Mary lifted her face and tried to smile; he brushed away her tears. A moment of sheer magic existed between them. She wanted to be kissed, he knew that. He wanted to kiss her, to taste those beautiful lips, to taste the salt of her tears.

Using every ounce of self-discipline he pushed her away gently and, embarrassed at his erection pushing hard against the towel, he turned away.

'I've got to see Francine first.' Ronnie was confused; he tried to think clearly. 'I've got to sort things out with my wife.'

He walked over to the bed, sat down and gently eased his legs between the covers.

'I've got to sleep now Mary. Please understand I've

never been unfaithful to Francine and no matter how much I want to do otherwise I'm not going to now; not until I know for certain there's no chance of getting my family back together.'

'She's truly a fortunate woman.' Mary got into bed and switched out the lights.

'Good night, Ronnie, I hope you feel better in the morning.'

Long after he slept she lay awake, turning the past events over and over again in her mind. When the time came it must be his choice and his alone. She determined to do nothing to influence that decision, other than offer her continued support. She must try to be less intense.

Having worked things through, she felt more at peace. She readjusted her pillows and allowed herself to drift away into the deep sleep her body, racked with physical and mental exhaustion, profoundly craved.

20

Ronnie tossed and turned, his breathing sounded forced and irregular. She switched on the bedside light and was amazed to discover it was already nine. She pulled the curtains; he was awake, tried to sit up but flopped back against the headboard. She helped him out of bed but he had difficulty in straightening up. He told her to ring down for some coffee and shuffled off into the bathroom.

The fever had come earlier than expected, his brow was burning. He ran a cold bath and clambered in.

By the time he returned to the bedroom he felt almost normal. The cold water had reduced his temperature, and the wound looked no worse. He sipped at the scalding coffee. 'Get ready as quickly as you can,' he said. 'I want you to go downstairs and see if you can find some proper bandages.'

Taking the lift to the ground floor, she walked up to reception. The girls behind the desk were busy making up accounts for the morning departures, and she had to wait.

'Can I see the front of house manager?' she asked. The girl smiled politely. 'Certainly, madam, I'll bleep him for you.'

'Can I help?' Mary turned to face the young manager.

'I hope so,' she said. 'My husband has just had an operation and we're flying back home today,' she paused and smiled warmly. 'I need to change his dressings and wondered if you might have some bandages. I also need lint and antiseptic cream. The hospital provided us with everything but I must have left it behind in the taxi. I feel terrible about it.'

The manager felt the full impact of her magnetism. 'Would you like our house doctor to attend your husband?' he asked.

'No, really, that won't be necessary.' She hoped to sound convincing, but had spoken a little too hurriedly.

'If you just wait a moment, madam, I'll see what I can do.' A few minutes later he returned carrying a first aid box.

'I think you'll find everything you need in here. When you've finished just leave it in your room. The housekeeper will return it when you vacate.' He gave a little bow, and Mary dismissed him with a devastating smile. Elated, she returned to the bedroom.

'Any luck?' Ronnie asked.

She placed the white plastic box on the bed, unclipped the two catches and opened the lid. 'Christ!' he exclaimed, 'where did you get this?' He took out a thick roll of crêpe bandage. 'Bloody marvellous.' He ripped open a package containing the lint and gauze dressings.

Mary smoothed the antiseptic cream over and around the wound. 'A bit too late for this,' she said, 'but at least it'll stop it sticking to the bandage.' Ronnie took the tube and squeezed the remainder on to the dressing. He pressed the lint gauze on to the wound, stood up, and allowed her to bandage it firmly in place.

'Does it feel more comfortable?' she asked.

'At least I feel clean,' he answered. 'Thank you, it's a great improvement.'

Ronnie dressed, packed their few belongings into the holdall and emptied the contents of the first aid box on top. Before leaving, and from force of habit, he took one last look around the room.

It was a miserable day; a fine drizzle carried with it a chilling dampness that found its way through to the bone. Ronnie shuddered and hurried as best he could to the waiting coach.

The flight was already boarding, and they were hurried through on to the waiting aircraft. The rush had left him weak; he felt alternately hot and cold.

Once airborne, he ordered two bottles of mineral water and drank greedily. Mary sipped a dry white wine; she could see he was beginning to suffer and wanted desperately to ease his pain. There was nothing she could do except keep quiet. There was a time to speak and a time to be silent. She reached for the inflight magazine and read it through for the second time in two days. Ronnie gazed out of the window, and tried to focus his thoughts. His mind refused to be disciplined and wandered incoherently. Disturbed, he tried to concentrate by looking for some landmark, some concrete link with sanity between the swirling cloud. He gave up and, with head spinning, closed his eyes.

He felt someone shake his arm . . . who was this woman physically assaulting him? He pulled away violently, looked at her shocked face and saw her flinch. Recognition suddenly dawned. 'Sorry, Mary,' his voice was coarse and rasping. 'Sorry, love, I was dreaming.' She touched his hand gently.

'We're there, Ronnie. Do you feel strong enough to carry on with this?'

'I feel better now,' he answered. 'I just went through a bad patch.'

She helped him out of the seat, collected the holdall and followed him out of the plane.

'If you want a hire care you'll need your licence. Have you got it with you?' He hadn't and asked her to find the Hertz desk.

Giving the receptionist his name and London address, the data was fed into the computer; credentials checked with his membership. He asked for a route map of Scotland.

The girl fumbled under the desk and handed one across. 'If you go through those doors there,' she pointed, 'I'll have the car brought round to you.'

Mary walked him out into the open air, and noticed a little more weight on her arm than previously. The sun was beginning to disperse the layers of cloud.

Ronnie breathed deeply, the cold air dampened the burning in his lungs. He opened the map, and re-adjusted the fold between Arbroath and Aberdeen. Mary peered over his shoulder.

'I hope you don't mind driving?' he said. 'The sister lives about eight miles beyond this little place here.' He pointed inland to the small town of Fettercairn. 'I've never been there myself,' he continued. 'When I was away during school holidays, Francine would bring the kids up here; they loved it.' He leant against the wall for support, and thought back to the time when he'd been waiting at home for their return. He remembered all three of them flinging their arms around him and hanging from his neck.

Mary noticed the sudden change. He seemed to have drifted off into a world of his own again. A white Ford Escort pulled up alongside the kerb, she caught hold of his arm and shook him violently.

'Ronnie ... Ronnie, the car's here.' From some deep resource he fought his way back to reality; he saw the car door being opened and climbed into the passenger seat. She was sitting beside him; the car moved forward. He felt a little better.

'Sorry, Mary, I thought I was going to pass out for a minute. Take the main road towards Dundee, fork left

242

around the city and pick up the A929 to Forfar.' Ronnie held the map on his knees and secured the safety belt. The weather had deteriorated again, and as Mary drove cautiously on the inside lane, they were shrouded in huge plumes of mist and spray from the heavy trucks thundering past. It was not until she turned into the minor road towards Forfar that she regained enough confidence to increase speed.

'These are more like the roads I'm used to driving on,' she said. 'Which way next?'

He made no reply; she looked across. He was asleep, with mouth open, his breathing erratic.

Pulling the car to the side of the road she studied the map before continuing on through Forfar, and picking up the A94.

The continuous rhythmic beat of the windscreen wipers made her feel drowsy. She opened the window a little, hoping it would clear both her head and the misted-up windows at the same time; it was now just after three o'clock. She passed through the small town of Brechin and drove on for seven miles before spotting the faded signpost to Fettercairn. She needed a break; her shoulder ached with tension and she was worried about Ronnie. Visibility was awful; the narrow road ahead twisted and turned, dipped and dived.

Before she recognised the little building on the left was actually a pub, she was already past it. She pulled up, reversed into the muddy car park and switched off. For a brief moment she rested, then shook Ronnie to waken him. His face looked flushed and red.

Placing her hand against his forehead, she felt the fever burning its way through and had to force herself to shake him roughly. He slumped sideways and hit his head against the window. He regained consciousness. 'Ronnie . . .' His eyes focused and he forced himself up.

243

'Ronnie, this is just crazy,' she pleaded. 'You've got to see a doctor.'

'Where are we now?' His voice was barely audible.

'We're almost into Fettercairn,' she answered. 'I've pulled up outside a pub. I need the loo.'

He looked at his watch. 'Well done, I haven't been much help to you have I?'

He undid the seatbelt. 'Come on then, lass, help me out will you? My throat could murder a pint right now.'

Mary got out and waited as he lifted his legs down on to the mud and pulled himself painfully to his feet. With his arm around her shoulders they picked their way between the puddles to the porch. He caught hold of the pillar to steady himself and removed his arm from her supporting shoulder.

'Don't want the landlord to think we're a couple of drunks,' he croaked. 'Just open the door for me.'

A fire burned in a tiled hearth, the sort one might expect to find in an ordinary suburban house. The room was brightly lit. Three men were playing darts in the far corner. An old man sat at the bar and had obviously been in conversation with the landlord. For a moment there was complete silence; all eyes turned towards the strangers.

Ronnie shuffled over to a small table farthest away from the fire and attention diverted to Mary. She was more than conscious of their scrutiny. Ronnie whispered something and handed her some money. She walked up to the bar, trying to appear bright and cheerful. To her surprise the landlord smiled through his bushy beard. His eyes twinkled, his sombre and awesome countenance changed to one of warmth and charm. She smiled back and ordered a pint of bitter and a vodka and tonic.

'On holiday are we, missy?' he asked. 'Terrible shame the weather.'

244

Mary picked up the glasses. 'We've come to visit a friend. We seem to have lost our way.' She turned to the old man to include him in the conversation. 'Perhaps you might know her, her name is Marjorie Dempster. I'm afraid we haven't got the full address.'

'I'll go through the back and ask the wife,' replied the landlord amiably. 'She knows everyone within a twenty-mile radius.' Mary offered her thanks and carried the drinks back to the table. 'Any luck?' queried Ronnie.

'He's gone to ask his wife. 'Scuse me but I've got to find the loo.' Ronnie pointed to a door next to the dart board. 'It's over there.'

'The wife says your friend lives in Glen Esk.' Ronnie looked up to see the Scot towering above him. 'Drive straight through the town and take the second turning on the left. About five miles on you'll see an old ruin; Miss Dempster's place is about a mile further up the track.' Ronnie thanked the man and offered him a drink. 'I don't drink, laddie. Thank you all the same.' The big Scotsman's ruddy face lit up in a crease of smiles. 'You can put a donation in the staff box on your way out. I'm sure it would be appreciated.'

Turning away he walked behind the bar to resume his conversation with the old man.

At any other time, a ruddy faced Scottish landlord, professing to be teetotal would have amused Ronnie greatly; right now he just felt too ill.

The short walk from the car had taxed his strength far more than he cared to admit, but it had made him realise there was little time to waste; his condition could only worsen.

He drained the glass, told Mary to put a couple of quid in the box, dragged himself to the door and walked out into the swirling mist.

She helped him into the passenger seat and leant over

to fasten his safety belt.

Satisfied that he was as comfortable as possible she got in herself and reversed into the lane. 'Shouldn't take us more than about twenty minutes at the most,' she said. Ronnie opened the window a little and laid his head against the glass.

Mary drove gently through the small town of Fettercairn and began to look for turnings to the left. All too quickly she had passed the first turning, or was it a cart track?

She decided she had better count it, and pulled the car off the road on to two concrete strips, separated by an area of tufted grass. Even at slow speed she had difficulty in keeping the wheels lined up with the bumpy meandering track. She switched on the headlights, but they didn't help. Torrential rain gusted violently across their path, the wipers could no longer cope.

From what little she could see, they were driving through desolate moorland. Every so often rugged hills loomed from the mist and cloud only to disappear again. Mary was frightened and unsure; she sought reassurance but Ronnie appeared to be asleep.

Suddenly, before she had time to return her attention to the road, the steering wheel spun in her hand; the car veered to the left, there was a solid bump and they came to an abrupt stop.

Conscious that her hands shook, she put the stick in reverse and let out the clutch. The front wheels spun but found no grip; she tried again; the car refused to move.

She switched off and, close to tears, slumped forward to rest her forehead on the steering wheel. A hand on her knee rescued her from despair.

'We'll have to get out,' Ronnie whispered. 'See if we can get it back on the road.'

He undid the safety belt and opened the door; the full force of the weather hit him face-on. He tried to push himself against it, but lacked the strength. Mary walked around the car and, making every effort to protect him from the weather, took his hands in hers. She pulled him upright and walked in front, one step at a time, as he supported himself against the bonnet. Slowly they made progress to the front of the car.

The car's wheels had slipped off the track and were hanging eighteen inches above the ground. The sump, set tight against the concrete, bore its full weight.

Ronnie rested both hands on the bonnet and bowed his head, water streamed down his face. He said something but she couldn't hear against the wind. He gestured that they get back inside.

'We'll never get it back on the road without help,' he said. 'We've got two alternatives, either we sit here and hope someone comes along,' Ronnie paused for a moment to collect his breath, 'or you must go for help.'

'But we could wait here for hours,' she said.

'Exactly.' Mary thought she detected slight amusement in his voice and marvelled at his coolness.

'Which way do you think I should go?' she asked.

'This track has to lead somewhere,' he whispered. 'We didn't pass any place once you turned off the road, did we?' She agreed but knew only that she was cold, wet, miserable and afraid.

She flung her arms around his neck and kissed him on the lips; they felt hot and cracked. 'I'll be back as soon as I can,' she said, and with one last lingering look, she got out and shut the door.

In an attempt to gain some protection from the weather she pulled up the collar of her sweatshirt, tucked her head into her shoulder and, taking a deep breath to give herself

247

courage, strode out resolutely towards the unknown.

☆　☆　☆

Ronnie watched her disappear into the gloom. Ill as he was, he marvelled at her resolve and courage. For the moment his fever had left him and he felt chilled. Reaching behind with some difficulty, he unzipped the holdall and pulled out Mary's rumpled skirt. He put it over his head, rubbed the surplus water from his face and hair, then folded it around his chest, tucking it behind his back like a blanket. Now he consciously made an effort to slow down his heartbeat and to regulate his breathing. He felt defeated and depressed.

For the first time he questioned the decision to come looking for Francine, and for what possible reason Mary had offered her help. Perhaps she thought she loved him!

Ronnie tried to analyse his own feelings. He cared for the girl, he cared for her a lot, but not .... His thoughts were interrupted.

The distant sound of a diesel engine carried to him on the wind. He strained to confirm the sound, it was getting closer. He leaned over to switch on the wipers and peered through the windscreen.

A pair of headlights set close together pierced the gloom. Seconds later the shape of a large tractor loomed out of the mist.

Mary, bent forward seeking shelter from the cabin, stood behind the driver. She jumped down. 'Are you all right, Ronnie?' He nodded and wound down the window.

'I met this farmer,' she continued, her teeth chattering. 'He says we are on the right road. Marjorie's place is about three miles further on.'

Ronnie watched from the car as the tractor was driven off the track on to the grass below. The farmer reversed up and, guided in by Mary, set his hydraulic platform neatly under the front wheels. With an increase of engine power and a whir of hydraulics, the platform rose. Ronnie could feel himself being tilted backwards.

Mary scrambled in beside him, eased the handbrake off and with a quarter-turn of the steering wheel, the car ran backwards on to the track.

'Bloody marvellous,' exclaimed Ronnie. 'Give him a tenner for his trouble.' He fumbled for a note.

'He won't take the money,' she said. 'He says he's glad he could help.' She put the car into gear and moved slowly away.

Every ounce of concentration was focused on the track ahead; she made no effort to increase speed and remained in second gear. 'This is where I'd got to when I met the tractor,' she said. 'Was I glad to see him! Do you know, I think it's stopped raining.'

Ronnie wasn't listening; he felt light-headed. It didn't matter. Nothing really mattered, not even life itself. He wouldn't fight it. If it was time for him to go, he'd let it happen and enjoy the peace. He was tired of the constant battle; the never-ending strain.

Who was this bloody woman with him, anyway? He wished she'd shut her mouth. What was she rabbiting on about; some ruin, only a mile to go. A million miles to go, more like. Perhaps he could see Francine and the kids; see them just one more time. That's it, he could remember now, only a mile to go, and they would be there waiting.

Mary switched off the wipers; the rain had stopped and the mist was clearing. She could see the hills ranging up either side of the valley. A patchwork of browns, yellows and from the heather, a predominant tinge of purple, contrasted wildly to outcrops of jagged rock and crags.

The track wound to the right, out of shadow into the light. A reddish sun, set between the valley rift, added

249

warmth to the surrounding countryside. She marvelled how one slight bend in the road could transform an alien and hostile atmosphere into one of peace and tranquillity. She could see the little stone cottage about 200 yards distant. Smoke spiralled from its chimney.

Mary pulled off the road into a beaten track; a flock of sheep looked up from grazing. Several goats, their bells clanging loudly, cantered to the far side of the paddock.

Easing the car past chickens and geese, she pulled up in front of the house. She felt that this was the end of her journey in more senses than one. Ronnie was only semi-conscious, pretty soon he would need a hospital. She caught hold of his arm and shook him gently. 'Ronnie . . . Ronnie we're there. You've come to see the children, remember?' He looked at her as if she were a stranger.

He opened the car door and with the safety belt still restraining him, fought violently to get out. Mary released the catch for him and wound down the window, her attention attracted towards the front door of the cottage.

A woman wearing an oversized jumper and baggy cords had stepped on to the porch; she was probably forty years old. A white apron, knee length, was wrapped around her waist; she lifted it to wipe her hands. She wore no make-up, her hair was pinned haphazardly away from her face.

She was a woman of striking appearance, but in Mary's mind it was not Francine.

Ronnie shuffled towards his sister-in-law; recognition dawned. 'Ronnie, it's you,' she said; her surprise quickly turned to concern. 'Whatever's the matter?'

He pushed his way past her into the house. Marjorie looked for some explanation from the young woman still seated in the car, but only received a sympathetic shake of the head and a weak smile.

Turning on her heel she followed him inside. 'Where

are they?' he rasped.

He moved to the staircase and with difficulty stepped on to the first tread, but his legs lost coherence and were unable to negotiate the next step. He looked up towards the landing to call for his family but the sound wouldn't come. He supported himself against the handrail, tears streaming down his face.

'Where are they, Marjorie? Please tell me.' She took a step towards him. 'They're not here, my love.' Seeing the pain in his eyes she paused. 'They went back to London two days ago.'

She ran forward and tried to break his fall. His weight was too much for her and she fell backwards on to the floor. Unhurt, she picked herself up, opened the front door and called for help.

The two women dragged the unconscious form on to a sheepskin rug in front of the fire. 'He's got a gunshot wound,' Mary explained. 'We've got to get him to a hospital.'

'I've no phone here,' Marjorie said. 'Do you think we can get him into the car?'

Mary thought for a moment. 'I don't think we should move him. Where's the nearest phone?'

'About three miles up the road; you stay with him then. I'll take the car and call an ambulance.' Marjorie started to walk towards the door; she stopped suddenly. 'What the hell is that?' Mary knew instantly.

'It's a helicopter. Quick, see if we can catch their attention.' She followed Marjorie outside. 'No need, my love, they're coming down here.'

A white helicopter with **POLICE** in large navy-blue letters across its side hovered fifty feet above the over-grazed paddock, livestock scattered in all directions.

The sound of a siren diverted the women's attention. Two panda cars, with blue lights flashing, sped recklessly up the track.

Four men leapt from each car and took cover behind doors flung wide, pistols extended menacingly. Two senior officers walked forward cautiously. 'It's all right, boys,' Marjorie shouted in a powerful voice. 'You can dispense with the dramatics.' The police stopped ten feet away. 'We have reason to believe that Ronald Brownlowe is here on these premises. Is either of you ladies Mary Verdusca?'

'I am,' said Mary, finding difficulty in getting the words out. 'But Mr Brownlowe is desperately ill. He needs to be taken to a hospital immediately.'

'Are you alone?' asked the officer.

'Mr Brownlowe's inside,' Marjorie answered. 'He's unconscious.'

'Stand away from the door, please.' It was more a command than a request. The women moved aside as the police sergeant, pistol extended at arm's length, kicked open the door. His companion, similarly armed, darted inside; a minute later he reappeared to give the all clear.

The sergeant's attitude changed; he now became warm and friendly. 'Sorry, ladies. We had to make sure you weren't being used to get rid of us.'

'What's all this about?' Marjorie asked.

Mary put fingers to lips, whispered she would explain later, and followed inside.

After a cursory examination, Ronnie was carried to the helicopter and strapped in.

Mary protected her ears from the noise and watched as it gained altitude, swung away to the south-east and disappeared between the hills. She felt a lump in her throat and turned away disconsolately.

'I'm afraid the authorities have asked for your co-operation in making a full statement,' said the sergeant. 'Some people are coming up from London tonight.

252

Would you kindly make yourself available at police headquarters Dundee tomorrow morning?' Mary nodded and accepted the offer of a lift to the hospital.

'I'll come too,' said Marjorie. 'Can you wait for us a minute, the poor girl's soaking wet. Come on, lovey, I'll lend you something to wear.'

Mary took off her drenched clothes, towelled herself dry and put on the clothes laid out on the bed.

'This is very sweet of you, Marjorie.' At last she felt able to talk rationally. 'We've been involved in a bit of an adventure. I'll tell you about it...' The two women walked back downstairs. They got into one of the waiting police cars and were driven away at speed.

21

Charles Verdusca smiled to himself and poured a heavy measure of Chivas; the ice crackled. He took a sip of the golden liquid and checked once more the share prices list in *The Times* against those written on the pad in front of him. Satisfied, he added up the extensions on the calculator. The figure was correct: £786,790 clear profit excluding fees, give or take the odd hundred pounds.

Even though it had come a little late he felt elated that his original decision to invest had been sound. He picked up the phone, punched in the code and waited impatiently as the number clicked its way across the Atlantic.

Asking to be put through to dealers, he had to wait another few seconds. 'Ben, is that you? Charles Verdusca ... Very well, thank you. Ben, I want to sell everything ... No, that's the way I want it. Sell on a rising market, today, Ben ... and Ben, transfer the money to my Swiss account will you? Thank you.'

Verdusca replaced the receiver and took a long, cool sip. The intricacies of life never ceased to amaze him. As things had worked out, he needn't have involved himself with this bunch of crooks in the first place, and now here he was with an even chance of having to face serious charges – charges even more serious than he'd ever contemplated. Violent killings had not featured in his reckoning. It didn't bear thinking about; Charles loosened his tie.

Closing his mind to disasters that might never materialise, he checked the time; it was approaching midday. If they were men of their word he could expect to receive payment sometime this afternoon.

He picked up the in-house phone and got through to extension twelve. 'Ah, Jane, Mr Verdusca here. I'm expecting a large transfer of money from Cayman. Yes, to my account. Send me up the confirmation please, as soon as it comes through. Thank you.'

Charles took his glass and walked over to the window. Looking across the town to the distant sea, he wondered about Mary. Where the hell was she? Would she talk? He thought not. Mary liked the good things in life far too much to rock the boat. But who was this bloke she'd gone off with? Henry's story that the man was a Government agent seemed most unlikely, but if it were true then all was surely lost. Perhaps she was trying to persuade him to keep quiet, perhaps that was it.

Whatever the outcome, his affairs would be arranged to cover all eventualities.

He took his coat and walked down the stairway to reception. 'Ah, Miss Raynes.' The young lady looked up from the word processor. 'I'm going to lunch. If anyone wants me urgently I'll be at the Capannina.'

At a brisk walk, it took just six minutes to reach the restaurant.

☆   ☆   ☆

Carlos, the *maître*, walked towards him and with a warm greeting took his coat.

'Would you care to take a drink, Mr Charles?' Verdusca nodded and sat down at the bar.

Aware that he had become the immediate topic of conversation, he stared into his drink. 'What had the

doctor said? No more than three whiskies a day ... balls!'
He drained his glass and ordered another.

'Nigel, what'll you have?' Verdusca greeted his young
lawyer and the two men talked trivialities until they'd
ordered. When the *maître* moved away, Verdusca reached
for the envelope from his inside pocket.

'Nigel, you've served me well in the past and I now
wish to offer you my complete trust. There's been some
trouble at the bank, I don't know how things may turn
out for me ... please take this.' He handed it over.

'If anything happens to me, I want you to act on the
instructions within this envelope.' The lawyer looked
shaken. 'No Nigel, I'm not going to do anything stupid.
It's just that the doctors have confirmed I have a serious
heart condition. What with the strain of the hijacking,
problems at the bank and, worst of all, the constant worry
as to Mary's whereabouts, I may not last the trip.'

'But what's in this?' he was asked. 'You've already
made a will.'

'In there,' Verdusca answered, 'is a detailed summary
of my personal holdings in three listings. My own un-
disputed assets, those that could be reclaimed by the bank
and, thirdly, details of monies that may be legitimately
frozen, pending investigations and possible charges being
brought against me.'

Here he was interrupted and they were shown to their
table.

'As you know, my wife inherits everything I have.'
Charles sampled the fine Burgundy and signified his
acceptance to the wine waiter.

'I don't want my personal estate frozen. If that were
allowed to happen it could take years to sort out. Do you
understand? Promise me, Nigel, that whatever happens
you won't disclose the contents of that envelope, or that
you have such a document in your possession, unless I am

256

dead.'

Charles Verdusca drank the remaining wine from his glass and held it up for a refill.

☆ ☆ ☆

Two hours later, seated in the office, he lit a large Monte Cristo cigar. He gazed as if mesmerized as the smoke swirled in intricate spirals above him. The buzz of the intercom snapped him out of the daydream.

'Jayne here, sir. Just to let you know we've received a transfer from the Cayman Bank for £1.5 million sterling.' Verdusca leant forward aggressively.

'Bring the confirmation up to me yourself, Jayne, and see the money is moved into our reserve account. Please inform Mr Larbalester and the chief accountant.' Smiling inwardly he replaced the receiver. It was amusing to think that part of the stolen money had returned so soon to Jersey.

No more pressure from those arseholes on the board. The bank would now be paid in full, weeks before he'd promised. He took a deep drag on the cigar; on the whole it had been a good sort of day.

☆ ☆ ☆

The drive to the airport provided an opportunity to read through a copy of his signed statement, the end product to four hours of interrogation at police headquarters. There had been no inference that he was suspect. Everyone had been treated equally and the thoroughness with which the police were conducting the investigation had impressed him.

He searched through his written version of events for any anomaly, anything on which he could be taken to

257

task.

On the short flight home he was content to look down into the bluish-green sea below, until there it was, his own beloved island. The white frothy waves beat against its pebbled shores; the heath speckled with colour. If ever he were forced to give it up there would be little reason to continue. It seemed likely that Mary had already gone. He could live with that, but lose his home – never.

Charles wiped a tear from his eye and cursed his own sentimentality. Stepping down on to the concrete pad, he thanked his pilot and walked slowly across the lawn. He entered the front door, placed his briefcase on the hall table and removed his coat. He folded it over the arm of the chair, went directly upstairs to Mary's room, and closed the door behind him.

☆　☆　☆

Martha heard the front door bell. She wondered who it might be and wiped her hands on the dishcloth. It wasn't often they received callers at five o'clock in the afternoon, or at any time for that matter. In the light of recent events she opened the front door with trepidation.

Two smartly dressed men stood in the portico, three uniformed policemen stood on the steps behind them.

'Good evening, madam. I'm Detective Sergeant Willis.' The man was polite but unsmiling. 'Is Mr Verdusca at home?' Martha nodded.

'Would you care to come in?' She held open the door, the constables politely removed their helmets. 'If you would just wait here, I'll tell Mr Verdusca you wish to see him.'

Martha started to run towards the stairs; suddenly realising she should not show her anxiety, she slowed to a dignified walk.

Charles was sitting on the bed looking relaxed and calm. 'Yes, Martha, what is it?' She realised she was gawping. 'Oh, I'm sorry, sir,' she swallowed hard. 'There's some police officers to see you, sir. They're downstairs in the hall.' He smoothed his hair into place with the flat of his hand. 'Thank you, Martha.' He stood up, smiling: 'I expect they have some news of Mary. Let's hope it's good news, eh?'

She waited a moment then followed him out of the room to watch from the landing.

'Good evening, gentlemen,' he spoke politely as he walked downstairs.

'Have you brought news of my wife?'

'Afraid not,' said the detective. 'We must ask that you accompany us to police headquarters, Jersey.'

'I've only just got back,' Verdusca protested. 'Surely it can wait till morning?'

'No, sir, it can't wait. We have reason to believe you are implicated in recent criminal events and wish you to assist with our enquiries.'

'Are you charging me?' Verdusca asked.

'Not unless you insist, sir. I would advise you to come voluntarily. We would suggest it might be advisable to pack a few things.'

For a moment there was a complete silence. The colour had drained from his face; he tried to collect his thoughts and asked how they proposed to travel.

'It's up to you, sir,' said the detective. 'Either we can go to Guernsey by launch and fly to Jersey or, with respect, sir, we can make use of your helicopter. That way we could outwit the media who are pressing us for a statement.'

'We'll use the helicopter. Thank you, officer.'

Charles called up to Martha to pack him a case, then asked permission to fix himself a drink.

259

For once, not bothering with ice, he filled the glass to the rim and took a long sip. He moved to the window and stared out over his beloved land towards the sea.

Martha handed him a small travelling case. She leant over and kissed him on the cheek, her eyes filled with tears. 'Good luck, sir.' She reached for his hand and gave it a squeeze. 'I'm sure everything will be sorted out very soon.'

'Thank you, my dear.' Verdusca straightened his back, drained the glass and stood tall. 'Now if you would like to call Henry, we'll be off.'

Verdusca walked steadfastly across the lawns to the helicopter; he had already made his momentous decision. The adrenalin pumped through his veins and caused a rapid increase in heartbeat. For a moment he had to steady himself. He took a deep breath, climbed aboard, and sat down next to the door. He buckled the seat belt and as the two officers settled themselves into the seats behind, Henry pulled the door shut and clamped the locking lever into the closed position.

Stretching his legs into the extra space afforded by exit seats, Charles reached into his lap and gently released the seat belt. He looked out of the window towards the house. Martha still stood at the front door and as the Sirkorski lifted from the ground he thought he saw her wave.

For a second he stopped to think. No matter what, he had never made a final commitment without pause for extra thought.

As far back as he could remember no one had ever got the better of him; no loss had occurred through impulsiveness. His decision must be calculated and rational. He could see no reason to change his mind now.

For the moment he lay back in his seat and clenched his fists. He took a long deep breath and closed his eyes. He breathed out slowly and opened them wide. Gritting his

260

teeth he hurled himself forward and, in one explosive movement, he was out of the seat and at the door, wrenching at the lock-bar.

The rush of air caught hold. The door flew open and smashed with great force against the side of the fuselage. The two detectives, temporarily stunned, struggled to release their seat belts. Verdusca, with a hand on either side of the open hatchway, paused. He looked up at the open sky and with a shout as loud as thunder hurled himself to freedom.

Feeling the wind cold against his face, he looked down and saw his island rushing to greet him. He had no regrets. It was as if he were a bird, already free from the shackles of life itself. Charles Verdusca spread his arms out wide and shut his eyes . . . .

22

Ronnie had already been to theatre and was now in intensive care. He was not allowed visitors. The two women, shocked by sister's blunt statement, asked if he were out of danger. She was non-committal and could only suggest they call later that evening.

Mary was determined to stay close by and decided to book into the nearest hotel.

Marjorie rummaged through her handbag. 'I'm afraid I must get back to feed the animals,' she handed over a piece of paper. 'This is Francine's address and telephone number. Ronnie's bound to ask for it.'

'Do you think she'll come up to see him?' Mary asked.

Marjorie smiled at her warmly. 'I shouldn't think so, my love. Now don't worry, everything'll be sorted out, you see.'

At nine o'clock sharp Mary called the hospital from the peace and quiet of her hotel bedroom. The night sister said that Ronnie was as well as could be expected, but was still not allowed visitors. There was nothing more to do except go to bed, and it was not until 8.30 next morning she walked to the hospital, and was told she could see him.

A nurse led the way to a small ward in which all four patients were wired to numerous machines and equipment. The room was a clutter of electronics; a policeman sat beside the bed.

Recognising her delicate perfume, Ronnie opened his

eyes. He smiled and without success tried to speak; she reached out and held his hand. She felt rather silly with the policeman there, but before she could think what to say, the nurse was pressing her to leave.

She kissed Ronnie on the forehead, and promised she'd be back. He managed a nod of appreciation and, giving him a loving smile, she was ushered from the room.

✩   ✩   ✩

The Midland Bank opened its doors for morning business, and Mary, impatient to see the manager, bustled through to 'enquiries'. She was granted an immediate appointment and, to an appreciative deputy manager, she stated who she was and, in brief, the circumstances in which she now found herself. She asked him to contact their Guernsey branch to authorise the withdrawal of £2,000.

Twenty minutes later, with the money in hand, she went out and bought herself a complete wardrobe. She changed out of her borrowed clothes into one of the new outfits and arranged for everything else to be delivered to the hotel.

She stood at the kerb and looked out for a taxi. For the first time in days, she felt presentable and normal, but she was already late.

Frustration and impatience increased as the minutes ticked by; finally she saw an obliging policeman who called in on his personal radio. Within minutes a patrol car had arrived to collect her.

✩   ✩   ✩

After a long and arduous interrogation, she signed her statement at 3.30. She did little to disguise her relief as she stepped out into the sunshine, and made her way to the

263

hospital.

Ronnie was no longer in intensive care and, not knowing what to expect, she felt like a nervous schoolgirl. To her surprise, he was sitting up in bed in a private room and, although still pale and drawn, he smiled and was able to talk.

She began to feel at ease, until he asked about Francine and the kids.

Without fully understanding why, she said only that they were in London. For the time being he could assume they had returned home; he appeared satisfied and asked whether she had made her statement to the police, and whether she'd told them of her husband's involvement.

'As the wife, I wouldn't be able to give evidence against him anyway,' she answered. 'No, I didn't tell them.' Ronnie reached for her hand.

'I've thought long and hard about this,' he said, 'but I'm afraid I'll have to. If I don't, it makes a nonsense of me ever being there. It's the only bit of concrete evidence I can give them.' Mary understood. Although she would never be able to forgive her husband, she still lacked any desire to incriminate him. 'They're coming to take my statement in the morning,' said Ronnie. She showed her surprise.

'There's nothing wrong with me now,' he added, smiling. 'They've got rid of the infection and I'll be up and out of here in two days.'

Mary met him at eleven in the morning three days later. They were driven to the airport, straight through security controls, and delivered directly to the aircraft.

It had been waiting on the tarmac for twenty minutes, and no explanation for the delay had been offered to the other passengers. The stewardess somewhat impatiently showed them to their seats.

'I have to go to Whitehall tomorrow morning,' Ronnie

said. 'As soon as we get to Heathrow I'm going to sort things out with Francine. You've got her address, haven't you?'

Mary blushed; she opened her bag and fumbled for the piece of paper.

'What she's doing at this place, God only knows. Why the hell didn't she use the house?' Mary could offer no explanation.

Met on the tarmac, they were shown to the waiting car and, without the fuss of normal formalities, were driven directly to London.

Ronnie caught hold of her hand as they pulled into the kerb outside the Grafton Hotel, Tottenham Court Road. 'I can't thank you ever enough for what you've done for me,' he said. 'Whatever happens I'll come back and see you this evening.'

'Do you promise?' Mary tried to hide her emotion.

She stood and watched as the car disappeared amongst the traffic. He hadn't even turned around to wave!

☆   ☆   ☆

The car turned left into Richmond Road and stopped outside number 33. Ronnie dismissed his driver and walked up the stone steps of the large terraced house. The number of flats were listed against an array of small window cards each displaying the occupant's name. Flat 2, Stoddard? Ronnie re-checked the address. He tried the front door; it wasn't locked.

His footsteps echoed on the marble floor of the elegantly proportioned hall; he knocked on the door to Flat 2, it swung open.

Two little girls sat on a settee watching television. They turned towards him; their faces broke into smiles of joy and excitement. Bouncing themselves to their feet they ran across the room: 'Daddy, Daddy! – Mummy, it's Daddy.'

He bent down to hug them, and they clung around his neck. He let out an involuntary gasp of pain. The two girls immediately let go and stood back.

'Daddy, what's the matter? Why have you got a stick?' Ronnie smiled reassurance. 'It's all right, darlings, Daddy hurt his side. It'll be better soon.' Kneeling down he opened his arms and gathered them to him. He kissed each in turn and stroked their fine delicate hair. Samantha pulled herself away. 'Daddy, Daddy, come and see my rabbit.'

'In a minute darling... where's your mother?' Ronnie leaned heavily on his stick and heaved himself upright. The girls were looking towards the dividing doors at the end of the room. His heart leapt; all he could think to say was to ask why the girls weren't at school.

'You'll never change, will you?' she said, not unkindly. 'No sense of time, or family routine.... They're home for the Easter holidays.'

'Oh,' said Ronnie weakly. 'Do you mind if I sit down?' Francine sent the children into the garden. 'Marjorie told me you've been very ill.'

'You might have come to see me, or at least telephoned,' he answered. 'Anyway what are you doing here? And who's this bloke Stoddard?'

☆ ☆ ☆

Ronnie joined his daughters in the garden. They seemed happy enough. Francine had gone out for an hour so he could be alone with them. He didn't know quite how he felt – numb really. He hardly felt anything except... except a great sadness over the children. They loved him, sure. But somehow, well perhaps he'd expected them to

266

have missed him a lot more; they seemed so content and excited with their new home.

He hadn't understood how resilient they were. However much it might hurt to be without them, his kids were happy and that's what really mattered.

He went inside, made himself a coffee, and sat down on the settee. Samantha climbed on to his lap and Jennifer sat at his feet. Together, as they had done so many times before, they watched TV.

Ronnie found it difficult to concentrate and was not sorry when Francine returned. She carried her groceries into the kitchen and called out asking whether he wanted anything to eat. He was hungry but wanted more than anything to get away.

Standing in the open doorway he said he might go to Portugal to convalesce. He paused, hoping for some reaction. There was none; she continued putting things away.

'If I find a decent place to live I'd like the children to come over for their summer holidays.' Francine stopped what she was doing and turned to face him.

'Ronnie, you can see the children whenever you wish to. Don't think I don't care or feel about all this. I've gone over it in my mind a thousand times. But I've found some peace for the first time in years.' She had tears in her eyes. He moved towards her but she held up a hand to stop him.

'No, don't use your charm and sympathy on me. Just leave me alone, please.'

He turned away. 'If you need to use the house' – he spoke from the other room – 'you can. I'll be in touch about the children.'

Kissing and hugging the girls, he walked over to the door and turned for one last look. The film had already reclaimed their attention and they seemed blissfully un-

267

aware of the tense situation. He closed the door quietly behind him and felt a dull ache in the pit of his stomach. He had never suspected. God, how naïve he was! He walked to the pub on the corner and wondered, over a cheese roll and half of bitter, what he might do next.

He had no wish to face Mary just yet. If she knew the meeting with Francine hadn't worked out, she would expect him to spend the night at the hotel. He wasn't ready for it; right now he was just too vulnerable.

If she wanted, she could come to Portugal. There he could take the time ... be given time. Time to sort things out; time to gain strength, time to become himself again.

Ronnie decided to spend the night at the house. He could pack what he needed for the trip and arrange to meet up with her in the morning.

Decisions made, he felt a lot better and, draining his glass, he gave a cheery wave to the barmaid and went out into the street.

☆   ☆   ☆

The house felt so empty; it looked drab and uncomfortable. Nevertheless the extreme effort it took to climb the stairs made him realise how much he needed to rest and to be alone.

When he woke up it was dark and cold. He switched on the light, it was 1.30. He had forgotten to phone!

Almost reluctantly he dialled The Grafton and was put through to her room. When she answered, her voice was full of sleep; as he spoke, she came to life. 'Ronnie, where are you? I was so worried. Are you all right?' Briefly he explained the situation.

'I've decided to go to Portugal.' He sensed a shock of disappointment, and tried to explain. 'I feel emotionally and physically drained; I need to get away from here.'

There was a pause and he thought she might be crying.

She said she thought it was a good idea. 'The sun will heal all your scars.' He noted the touch of sarcasm, but sensed her utter desolation. 'Can you be ready to leave tomorrow evening?' he said.

Completely taken aback, she broke down and sobbed out loud. Immediately he felt ashamed for playing with her emotions, and waited for her to gain control.

'Well,' he said. 'Can you?'

'Oh, Ronnie, you know I'd like nothing more,' she almost exploded with happiness, 'but I haven't got a passport and we can't risk using the forged one again.'

He told her it would be no problem to arrange with the Department.

'First thing in the morning I've got to have my dressing changed. After that I shall be in Whitehall for the rest of the day. Can I leave you to get the tickets – yes, Lisbon – and don't worry about money, I've got plenty. Meet me at the Ministry of Defence at 4.30, by the front desk in main reception. Yes, I am too.'

He replaced the receiver. Why was it that women in tears always turned him on? Had he really wanted to take her with him? He thought not, but now it was done . . . .

23

Members of the Government and particularly those of the opposition were in outcry over what they saw as 'an affront to the very foundations of democracy' and 'this assault on our beloved Channel Islands.' The House had demanded satisfaction and that no cost nor effort be spared in bringing those responsible to justice.

Ronnie had not expected the debriefing to be routine, but something more of an inquisition, and he was right.

Escorted to the eighth floor, he was shown into a large suite of offices and ushered through into an oak-panelled room overlooking the Embankment. It immediately became obvious that much importance was to be placed on the evidence he was about to give.

The gentleman at the head of a baize-covered table stood to welcome him and asked after his health. Ronnie took the seat offered at the opposite end, and introductions were made around the table. One or two names were echoes from his past, but he recognised no one.

In addition to seven members of the Special Committee were the Minister of Defence, the Under-Secretary of State, a senior police officer and two senior detectives. Each had transcripts of his statement.

A middle-aged female secretary seated to one side of the Chairman, Colonel Radley, made ready to take minutes. The Colonel cleared his throat and asked that they proceed.

It was a slow process. Ronnie read out his statement a paragraph at a time, and was taken to task and questioned on each contentious issue. By the time lunch was called they were a third of the way through and the meeting was adjourned until two o'clock.

Feeling stifled and tense, Ronnie found his way out into the rear gardens and crossed the main road on to the Embankment; he walked along beside the river. Only another few hours and it would virtually be all over. He could expect to be recalled should someone be charged, but he would never be summoned to appear for the prosecution. His identity would be kept secret; the unwritten law of his volatile profession would be respected.

By the time the Palace of Westminster chimed two he had already taken his place at the table; at four minutes past, the meeting was reconvened.

The afternoon dragged on, word by word, sentence by sentence, question by question. The four most contentious, that would test the very core of his credibility, remained:

Why had he not kept in regular contact with operations?

Why, when Hammond was killed and he consequently gained control of the helicopter, did he not report to base?

Had he not known at the time that Jersey was the ultimate target?

And finally, why did he return, at great personal risk, to attempt the rescue of Jackson Rae and engineer the escape to France?

Ronnie, trained in all aspects of interrogation himself, had known these questions would be asked and had ready answers prepared: a reason; an excuse; a purpose. After several requests from around the table for additional clarification, his actions appeared to be accepted. The document had now been examined in its entirety, and he

271

was asked to sign it.

Three folios were now produced and Ronnie flicked through pages of photographs searching for some recognisable face.

He paused several times when recognising some ex-companion or adversary from past assignments, but it was not until the second page of the third volume that he pointed to a picture in the fourth row.

'Here's one of them,' he said. 'It's the German, who called himself Mueber; the photograph is referenced CX 726.'

Two pages on he saw a picture of Rae and, thinking there was little to lose, he identified his dead comrade; the Colonel jotted down the reference and indicated he should continue.

Ronnie reached the final page, breathed an inward sigh of relief that Franco's picture had not been included, and pushed the files away from him.

A fourth folio was now presented and he was asked if he could recognise the country house used as the mercenary headquarters. The Colonel explained that every estate agent in Wales had already been contacted and asked to provide details of any large country property, disposed of or rented within the last six months. Particular attention had been placed on properties that may have once been schools, health farms, rest homes or public buildings.

Ronnie turned the pages, looking carefully at each photograph, and halfway through he found it.

Leaving the page open he pushed the folio across the table. 'That's it, Featherstone Manor.'

'Are you sure beyond all reasonable doubt?' asked the Colonel.

'Absolutely positive. That's where I was taken, there could be no mistake.'

Colonel Radley thanked him and made a short speech

commending him on his achievements.

'It is easy for us, sitting within the safety and confines of Whitehall, to criticize or make unreasonable demands of our agents in the field.' He paused to look around the table.

'Those of us here today wish you to know that we understand that allowances have to be made for decisions taken under duress. You are now free to go, but please leave your address with Captain Wallace in the outer office. We may need to contact you in the course of further enquiries.'

Ronnie thanked the tribunal for its courtesy and was shown through to the outer office where he gave details of his intended travel arrangements to the young man seated at one of the desks. When mentioning that Mrs Verdusca would be going with him, Ronnie detected a hint of disapproval and fought to keep the contempt from his voice. 'Mrs Verdusca has left her passport in the Channel Islands,' he added. 'Could you arrange temporary clearance between here and Lisbon?'

The man looked through a file already on his desk. 'That can be arranged, sir. I'll have the necessary documentation drawn up and left for your collection at passport control. Heathrow or Gatwick, sir?' Ronnie checked the time.

'Can I call down to main reception from here? Mrs Verdusca should be waiting.' Within a minute she was on the line. 'It's Heathrow, and her full name is Mary Louise Verdusca; maiden name Cartwright.'

Ronnie felt as if a ton weight had lifted from his shoulders; the doors opened and he stepped into the empty lift. Before he had time to push the ground floor button it started to descend, stopping at the third.

A dapper little man entered. He wore a navy-blue overcoat and carried a bowler hat, an umbrella and a black briefcase. He peered over the top of circular metal-rimmed spectacles, nervously mumbled a 'good afternoon' and shuffled his feet.

The doors opened, and the two men made to step out at the same time. The umbrella caught between Ronnie's legs, he stumbled forward, accidentally wrenching the briefcase from the little man's hand. It fell, scattering it's contents over the marble floor.

Ronnie apologised and knelt down to help. He placed the two girlie magazines between the folds of *The Daily Telegraph* and as he slipped it into the case, noticed the calling card attached to the lining.

'I'm very sorry, Mr Mullings. No damage done.' Across the hall Mary smiled at them. Ronnie thought she looked wonderful. Mullings averted his eyes, furtively glanced at his watch, and head bowed hurried on.

✿　　✿　　✿

On arrival at Heathrow they checked in their luggage and went upstairs for a light meal. It was so good to be with her again and yet her dazzling appearance made him feel a little uneasy.

Obviously excited with her day she'd bought a complete summer wardrobe, had her hair done by a fashionable London stylist and had spent at least two hours at a beautician's. Ronnie was unimpressed, would a woman like this ever be able to accept his own simple life-style? If she didn't, she'd leave soon enough. He would simply enjoy her whilst it lasted and why not?

He looked up at the departures monitor screen; their flight was boarding through gate 14. They walked downstairs and joined the queue moving rapidly towards passport control. Ronnie gave their names, and asked for Mary's papers; the officer was most polite. He called an

274

assistant to take his place, and escorted them into a small office. He offered them a seat and asked them to wait. Two minutes later Mary was handed her documentation.

'Mrs Verdusca,' the administrator looked at her intensely, 'I am afraid I have some bad news.

'Earlier this evening – I regret to have to tell you this – your husband was involved in a tragic incident . . . .' Mary looked at Ronnie and back to the official.

'How tragic?' she asked.

'I'm afraid he was killed. Apparently your solicitor,' the man looked down at his notes, 'a Mr Nigel Le Seeleur? . . . wants you to contact him immediately. He says it's imperative you return home. Here, I've got his number. You can telephone from here if you like.' The man stood up and addressing himself to Ronnie offered to hold the flight for thirty minutes. He smiled sympathetically and left them on their own.

Mary dialled Jersey, and by the time she replaced the receiver was in tears.

'Oh, Ronnie, I was so looking forward to being with you . . . I've got to go back, there's too much to sort out. Poor Charles – he was killed instantly. Apparently he jumped out of the helicopter after being arrested.' She opened her handbag and took a handkerchief to dry her eyes.

'If I'm quick I can catch the 8.30 flight to Jersey.' She flung her arms around him. 'I love you Ronnie, I really love you.' Opening her handbag she gave him a printed card.

'This is Lucy's address, I'll be staying with her. Ring me, Ronnie, you will, won't you?'

He promised to call within the next couple of days. 'You'll have to come over to collect your luggage,' he said smiling.

'Keep it for me darling; keep it really close to you.' She

275

opened the office door and led him out as if he was a small boy. He pulled her to him roughly and kissed her full on the lips, then holding her away looked her straight in the eyes.

'I'll give your love to Franco. We'll be waiting for you.' With a last meaningful smile he turned on his heel and without looking back walked away.

☆   ☆   ☆

Ronnie was met at the departure gate and escorted to the waiting aircraft; he boarded and the doors were closed from the inside.

He buckled his seat belt; lay back and shut his eyes. She was so beautiful... but now he had the time he really needed. Time to be on his own... Franco would understand. Ronnie smiled, for the moment content....